SUNDOWNERS

SUNDOWNERS BOOK ONE

R.L. MERRILL

CELIE BAY PUBLICATIONS LLC

For my baby Simi...You were such a great writing buddy. I miss you so much every day, but I know you're acting as a Canine Intervention Specialist for all of those good pups who passed during these dark times.

For my dear friend and inspiration Jojo...I miss your smile every day. We've all lost so much these past few years, and losing you has been so hard. Thank you for the years of beauty and love you shared with me. Pet Simi for me and peace be with you. I'm sorry you aren't here to read yet another character you inspired.

For my readers who suffered losses during these dark times, my heart is with you. Hang in there, we're going to be okay.

Sundowning: Late-day confusion
From the Mayo Clinic:

The term "sundowning" refers to a state of confusion occurring in the late afternoon and lasting into the night. Sundowning can cause different behaviors, such as confusion, anxiety, aggression or ignoring directions. Sundowning can also lead to pacing or wandering. Sundowning isn't a disease. It's a group of symptoms that occur at a specific time of the day. These symptoms may affect people with Alzheimer's disease and other types of dementia. The exact cause of this behavior is unknown.

PROLOGUE

S eptember

Donna Hicks smoothed the fine silk skirt she'd picked out for her husband's event and fidgeted in the front seat of their McLaren. "Are you sure we're dressed all right?" She gave her husband's attire a onceover, grinning at how well the Hugo Boss hugged his lines.

"Of course, darling. You look stunning," her husband Timothy said, taking her hand and kissing the back of it. "Grant assured me that casual-nice was the dress code. Oh, honey, this is huge. I thought we'd have to wait at least a year before getting this invitation."

The McLaren handled the curves of Highway 17 with ease on the dark January night. They took a blind turn onto a two-lane road and then another onto a much narrower one with no street signs. Donna wasn't sure how Timothy knew where he was going, as it was pitch black outside. The private drive was only wide enough for one car. Thankfully it was paved. Timothy had already had to take the new car into the shop because he'd run over a concrete parking barrier in the lot at the gym, scraping the underside of the luxury car.

"So tell me more about this group," she asked her husband of sixteen years. "Am I allowed to discuss my research or should I simply play the trophy wife tonight?"

Timothy chuckled. "They know about your work," he said. "I brag about you all the time. Just be yourself. They invited us because we meet their requirements for membership, I guess." He laughed nervously. "I just didn't think it would happen so soon."

"Timothy, you made your company over a billion dollars last quarter. You've revitalized the processes for your team and you've already been promoted twice despite only being there for a year. I think you've shown these people that you are absolutely worth their investment."

When Timothy had told Donna about the opportunity to join a private club for influential Silicon Valley businesspeople, she'd been intrigued. He hadn't had a lot of details, but he'd been so excited. She'd grown up on the Peninsula, but he'd been raised in the Central Valley, and had spent his career in finance trying to make people forget he was the son of farmers. They'd met when his original company invested in her medical research program and he'd checked all the boxes on her suitable-husband-qualities list. He was younger than her, independently wealthy, no children and didn't care to have them, and more than happy to let her rule the roost in their Palo Alto mansion.

"Here we are," he said, and they both took a moment to breathe.

The magnificent structure before them was all glass, redwood, and steel. It was illuminated from within with soft lighting that only went as far as the thick copse of trees surrounding the house. The roof appeared to be...moving?

"It's got a green roof even," Timothy breathed. "It's just like the Meta offices. I bet you can't even tell there's a home here from above." He parked between a Ferrari and a custom Tesla and shut off the engine. "I can't believe we're here."

"Timothy, just promise me one thing?"

"Anything, darling," he said, taking her hands in his. "I want you to be comfortable with this too."

With great wealth comes great opportunities.

"Let's not get in over our heads, you know what I mean? If they start asking for us to commit money or time...talk to me before you make any decisions? We've worked really hard to pay off the houses and cars. I want us to have something to show for the sacrifices we've made."

"Absolutely," he said, but she knew he'd probably forget the moment they were inside. "I want us to have all the things we've dreamed of. A long, happy, and healthy life together."

He pulled her forward and their lips met. He really was a sweet man. Hardworking, decent. Took good care of his body, and took excellent care of her in bed. They were a team, and if all they'd heard about Elite Ventures Enterprises was true, they were going to be a part of something important.

"Let's do this," she said, kissing him once more. He pulled back and growled a little before moving back in for a deeper kiss. She laughed as he slid a hand under her skirt.

"There will be time for that later," she purred. "All you want."

They left the car and climbed the steps up to the front door, which opened as they approached. Timothy took her hand and smiled at the tuxedoed man at the door.

"Mr. and Mrs. Timothy Hicks," the man said as he gestured with his hand. They stepped inside and the door closed behind them with a whoosh. Donna's heels clicked loudly on the concrete floor. The foyer was wide and empty save for a few sculptures and paintings. Two tall vases stood on either side of a vast entryway before them that was completely dark. Timothy hesitated and the man from the door called out, "Please, step inside."

Donna felt Timothy squeeze her hand, and then they stepped into the darkness, ready to take their lives to the next level. For a split second before her heel connected with the floor, she thought perhaps they were pushing their luck, that they'd already been so fortunate. Was joining the organization more than they deserved?

The darkness enveloped them, and with it, Donna felt hands on her arms and shoulders. Timothy's hand was pulled from hers and replaced with a stranger's. Bodies pressed against her and she tried to fight the panic. She whispered her husband's name but only heard muffled voices around her, attempting to sooth her, quiet her. Prepare her.

The light came on—and she gasped at what she saw.

It was too late to turn back now. She knew that, and yet she dug her heels in, afraid to move any closer. She'd lost sight of Timothy and was now on her own, and yet she wasn't alone. More bodies closed in on her, like people crowding a full elevator heading to the lobby at the end of a long workweek, everyone excited for the weekend.

And just like in an elevator, the floor began to lower.

"Welcome, guests." The voice that came over the loudspeaker reminded Donna of something out of a sci-fi movie. "The Source is grateful for your work and dedication. Please prepare to pay tribute, and then we shall begin your introduction."

Donna sucked in a breath and before she could exhale, the press of bodies came even closer. She felt like screaming, and then she was bathed in a warm light from above, until everything was...fine.

She sighed, letting her body go slack, and heard sounds of approval around her. Everything was glorious, everything was wonderful. She'd never felt better...

1

CHAPTER ONE

C reed

January

"Well, Mr. Lowell, I think we have everything we need. Your references all check out, and you passed your background check. Can you start on Friday?"

What a relief! I smiled and leaned against the wall of my dingy hotel room. *Thank goodness for excellent references.* I inhaled the combination mildew/chlorine smell caused by the permanent dampness from the ocean and the indoor swimming pool below my room. This was the break I needed, or my current accommodations would soon go from bad to worse.

"Thank you, yes. What time does the evening shift start?" I kept my fingers crossed while I waited for the answer.

"Six o'clock. Just come to the front desk and our evening supervisor will get you set up. Lexi's great. She'll show you the ropes."

"Wonderful. Thank you for this opportunity."

"We should be thanking *you*, Mr. Lowell. You're overqualified for the position, and we've had a difficult time keeping our evening staff. I hope this works out for the both of us."

I thanked Yvonne, the Human Resources director, once more before disconnecting. Then the victory dance commenced.

"Did you hear that, Rhonda? We're in!"

My red Doberman rested her jaw on her paws and made an old lady noise, indicating that she'd rather be napping than dancing.

I would not be thwarted, however. I danced a *West Side Story* routine across the room to the kitchenette and reached into the fridge with panache. There was one last bag of A-positive that I'd been sipping on since arriving in Santa Cruz, and now I could finish it off since I'd have a steady supply in just two days' time. Not that I needed much—especially not when I was working—but it was important to never let my energy stores deplete. It affected my judgement and my ability to do the work that was so desperately needed.

I did a spin and a box step before kicking my leg out, and throwing my arms back in a layout. Hopefully I'd find a patient who knew the old dances at Puesta Del Sol, my new place of employment. They were the most fun to work with.

I reached into my lone duffel bag, which contained seven sets of scrubs, a suit, three white t-shirts, a pair of jeans, a Harvard hoodie, two pairs of shoes, and a small photo album that contained cherished pictures of my parents and younger siblings. The rest of my belongings and resources were hidden in pre-paid storage facilities around the country for when I got desperate...or had to run.

My family was all gone now. My little sister was the last, and she'd passed away four months ago according to the hometown newspaper in Macon County, Georgia. I read every copy that I could get ahold of through the local libraries. The internet had been such a great invention. Even though I hadn't been home in nearly forty years, I'd managed to keep tabs on everyone. They'd all lived mostly happy, satisfying lives and died of natural causes at advanced ages, which was the best I could have hoped for.

But now that I had no worry of repercussions for my family, I could finally seek out the truth.

Puesta Del Sol was hopefully the end of the line. The last assisted-living home where I'd worked in Albuquerque had led me here, to Santa Cruz, California. "Go west, young man," turned out to be the advice I'd needed all along.

I was determined to find those responsible for sending me on this decades-long exile. It wouldn't be long now. It was time to set things straight, and it seemed fitting to be back near where it all started.

MARCH

TWO MONTHS LATER, the trail of promising leads had gone cold. Still, I loved my new life in California. I was surrounded by a competent and diverse staff at Puesta Del Sol that knew how to run a place of healing and hope with patients who were happy and well cared for. And I loved Santa Cruz. It was almost enough to make me consider letting go of the past.

What a great place for a guy like me. It was easy to fit into the college town that was also a magnet for transients, tourists, and folks who were followers of alternative lifestyles. Not only were there prac-titioners of Eastern religions and schools of thought, but also those who claimed to be creatures of the night, a holdover from the vampire craze that swept the area after a hit movie in the '80s made them cool. I occasionally even found folks who didn't mind a little role play.

My love of music meant I was a frequent guest of The Catalyst, a large music venue, bar, and eatery located downtown that drew fans from all over the Bay Area. One night they'd feature punk, the next rap, and sometimes even classic rock bands made their way to the club.

Tonight was a perfect opportunity to blend in as a lineup of alternative bands from the eighties was playing. I'd worn my black suit, skinny tie, and black Dr. Martens. I'd even slicked my dark auburn hair back and donned black eyeliner for the hell of it, the makeup highlighting my eyes, an unusually bright amber shade that often made people stop and stare. Of course, the rest of the package could also be to blame for that. My pale, freckled skin fit the role of a night walker perfectly to round out the look.

I made my way through the crowd to the bar and ordered a beer. A willing playmate soon appeared, and the game was on.

The young man, dressed in a velvet waistcoat and ruffled poet's shirt, saw me approach the bar and immediately perked up. I took a swig of my beer and nodded at the Goth. When I moved away from the bar, I felt him at my back as I headed to a dark corner. Once there, I leaned against the wall and waited.

The young man approached with a sly smile, and I took it as an invitation. I reached for his shoulder, turned him around slowly, and pulled him back against my chest, enjoying the way his body fit against mine.

"I have your permission?" I whispered in the young man's ear. "I promise you'll enjoy it."

The young man turned to face me and his eyes widened in surprise. "Here?"

I smiled at him and ran a finger down his neck, enjoying the way he shivered. The energy from his excitement would have been enough to nourish me, but I was feeling greedy tonight.

"Yeah, just um, be safe about it."

I bathed him in a wave of calm. The manipulation of energy was effortless for me now. "You're in good hands, my friend." I turned him around and stopped him when he went to loosen his belt. "Relax, I've got you."

I slid his long, curly blond hair to the side. I had ways of making the experience pleasurable, so I poured energy into giving this guy one helluva good time, one he'd remember for years to come. He just wouldn't remember that a man sank his teeth gently into his neck and took sustenance from his body.

Give unto them what they require.

Take only what you need to survive.

I would never forget what I'd been taught.

"Blessed be."

After a few sips, I felt my playmate shudder against me and let out a satisfied moan. A few more pulls and his body tensed, gasped, and shuddered once more. It was nice to know I hadn't lost my touch.

It had been a long time since I'd chanced feeding in public, but I felt safe here. Santa Cruz had welcomed me with open arms, and I wanted to stay.

The young man raised his arm and cupped the back of my head. He pressed his ass back against me, and I knew it was time to end this tryst.

"Thank you," I whispered against his ear, and then pressed a kiss to his neck.

"I should be thanking *you*," the guy said. "What's your name?"

I disappeared into the crowd before the young man turned to look, and I was out of the club before he could wonder what happened.

I rarely drank blood—it was an infrequent need to maintain my existence as long as I had plenty of human energy to manipulate—and I always made sure my partner enjoyed it. But the act often left me feeling...empty. I worked hard to help others live a more satisfied life, and after all this time, I sometimes resented that I couldn't pursue happiness of my own. I would have loved to take that young man home and enjoy more than just an Exchange. Someday I would find...someone. But not until it was safe. Not until I'd done what I came here to do.

2

CHAPTER TWO

R oman

MOST PEOPLE WOULD BE unnerved being picked up from the airport by a patrol car, but I was used to it. I'd spent much of my teenagehood in the back of patrol cars driven by my aunt Vanessa or my uncle Reynaldo. They were both cops in Santa Cruz, and therefore there'd always been eyes on me. It was Reynaldo's turn to pick me up, and apparently to play bad cop.

"I have news you're going to hate, but I want you to listen to me before you lose your shit, okay?"

Here we go. "Thank you for treating me like teenaged Roman and not giving me the chance to respond like the mature adult that I am."

Rey snorted. "Yeah, right. At twenty-five you're a mature adult. Got it."

"Come on, man. Give me a break. I've been on a plane for twenty-three hours. I'm funky, I'm tired, and I just want to go home. Not get the Tito Reynaldo treatment."

Rey didn't laugh, and that made me nervous.

"It's Lola Frances."

I hadn't spoken with my grandmother for a couple of weeks. The village where I'd stayed in Spain for the summer had shitty Wi-Fi and terrible cellular coverage, but I'd texted my aunts and uncle as often as possible and traveled into a bigger town to call home once a week. Lola knew I was coming home today. Tonight. What the hell time was it?

"What's going on?" I took off my jacket and ran my hands through my too-long black hair. I shoved the jacket in my backpack and slumped in my seat. Reynaldo was uncharacteristically quiet. "What is it?"

Rey signaled and then merged onto Highway 17 from the San Jose airport. His gaze darted around and the crease in his forehead deepened. I was ready to tell him to spit it out when he exhaled and finally began to speak. I'd aged ten years in the time it took him to start talking.

"Vanessa and I moved Lola Frances to the assisted living center where Stella and Phyllis live. Puesta Del Sol." He glanced at me as though he hadn't just hit the ejector seat and sent me flying sickly through the air. "She had a rough summer, and she wanted to be there with her sisters. A spot opened up two days ago and we moved her in yesterday."

"A rough summer." I ground my teeth together and counted back from ten. I would not lose my shit and let him win. "And no one thought to tell me this?"

"It only happened two days ago."

"But you had it planned, you'd been researching places. This isn't like an impromptu trip to the beach or the craft store."

"Here we go," Rey muttered.

And I bit.

"Who made the decision, really? You guys couldn't have called me when things got bad? I would have come home. She's my grand-mother, Rey. Don't you think I should have been involved? And don't even *think* of calling me a kid right now, because cop or no cop, I will kick your mother—"

"Time out." He held up a hand, and I wanted to break his damn fingers. *How dare they?*

I took a moment to let the anger bleed out so I could listen to what he had to say.

"I'm done. Tell me."

Rey nodded, checked his mirrors, and then pulled into the left lane. We'd entered the two-lane section of the mountain pass, which was harrowing at any time of day. This late at night it was mostly empty but that was a false sense of security. A wasted driver could come along at any minute, or in the winter you could run headlong into a mudslide, or in the summer a traffic backup from folks headed to the beach. It was a treacherous, winding road, and I would do well to remember that Reynaldo was always careful and therefore he needed to concentrate more than he needed to placate me.

"About two weeks after you left it was my night to stay with her, and when I got home, the fire was left on the stove. Lola was outside standing in the garden in the mud, freezing cold in the rain, looking for her cat that died twenty years ago."

That was a gut-punch. She'd had a lot of forgetful moments before I'd left, but they hadn't been life-threatening. I'd foolishly thought it was just the subtle beginning of a drawn-out process and that I'd be back in time to be there for her when she needed me.

"I shouldn't have taken that internship."

"Roman, you had to go. It was a great opportunity. We all thought we had it under control. But even with the two of us splitting the weeks and staying with her, it wasn't enough, and she wouldn't have anyone else come stay. She refused."

"You could have told me. I would have come home. I can with-draw from the Ph.D. program and resign my position this year—"

"No way. You have to finish your dissertation. *No way.* Plus, she wouldn't have it anyway."

"I'll talk to her. I'll make her listen."

"She *wanted* this. It was her idea. We confronted her, and she said she wanted to be with her sisters. And since when did she ever change her mind based on anything we want when it comes to her? When Tito Armand died, we tried to get her to sell the house and move in with us, and she refused. When your parents died, we tried to take you in because she was going through a tough time, and she refused, said you belonged with your lola. You're her baby, and she's not going to let you do anything that puts your future in jeopardy."

I crossed my arms and wanted to throw a bunch of angry statements his way, but he was right. There's no way Lola was going to let me defer. She fought tooth and nail to convince me we would be able to afford for me to go to college as far as I could, and for me to take advantage of all the educational opportunities my program offered. Every time I said no, she said, "yes you will!"

"She knew I was coming home today. I have to see her."

"I'll take you by there."

"Where is it?"

"It's on the hill near the Boardwalk. You know that really big Victorian-style house?"

"I know it." I hated it. I hated this whole idea. "Isn't she miserable not being in her house?"

Reynaldo laughed for the first time since he'd picked me up. "You can see for yourself. We'll be there shortly. In the meantime, how was Spain? You fluent in Spanish yet?"

I clucked my tongue. "I was fluent before I left, asshole. Learned some Euskara while I was there." Also got too close to a Basque musician, but Reynaldo would give me shit about it if he knew. Basajuan was a blond bombshell and a helluva good dancer, but a Filipino-American grad student was just a dalliance for him. I'd almost been ready to say screw my degree and stay, but he'd cut out before I had the chance to be young and foolish. He'd done me a favor for sure.

"Heard you had a boyfriend. What's up with that?"

"Shit. Don't you and my tita have anything else to do other than gossip about me?"

He shrugged. "Our lives are boring. Vanessa's married to Bernadette and they're settled down being moms, and my last boyfriend was more interested in DJing parties and getting high then hanging out at home with me." Reynaldo growled and thankfully unleashed his tale of woe on me so I could smile, laugh a few times, and pretend to listen.

Lola was gone, moved a few miles away, and soon would be beyond reach. School or no school, I was going to spend as much time as possible with her. I didn't want her to feel alone.

Twenty-minutes later, Reynaldo pulled up in front of Puesta Del Sol.

"I used to ride my skateboard on this street. Crashed in front of this place plenty of times."

"It's a beautiful place, very well maintained. She's got a private room on the same hall as Stella and Phyllis. There's TV, Wi-Fi, activities daily, exercise classes... She'll get assistance in the morning and evening with self-care and medication. Meals can be taken in her room or with the other residents. And for night owls like her, the evening staff keeps them thoroughly entertained."

"Sounds like a resort."

"It might as well be. You'll like it. I wasn't sold at all until we came here to visit her sisters. Their bingo is a class act, which is of the utmost importance."

"I heard that," I said. We both climbed out of the patrol car and made our way up the ramp to the front entrance.

Rey and Vanessa were Lolo's brother Emmanuel's kids, but they'd spent a lot of their childhood with Lola Frances. Her house became home to the three of us at one point or another.

"Her insurance pays for part of it and she has a supplemental plan that covers a bit more. We're looking into a reverse mortgage on the house to pay the rest when the time comes, but her savings will last for quite a while."

"The house? But you can't—"

"Don't worry, Junior. We won't leave you homeless—"

This time I punched him in the shoulder. "That's not what I meant, asshole." I pulled my hand back and didn't miss his raised eyebrow admonishment.

"I'm in uniform, twerp. Don't pull that shit with me."

"I'm sorry. I only meant that we can't sell her house. It means everything to her."

Reynaldo put a hand on my back and pushed the door open. "Don't worry about it. I was only telling you so you wouldn't worry about it."

"Well, I am worried," I muttered as we stepped inside.

"Ah, good evening, Officer Cabral."

The nurse at the counter was full of smiles for Reynaldo. He had that effect on people. He was a damn handsome guy and the uniform really did it for men *and* women.

"Lexi, good to see you. This is my nephew Roman. Frances is his grandmother."

She laughed and shook her head. "Are you as much trouble as her?" She might have been flirting, but I was ready to drop. I wanted to see Lola and then go home, shower, and go to bed.

"He's jetlagged, so you won't get any trouble from him."

She smiled and gave me the sympathetic head tilt. "Okay, you can go on back and see her if you'd like."

Reynaldo tipped his ear toward the radio clipped to his shoulder and then walked away, holding up a finger to us.

"Oh, um, I can take you back," Lexi said.

I followed her down the hall and heard laughing that sounded familiar.

"Yeah, she and her sisters are really happy here, Mr. San Angelo. I wouldn't say it if it wasn't true." She paused outside the door and leaned close to me. "We had to bring my grandmother here for the last three years of her life, and she loved this place."

"I'm sorry for your loss." I looked down at my rumpled self and wished I'd had time to clean up for Lola.

Time to suck it up, Junior.

I thanked Lexi and went inside to find Phyllis, Stella, and Lola sitting together in Lola's bed, watching the TV.

"Frances, you have a visitor."

"Can't you tell them to come back later? I'm watching *Magnum P.I.*"

"Lola, it's me."

She glanced at me and grinned really big, and then she waved me over, shushing me as I came closer. "He's no Tom Selleck, but this guy is pretty good. Give me a kiss," she said, sticking her cheek out.

"Nice to see you, too, Lola. I only traveled for twenty-three hours to be shushed."

"Shhh," she said, grabbing for my hand. "We're about to find out which one is the killer."

"I still think it's the other one," Stella said.

"Hello, titas," I said, getting the same shushing treatment. But they waved and smiled. I knew better than to interrupt their shows, even if I'd just returned from my longest trip ever away from home.

"It's probably the quiet one," I said, just as the big reveal happened. All three ladies shouted at me in Tagalog and then climbed off the bed, grumbling. I got kisses from Stella and Phyllis as they left.

"Remember we have our Pilates class at eight tomorrow," Stella said as she walked out the door.

"I'll be there," Frances said. And then she turned her full attention on me. "Come sit down, Roman. It's so good to see you."

"Lola...why?" I sat down next to her and took her hands. "I would have come home to be with you."

She waved me off before I could get any more words out. "Nonsense, you had an important job to do over there, learning about serial killers."

"Cult leaders, Lola. And nothing is more important than you," I told her, and I meant every word. If she hadn't taken me in when my parents died, I don't know what would have happened. My aunt and uncle weren't in any position to raise a rowdy teenager like me. I probably would have ended up in jail. Or worse.

"It's so fun here," she said. "The staff is wonderful, the food is okay, not great, but they have so many activities. I am busy all the time and I am with my sisters. It's been hard without them."

It's been hard for her since you were gone and couldn't give her rides. She was alone at home. After all she's done for you, you should have stayed.

"Lola, I can take care of you—"

"You can take care of yourself, now, and that's what matters. It's nice here. They have people who know how to clean a room."

I barked out a laugh. Her smirk let me know she was ready to change the subject.

"I learned from the best," I said, hugging her once more.

"You learned nothing. I've never seen such sad hospital corners."

It's good to be home. "What can I say? I was meant for academia, not hospitality."

"You were meant to be pampered, my sweet boy. What happened to that boyfriend you met? Where is he?"

I sighed. "San Sebastián. Where he lives."

She shook her head. "His loss. Now, I have to go to bed. We have Pilates in the morning," she said as she led me to the door, where Rey was lurking.

"Hello, Tita." Reynaldo gave her a kiss on her cheek and she patted his shoulder.

"You better be careful out there and make sure Roman gets enough to eat. He's too skinny."

"I got it, don't worry. I'll get him settled in and grab some groceries."

"And I'll see you both tomorrow night for bingo."

"Yes, ma'am," Reynaldo said.

"And bring me my picture albums when you come back."

"I told you, Tita, you don't have room for all twenty of your albums. Bernadette is scanning them and they'll all be on your computer."

"As long as I have them all. I want to have my family with me."

Her smile faded, and I wanted to throw her over my shoulder and make a clean getaway.

She wanted her pictures so she didn't forget. We'd talked about them before I left. I'd tried to put them in one of the spare rooms and she shouted at me and cried. I'd made my grandmother cry, and I'd felt like the lowest of low. Kinda how I felt now, leaving her behind in an unfamiliar place.

"I love you," I whispered to her as I hugged her once more.

"You're a good boy. I'm glad you're home. Now go take a shower, you smell bad and your hair is too long."

Yeah, it was good to be home. Even if it hurt like hell to see my lola in assisted living.

"The place is really nice," Reynaldo was saying as we walked out to the car. "Phyllis and Stella keep her busy. She'll get back her sass."

"I feel for the staff with those three."

"They definitely have their hands full."

I followed him down the steps to the patrol car and we climbed inside.

"I'll get you home and then I'll come back over tomorrow. I'll have to jump your car, the battery's probably dead."

"Oh, thank you. I guess I thought Lola would be driving." My throat was sore and my skin hurt. I really wanted to get home before I ended up crying in front of my uncle.

"She had a near-miss after you left, and so she decided on her own that she wouldn't drive anymore."

I blew out a shaky breath as my chin quivered. No, I would not cry.

"Anyway, you need to come over soon. Vanessa and Bernadette miss you, and Emmanuel Jr. is driving us all crazy."

Reynaldo lived with his sister and her wife, and also kept a room at Lola's. He said it was to save money to buy a house, but really he liked the attention and not having to cook. Vanessa and Bernadette had been really good to me and were the main forces pushing me to go to school.

"Yeah, I wonder why. He's eighteen. That's his job."

"He's looking forward to having you back. I think he misses playing video games with you."

"Right. Yeah, sure."

It was good to have family, but with Lola gone, I'd be alone for the first time in my life. I didn't like the idea. Not that I was a big people person or a talker, but just knowing Lola would always be there with a hot meal and a funny story made it easier to deal with the stress of school instead of doing something self-destructive like so many other guys I'd grown up with.

"Shit. What the hell is this?"

Reynaldo pulled the car over downtown, just a few blocks from the house. Two other police cars were there and a small crowd of people.

A young woman sat wrapped in a blanket at the rear of a fire truck, trembling, black mascara running down her face.

"I'm going to see if they need anything," Reynaldo said.

"I'm coming with you," I said.

"You know the rules," he said as we both climbed out of the car.

I'd done ridealongs with my aunt and uncle since I was eighteen. I knew to stay back and observe. I also knew not to tell anyone that he'd taught me how to disengage his shotgun in the patrol car, and that he'd told me to use it if he ever got in a jam and needed me to. I enjoyed a lot about police work, but I was more interested in *why* people did the things they did, which is what led me to my degree path in psychology and criminal justice. I dreamed of a job at Quantico someday, but I wanted to keep my options open.

"They just kept...scaring me. They laughed the harder I cried. They wouldn't let me go. I tried to get away, I screamed, but they had me cornered next to the building and surrounded and...I've never been so scared in my life."

The victim pulled the blanket tighter around her as Reynaldo and I approached Officer Megan Fuentes, a female cop I recognized from a previous ridealong. We hung back while Megan spoke to the victim in hushed tones. I subtly glanced around at the onlookers.

Why *here*? Why *her*? The woman was wearing a business suit with a skirt and tennis shoes, and said she was walking from the bus to her home after picking up dinner from a restaurant downtown. She was still in a fairly crowded area, meaning there were witnesses.

When she was finished, Rey spoke to Megan while I looked around the area. I'd learned what to look for in a crowd after a crime had been committed, that perpetrators often hung around to see their handiwork. There weren't many folks around at this point.

Rey joined me a few minutes later.

"Megan's already interviewed two of them who said the same thing the victim did," he said. "So weird."

"What did they say?"

"Guy over there said it was like something out of a movie. They pushed her back and forth between them and crowded her against the wall, just laughing. And staring. Until one of them bit her on the neck where it met her shoulder."

"Like some sort of fucking vampire?"

"Guess so. Damn. I've seen a lot of weird shit as a police officer. Disturbing shit. Disgusting shit. Hilarious shit. It's the weird shit I can't stand."

"You mean because weird shit has no rhyme or reason?"

"It's harder to solve. Someone attacks a person they love out of anger? Simple. A person robs a bank? Cut and dry. Two persons fight and one is killed? Sad but predictable. But four grown men, well-dressed, who corner a woman against a building and taunt her like high school bullies? Who could even make up this shit?"

"The group I was researching in Bilbao had a whole mythology around blood. It was intense. And there are definitely blood drinkers out there who do it because they think it has medicinal benefits, and they have rituals around the ingestion of another person's blood, but this situation doesn't seem like your average vampirism."

"Yeah? *Average vampirism*, huh? Well, once you've caught your breath, you can tell me all about it. This ain't the weirdest thing I've ever seen, but it's pretty fucking weird, and this isn't the first incident."

"No? Now I'm intrigued."

I'd returned to UC Santa Cruz to complete my dissertation and doctorate degree on modern cult behavior and crime. It seemed oddly coincidental that the moment I returned home; my two worlds intersected.

Rey got me home after midnight and thankfully I was too tired to do anything more than strip, shower, and crash. There would be plenty of time to mourn in the morning.

3

———————

CHAPTER THREE

C reed

"HELP ME, RHONDA!"

Normally I loved singing along with the Beach Boys, but today I growled my favorite lyrics to my beloved dog.

"Where the hell are they?"

I came to Santa Cruz after getting a tip that my enemies were here and then...nothing. Nothing out of the ordinary. Until a strange news article caught my attention.

A woman was bitten on the neck on a busy street. In front of witnesses. Strange...and possibly not related to the people I was looking for, but something I needed to keep an eye on. It could have been kids being dumb. Or it could be the break I needed.

I spent all of my time off from the nursing home scouring the internet and the local library files for something...anything. I'd been away for so long, I had no idea how to find who I was looking for anymore. I searched for certain words or phrases that the group I studied with— my cohort—used, or names, but then they could have easily changed them in the last fifty years. I needed to find the people responsible for the destruction of my way of life and the death of my mentor.

How that would happen, well...perhaps it would be some strange news story that was the key, so I continued to look.

I finished my afternoon smoothie while looking through some of the financial magazines I'd picked up at The Bookshop and was doing some more research on local spiritual groups. I'd come here after hearing about some folks who were living together and practicing the healing arts, and I thought maybe I'd found them. Instead, they'd turned out to be a Wiccan coven. There were more, I was sure, but they weren't out in the open, these groups.

It wasn't like the group I was looking for would be posting on the internet and inviting folks. No, they'd gone underground fifty years ago and it was highly unlikely that they were practicing out in the open. If they were still practicing at all. They could have ditched The Way after the mutiny; I had no way of knowing.

I was about to toss all of the papers out the window when Rhonda gave a deep woof.

My beloved dog waited by the door, her floppy ears perked with interest and her expression scolding me for letting my frustration get to me. She'd been my companion so long, she knew just what I needed.

"You're right. I could use some fresh air."

She turned her gaze toward her leash on the table and sighed heavily as though she were put out by my slow response time.

"Yeah, yeah. I'm coming."

I hooked the leash on her collar and she waited for me to open the door before she stepped gracefully outside. She climbed the concrete steps that led from the door of my basement apartment to our quiet street, pausing to glance around before stepping onto the sidewalk.

The sky was filled with popcorn clouds and the hazy orange glow of sunset. We walked the couple of blocks to Lighthouse Point and I breathed in the ocean air. For so long I'd wandered the interior of the country, looking for signs that those I pursued had passed through, and I'd felt stifled. Coming to Santa Cruz was like arriving in paradise. I didn't want to think it was temporary.

I watched the surfers finishing up their evening sessions, and Rhonda and I attracted attention as we walked by. She made heads turn, for sure, and then when people spotted me, they'd have a secret smile. I'd been told for years that I had a "youthful aura and naturally handsome features." I didn't necessarily disagree; it allowed me to attract folks when I needed to.

I didn't require an Exchange at the moment, but I frequently toyed with the idea. It would be so easy to succumb to temptation, but the skills and traits that I'd learned from The Source were meant for a higher purpose. Celibacy wasn't required, but I'd spent a long time living like a monk to protect myself and remain strong enough to provide for those who needed my gift. *Look but don't touch...*I needed that reminder.

However, an opportunity to glean a little positive energy presented itself as we walked down the hill towards the pier and the beach at the Boardwalk.

Nestled inside a sleeping bag, a couple giggled and fumbled in the increasing darkness. I always tried to be discreet, but I was drawn in by the energy their bodies produced like a junkie looking for my next fix. It wasn't one of my proudest life hacks. The excessive amounts of dopamine and adrenaline released during sex gave me a high that would carry me for days. I wouldn't need an Exchange to keep up my strength for some time.

I lingered for just a short time before moving on. Rhonda and I strolled along the water's edge, and I was totally lost in thought. Rhonda pulled as far as she could to the left, staying out of the water and sneering at the waves as they came close to her. Several groups gathered, wrapped in blankets to ward off the chill. Joints were passed, songs were sung, and I enjoyed the vibe.

Then I stopped short as we neared the southern end of the beach.

I'd seen this group of spiritualists before, and at first I'd thought I'd found what I was looking for. They dressed in white linen and prayed together, combining yoga and meditation in their practice. I'd even been approached by the group, and I'd unintentionally drifted near enough this time to be noticed.

"Would you like to join us?"

I pulled Rhonda a little closer, as she was on high alert. She wasn't too fond of people getting close to her master.

"Thanks, I'm good. You have a pleasant evening."

The man grinned. "I've seen you around. You're welcome to watch, if that feels more comfortable to you. Namaste."

The man pressed his hands together and bowed. I nodded back and tugged Rhonda over to some rocks that butted up against the base of the Boardwalk, where we sat down. I watched the waves come in and out and tried to focus my breathing, anything to slow my mind down.

Memories washed over me like the incoming tide.

1970

"Come on, Creed. It'll be great. I talked to the guy this morning. I'm ready to get out of this hell."

My best friend Muse and I had worn out our welcome at the flophouse in the Haight. It was time to move on, anyway. More people were overdosing on heroin than fighting for peace, love, and happiness, and I couldn't take the heartache. I'd watched several of my fellow runaways go that way over the past year, and I'd sworn I wouldn't be next. Me and Muse were the only two who'd stayed away from the hard stuff, but Muse had been spending time with a dealer who was known for using his girls for profit, and I didn't want to see that happen to her at sixteen years old. I wanted to protect her.

"There's a van leaving for the compound soon. I guess it's up in the hills about fifty miles south of here. I talked to the guy and he said we could both come as long as we were open-minded, willing to work, and discreet. It sounds really cool, man. They play music and study spiritualism."

I was uneasy hearing her plan. I'd had my share of religion as a child. My mother was Baptist, my father Catholic, their own parents refused to sanction their marriage, and then the two of them fought over which faith they would teach their children.

I saw the hypocrisy of both, but learned enough to use it as a weapon. When it came time to register for the draft in 1968, I knew exactly what to say to receive a Conscientious Objector status. Once I was clear, I hit the road and never looked back. Well, never wasn't exactly true. I looked back on my decisions plenty.

"I don't know how I feel about this," I said to Muse. "I've done my time with religious oppression."

Muse tugged on my shirt. "It's not like that, man. They teach a higher level of consciousness through meditation. Cross said they'll teach us about healing people and stuff. Come on, it'll be great."

I could still see her smiling face urging me to join her. The decision to board the van changed both of our lives irrevocably. I wished she were here with me right now.

Instead, I was hunting those who were responsible for all we'd lost.

THE SKY HAD GROWN dark while I was caught in a loop of memories and the spiritualists were wrapping up their evening prayers. The man who spoke to me waved and trotted over.

"Here," he said, handing me a business card. "If you ever want to visit. Our temple isn't too far from here."

I looked at the card. *Fellowship of the Setting Sun.* The pain in my chest was nearly overwhelming. The name was similar, but these folks were innocent. They weren't following The Way.

"Thank you," I said quietly. I wanted to tell this young man my story, wanted to tell him everything, wanted to tell him to be careful. "I'll keep you in mind."

The young man looked me up and down with a shy smile. I was tempted to push for more, but I had things to do, and getting involved with someone wasn't one of those things.

First on my list was learning more about the bizarre attacks taking place in my town. If some kids wanted to pretend to be vampires, I'd certainly show them how it was really done, and they'd live to regret their foolish activities.

Then, I needed to press on in my quest of finding the usurpers. I vowed I would find them. And make them pay.

4

CHAPTER FOUR

R oman

COMING BACK to UC Santa Cruz as a doctoral candidate was surreal. It was sort of like going back to visit your elementary school when you were in high school and everything seems so small. I'd gone directly from my undergrad into the master's program, then into the Ph.D. program and then spent the past several months in Spain, so even though it had only been a few months since I'd stepped foot on campus, everything felt different.

Muscle memory led me to the Psychology department and the desk of Maria Ferelli, the secretary to the department chair.

"Roman San Angelo, it's wonderful to see you," she said in her thick Italian accent. She stood and came around the desk to give me a hug. "I always knew that you would make it."

"I'm glad one of us had faith," I said with a laugh, appreciating the hug on this morning where I felt like I was on a tilted stage. It took all of my concentration to stand up straight and pretend like I had my shit together.

"Oh, you were a pesky thing as an undergrad, but I knew once you set your mind to becoming a professor one day that you would make it."

It was true. I'd get so frustrated with my professors, always fighting with the old white men who thought they knew everything, and I'd often vent to Mrs. Ferelli. I had no one else. No one in my family had gone past a bachelor's degree—Vanessa earned her undergrad degree after she'd had Emmanuel. Whenever I tried to talk to Reynaldo, he vacillated between giving me shit and being a little put out that his nephew was more educated than him, even though he had just as much intelligence.

"If it weren't for you, I might not have, so thank you."

She pinched my cheek, which set us back a few steps in our conversation, but that was fine with me. I'd allow it. She walked me to my office and introduced me to the other graduate student, Marvin Liu, who would be sharing space with me. We went over the schedule, my responsibilities, and I was given a manual to read and memorize. It was official. I was a university professor. A doctoral candidate. All but dissertation. Then, who knew? Maybe I would go the teaching route. I had a lot to do before that was finished.

I left the school in a bit of a daze, and I was dreading going home to a house without Lola, so I turned around and drove to Vanessa's. Her car was gone, but the porch light was on and the garage door was closed, so I figured Bernadette was probably home.

"B? You home?"

I let myself in the front door and immediately kicked over a pile of Emmanuel's shoes.

"That you, Roman? Watch out for the shoes."

"Too late for that," I muttered.

"Come taste this," she said as I rounded the corner to the kitchen. Bernadette stood at the stove with a spoon of bulalo in her hand.

I leaned down and inhaled, instantly salivating at the scent of one of my favorite dishes Lola used to make for family dinners.

"I'm trying to get Frances's recipe right. Vanessa and I want to take her food that she misses, but I'm a poor substitute for her cooking."

I smiled at my tita's wife. "It's good. Real good."

She sighed. "Good. I've been working on it all afternoon. Last time I made it, Emmanuel said it tasted like dishwater, the little shit."

"He can't help it, he's eighteen."

I grabbed a bowl and spoon and turned to ask her permission, but she gestured for me to hand it over and she gave me a heaping bowlful. I sat at the table with her and finally got to tell someone about my trip to Spain.

"I'm so excited you were able to go, Roman. What an amazing experience. I hope Emmanuel will get to travel. I've got to get him through his first year of college, though. He might not survive it. *We* might not survive it."

"Survive what?" Emmanuel came sauntering in wearing sweaty workout clothes and carrying a water bottle.

"Your stench. Go shower before you eat," Bernadette said, swatting his hand away from the ladle on the stove as he attempted to eat right out of the pot.

"Is it right this time?"

"You'll find out after you shower—"

"Unless I eat it all," I said with a grin.

Emmanuel shook his head but he gave me a pleased grin. "Good to have you back, Roman." He walked through the doorway to the hall and hopefully the shower beyond. "I missed kicking your ass at Madden."

"Anytime," I said as I heard the door close to the bathroom.

Bernadette sighed and poked at her food.

"What's wrong?" I asked her.

She shrugged. "Nothing. I just worry. He's just been moody. College is harder than he thought it would be and it's been a fight. I hope you can encourage him, you know? Let him know it doesn't suck forever."

I laughed. "Who says it doesn't?"

She frowned at me and pulled my bowl away.

"I'm kidding, I'm kidding. Please, this is the first real meal I've had since I got home." She shook her head and laughed as I shoveled in a few more bites. "Honestly, the early parts of general ed do suck just because it feels like a continuation of the shit you hated in high school, but once he gets to the subjects he likes, and once he chooses a major, it will be better. I swear. And I'll talk to him."

She nodded. "I wish he was at UC with you. Then you could at least keep an eye on him."

"He's going to be fine. You don't remember how much of a mess I was."

Her focus narrowed on me and I quickly realized my error.

"Was? I heard from Rey you were pretty upset about Frances. I'm sorry, Roman. We really tried—"

I held up a hand. "I know you did. It's just weird, you know?"

She gave me that side-tilt-pity-smile thing and I was torn between crying on her shoulder or throwing another tantrum. Instead, I cleared the table and started washing the dishes. "I'm okay. I'll get used to it. Besides, I gotta grow up sometime, right?"

My smile wasn't fooling her, but she patted me on the shoulder.

"Don't worry. I promised I wouldn't let you starve. Come by anytime. Guess I'm going to be a domestic goddess after all."

"You weren't already?"

She flicked me with a towel and then we spent the next hour talking shit about Rey and his messy life. It was nice. Almost nice enough to fill that hole in my heart that wondered what the hell I was going to do without my lola at home.

5

CHAPTER FIVE

C reed

"WE GOT a new gal in twenty-six while you were off. Frances Josephine San Angelo. Age seventy-two, diabetic, mild COPD, mild dementia. Sisters are Stella De Leon and Phyllis Jackson. I was here to check her in and she's hysterically funny."

I pulled up my new patient's chart and read through the notes.

"Says her emergency contacts are her nephew Reynaldo Cabral, niece Vanessa Cabral, and her grandson Roman San Angelo." I frowned. "Occupation for Reynaldo...police officer. Interesting." *Interesting, indeed.* An officer of the law could be dangerous. I'd have to proceed with caution. I planned on staying here for several more years, if all went according to plan.

"Yes, and Roman is a grad student up the hill. He's *cute*," Lexi said with feeling. She placed a hand in the middle of my back as she passed by. "It will be nice to have a cop around. Maybe we'll stop having so many break-ins in the area."

I turned to face her. "Break-ins?"

"Yeah, they got Jamal's truck two days ago, and Lisa's car last week. The police said it was probably a displaced person, but I don't know. They haven't been staying around here lately."

"Well, maybe we can talk to management about security. I know we have Old Moe and a few cameras. We can have him look at the footage. I'd hate to see anyone get hurt." And I was very curious to see who was poking around.

Lexi made a face. "I really hope they catch who's doing it." She wrapped her arms around herself and shivered. I pulled her into a hug.

"Don't worry. I won't let anything happen to you. I'll walk you to your car after your shift, okay?"

Lexi nodded and covered her mouth as she yawned.

"Looks like someone needs some more coffee." I tugged on the end of her long braid.

"You're probably right. I'm going to grab some." Her gaze was inviting. "You want anything?"

I smiled at her. *Nothing from you, dear.* "I'm fine. I think I'm going to go meet Frances."

Lexi gave me a finger wave. "Say hello to Officer Cabral for me," she said with a wink before turning and walking down the hall.

Lexi and I had become close, and she frequently hinted she was interested in more than friendship, but she wasn't quite the flavor I preferred. It wasn't just a sexual thing. I preferred the taste of men. In and out of bed. Their blood had a different kick to it. Hard to describe. Not that I was partaking of anyone lately, nor did I need that in my life after all these years...

Which sounded pathetic, even to me.

I used my key card to log out of the patient information system and went down the hall toward my new patient's room. I heard laughter as I approached the open door.

"Roman, you need your rest, you're getting grumpy. Go get some sleep. You have to teach tomorrow."

"Not until the afternoon. Now, do you have everything? Can I bring you anything when I come back?"

I turned the corner—and stopped in my tracks.

A flustered young man stood with his back to the door, reeking of stress and...pain.

"I hear we have a new neighbor?" I said as I leaned in the doorway with a smile. "May I come in, Mrs. San Angelo?"

The man turned, and I noticed the UC Santa Cruz logo on the front of his shirt. Stretched across a well-sculpted chest, no less. Roman, I presumed. He was a tad shorter than me, and while I may have outweighed him by twenty or so pounds, he definitely had an athletic physique. With toned arms like his, and smooth, tanned forearms lined with thick veins, I imagined he was into weightlifting. How nice.

I gave him a polite nod and somehow managed to pry my gaze away and turn my full attention to the lovely lady before me.

"Yes, come in, please," she gestured with her hands. "I remember you from bingo nights with my sisters. How do you do?"

"Very well, thank you. Welcome to Puesta Del Sol. I apologize for not being here to greet you when you moved in, but they make me take nights off sometimes, can you believe it?"

Frances gave a girlish chuckle. "You kids all work so hard. In fact, can you tell my grandson I am *fine*? That he should go home?"

Frances was sitting in the wingback chair at the foot of her bed. The room, which was minimally furnished, looked lived-in already. There were framed pictures on the walls, a handmade quilt on the bed that was littered with pillows—which weren't regulation but I'd let them slide.

"Your grandson probably wouldn't take orders from a lowly night nurse like myself. You, on the other hand...are you going to give me trouble?"

Frances batted her eyes as I approached and took her hand. I bent and kissed the back of it like the southern gentleman I was. Or had been.

Her grandson scoffed. "Probably she *will* be trouble. Especially when she gets together with her pack."

I winked at Frances and then turned to shake hands with—

"Roman."

I would remember the moment our skin brushed for the rest of my existence.

Soft skin with the hint of calluses, strong, thick fingers. The scent of the ocean breeze clinging to him. And the pain that emanated from his soul flooded me.

"Creed Lowell." My voice cracked when I spoke. "Pleasure."

Roman pulled his hand back faster than was socially acceptable, unless you were trying to let the person know you found them displeasing. His heavy brows lowered and he cleared his throat. I sometimes had that effect on people. A little too probing...a bit much.

"Roman, give him your phone number. You never know, he might need to get in touch with you." Frances folded her hands demurely over her knee and pointed her toe.

I fought to keep my smile appropriate and not too smug. Good to know Mrs. San Angelo was into playing matchmaker. If I *were* looking for a match, Roman would certainly fit the bill.

Roman rolled his eyes. "Lola, I'll be back tomorrow. You can stay out of trouble until then, right?"

Frances shrugged. "It depends on how good the food is tomorrow."

I barked out a laugh. "I'm in tight with the person who oversees the menu choices, and I can be bought." I winked at her, and then I got down to business. "My assistant on this floor is Lexi, she was here when you moved in, I believe? She'll be in shortly to check your blood sugar and go over our procedures with you. I know you've had a long day, so we'll be going over a lot of things with you daily for a while. But for now, is there anything I can get you?"

She smiled and shook her head, but I could see the reality was starting to set in.

"I'll leave you two. I'm just on the other end of that phone, okay?"

"Thank you…"

"Creed."

"Creed? What sort of name is Creed? Are you Catholic?"

"I have a relationship with the church." *A complicated one at best, but that's a conversation for another time.* "Creed is a family name."

"Oh, just like Roman. He's named for his father, my son."

"Isn't it time for you to go to bed, Lola?" His voice wasn't exactly hard. He sounded as if he were trying to get her off her current subject.

"No, but it's time for you to go home," Frances said. "Kiss your grandmother and go on."

Roman rolled his eyes. "I'm twenty-five-years old and my grandmother still tells me when to go to bed." He bent and kissed her cheek, and then grabbed a sweatshirt from the foot of the bed.

"Nice to meet you," Roman said to me, looking a little lost. Saying goodbye seemed so painful for him. I wanted to find out more about their relationship. "Is there, uh, a curfew? Any particular time you close up?"

I followed him to the door. "Officially, visiting hours are done at ten, but I have a feeling you'll get a pass."

Roman nodded, but he didn't seem to find my crack very funny. *Everyone thinks I'm funny.*

"Thank you. I'll be back tomorrow night for sure."

"Mr. San Angelo? I know this is difficult—"

"You think? I just came back from being out of the country to find my aunt and uncle had put my grandmother in a home. You can't possibly understand."

Roman's grief washed over me, leaving me breathless. *So much pain.*

"I promise. I'll make sure she's well cared for and entertained. She'll be very happy here."

Roman looked down at his feet and nodded once more before heading toward the exit. I watched as he pushed the doors open with more force than was necessary and it took all the self-control I'd gained over the past decades to not follow him.

There goes a man who just lost the last thing keeping him from a lonely existence. But it wasn't just his grandmother he felt grief over.

I returned to check on my new patient and saw she'd fallen asleep sitting in her chair. Thankfully I was quite adept at the whole sneaking-around routine.

I gently lifted her from the chair and shared a bit of healing energy to ease her. Her blood sugar was high—I could sense it—and her lungs were working harder than they needed to be. Soon I would treat what ailed her and make her more comfortable, but for that, I needed her lucid permission. I'd have to earn her trust...and that of her handsome grandson. I'd had to leave more than one nursing home previously due to a concerned adult child.

When I returned to the nurses' station, it was time to walk Lexi to her car. She was shaking by the time we got to the back lot, which had me on high alert.

"I just don't want to come across someone in the act, you know? What if—"

"Lexi, you're safe with me. People who are breaking into cars are looking for a quick buck. They're not interested in hurting people. Most of the people out here are suffering. They're hungry, and they're looking for a little comfort. Aren't we all?"

Lexi turned to smile up at me. "You need some comfort?" She pressed her chest against mine and bit her bottom lip.

Sigh. I really hated to set boundaries with her. I never liked letting anyone down. "Your friendship *is* comfort, Lexi." I brushed her hair back from her face.

She frowned and rested her hands on my waist. "Friendship? We've been friends for a long time, Creed. Ever since you moved to town. You've never talked about anyone, been with anyone..."

I kissed her forehead. Then I looked into her eyes and tried to send her some reassurance. "It has nothing to do with you, Lexi. I prefer the company of men."

Her eyes widened and then she blushed. "Oh. I'm sorry, Creed."

I gave her my warmest smile. "No reason to be sorry. You're my best friend, Lex. I hope we can remain that way."

"You're mine, too," she groaned. "But you're also really hot." She pouted up at me, and I tweaked her nose.

"Thank you. Now you be safe. Go straight home."

I swayed on my feet from the emotions Lexi was letting off. She was a brilliant woman and her energy felt like a two-beer buzz. It wasn't a lot, but she'd be enough to get me through the night. It was too dangerous to use her for anything else. She was too close to me. Thankfully I had plenty of energy for the time being.

"You be safe, too," she said. "You seem a little off tonight."

"Nah. I'm fine. Just a lot on my mind. Good night, Lexi."

She climbed into her Honda Civic. "Good night. Thanks for walking me."

I closed her car door behind her and stepped back as she pulled away.

The ocean breeze caressed my skin, and I closed my eyes to embrace the night. The distant screams and roars from the roller coaster at the Boardwalk had become a comfort, the thumping of music from the nightclub downtown a welcome soundtrack. I rented a basement apartment a few blocks' walk from the home and downtown Santa Cruz provided everything I needed. Food, entertainment, and reserves of residual energy from those who frequented the area. I learned early on that living around people was important to keep up my energy. Which was necessary until I finished my task.

Santa Cruz had been my favorite stop on this long journey. I'd never thought of myself as a beach town kind of man, believing I preferred the magnolias and green fields of Georgia. But now that I'd finally made it back out west, after many stops over the past fifty years, I felt at home. The second phase of my life started near here, and it seemed fitting that my search had led me back. The energy in this place called to wherever the power within me lay. Some nights I thought about giving up the search for those who'd wronged me, but I knew I'd never rest until I'd put an end to their misuse of power.

The peaceful feeling wavered, and I felt something brush against my psyche. Just a nudge. A test.

I wasn't alone.

Someone trained in The Way was scanning me, testing my power, psychically approaching me in a way that brought back some painful memories.

I hadn't felt the presence of others like me since I'd fled my commune fifty years ago.

I've come to the right place. Finally, a sign that I'd found what I was looking for.

I concentrated on blocking access to my energy and waited, alone and vulnerable in the darkness.

Where were they? My hair stood up on my arms for a moment and then it went away. Whoever it was must have been passing by. I moved toward the street out front and saw several groups of young folks talking and laughing as they walked to and from the Boardwalk, but no one stuck out. No one looked my way.

I was close. I would find them. I knew I'd recognize the ones I was looking for when the time came, and that time *was* coming. Until then, I would live by the beliefs I'd committed myself to so long ago.

Give unto them what they require.

Take from them only what is necessary to survive.

I was tired of running. For some time now I'd wished it was possible to set down roots. But sins of the past have a way of catching up to you once you got comfortable, and I wouldn't rest until I found those who destroyed the people I loved. Now that they'd shown themselves, that time was at hand.

6

CHAPTER SIX

R oman

IT HAD BEEN a month since I'd failed as a grandson, and I was feeling remarkably good, which in turn made me feel guilty as hell. I'd had more sleep than in the past year since my lola's health had declined. Other than school and work, which was grueling this year, I had nothing to keep me grounded other than visiting Lola nearly every day. I worked out at the gym with Tito Reynaldo three times a week, I picked up an extra TA assignment, and I had beers with Reynaldo, Vanessa and Bernadette once a week. But I missed my lola even though I saw her daily. I missed having her home with me. Staying busy was key to not losing my mind.

My research project was not going well. I'd spent the last term and the summer researching a particular cult in Northern Spain that had ties to some of the wealthiest citizens of the coastal towns, as well as other countries in Europe and even the United States, but since I'd returned, I'd been distracted.

Besides Lola being gone, Reynaldo and Vanessa shared more about the weird series of car break-ins and an uptick in assaults downtown, which had me intrigued. They'd both been working extra shifts as they tried to catch the perpetrators. So far they'd identified a group of four men, late teens/early twenties, clean-cut, all white with foreign accents, who cornered their victims—both men and women—and terrified them before one of them bit the victim on the neck.

"It's fucking *The Lost Boys* all over again," Reynaldo said over beers one night. "Every few years since that damn movie came out in the late eighties, some copycat wannabe vampires do stupid shit that the cops have to clean up."

So while I should have been thinking about La Mente, the organization I'd studied in Northern Spain, I was going over the Santa Cruz PD reports and digging for more information on these attacks. There was something about the randomness of the victims, and something one of them mentioned about blood that had echoes of the case in Spain. Could there be a connection?

"It's pack behavior. You haven't made any arrests?"

"Nah, man," Reynaldo said. "They're slippery bastards. They disappear before anyone can get a good ID or anything. No surveillance cameras. Nothing. It's fucking weird, man. And I hate weird."

"And there have been how many so far?"

"We're up to four now." Vanessa handed me another beer. "We're working on putting some plainclothes folks downtown and at the Boardwalk to see if we can catch these guys." Vanessa had recently been promoted to detective, which was a bone of contention between her and Rey, who'd chosen not to climb the ranks in the department. He was happy being a patrol officer even though Vanessa pushed him to at least test for sergeant.

"Good. In San Sebastián there were a couple of reports from people who had attended meetings for this society called The Order of the Mind, and they talked about scare tactics. I don't know, maybe there's a connection. I'd like to ride with you again, Rey."

My uncle shook his head. "I don't want you down there until we catch these weirdos."

"But maybe Roman can see patterns we don't see. Or if you still have some connections with the law enforcement in Spain—"

"Yeah I can email and see—"

"Fine, but you stay with me, I don't want you out by yourself until we catch these guys."

I flinched. "I'm sorry, what? I can take care of myself." He could talk all he wanted. I wasn't about to hide from whatever was going on.

He threw an ice cube at me, I tossed an empty can at him, and then it was on, and we were wrestling on the floor while Vanessa and Bernadette moved the breakables.

"Damn, you're strong, Junior," he said as he pinned me to the floor with my hands behind my back. I should have learned by now that he could still take me, but it was fun making him work for it.

"Just making sure you still got it," I said, my face smushed into the floor.

THE EVENING ACTIVITIES were usually over by the time I arrived at Puesta Del Sol, but some nights I got there in time for the fun, and man, it was not what I'd expected an old folks' home to be like. Lola had been more awake and alert than ever. It was as if the move had been a miracle for her. Phyllis and Stella, too. The three of them were chatty and happy, like back when I was a boy and they'd throw big parties.

They were the life of the place, and they sure loved their night nurse.

Creed.

The guy was something else. He was like a camp counselor for old folks. Watching him with the patients reminded me of *Twilight Zone: The Movie*, where the old guy comes in and gets the other seniors to play Kick The Can and they turn into little kids. The smiles, the laughter...I'd almost accepted that the move was a good thing for Lola Frances. Almost.

Over the past four weeks, he'd become more than just my grand-mother's nurse, though. I found myself becoming way too interested in watching him with the residents. He was kind, he was always smil-ing, and he was way too charming. Never in my life did I imagine my type would be a guy in scrubs singing Tony Bennett songs and playing piano.

My infatuation with Creed was cemented that fourth week. Reynaldo and I showed up for Tuesday Bingo and were subsequently coerced into staying for a singalong. Creed was quite the piano man, and he had a great voice. He had a great everything. *Too* great, actually.

"Oh, Creed, dear, do that one again. The Tony Bennett one."

"You mean 'The Best Is Yet to Come'?" He ran his fingers deftly over the keys and wiggled his eyebrows at Stella.

I sat next to Reynaldo and Lola Frances, who clapped her hands together. She was practically vibrating with excitement. "Isn't he wonderful?"

"If you like the talented, handsome-guy type," I muttered. I was still salty about her being there. And as much as I agreed there was... something...about this Creed guy, I still couldn't be as excited as her.

Lola Frances turned toward me. "Seemed to me once upon a time that *was* your type."

I stretched out my legs. "Please tell me you're not getting ideas."

"So what if I am? You're all alone in that big house, you work too much. You need someone to take care of you, and Creed is a very nice man. A little younger than you, maybe—"

"You mean still in diapers?" Reynaldo chimed in.

I punched him in the arm. He wasn't in uniform so it was fine.

Frances's nostrils flared and she squinted at her nephew. "Just because you keep chasing the good ones away," she said to Reynaldo. "Besides, I am talking to my grandson." She patted my arm and stuck her tongue out at my uncle.

"You're right, Lola," I said, raising my hands in surrender. "But if I start dating, that means I'm going to have to clean up the house, pick up all the beer cans and dirty socks—"

"Roman Emmanuel Armand San Angelo! You had better not—"

"Oh, did I tell you? I moved all of your sewing stuff out of Vanessa's old room and I'm setting up a home gym."

"How dare you!" she exclaimed, while Reynaldo had a good laugh. Lola had encouraged a way of teasing each other that others often remarked was cruel, but it was how we knew we were loved.

"Frances? Would you like to sing with me?"

She turned and placed her hands on her knees, faux-gasping as if she were shocked.

That damned Creed. He had Lola Frances preening like a schoolgirl.

"I haven't seen her flirt like this since her failed attempts at dating after Lolo passed away," Reynaldo whispered to me.

"Oh, I couldn't," she said, pressing her hand to her chest.

"Never stopped you before," I muttered.

Frances stomped on Rey's foot as she stood to sashay over to the piano.

"Ow!" He looked shocked "Why me? He's the one who said it." Reynaldo shot me a comical ugly look he didn't really mean. He rubbed at his foot. "Damn, you got lead in your shoes or something? That's gonna leave a bruise."

"You deserved it," Lola said, and then she curtseyed to Creed.

Creed smiled and shook his head. It seemed as though he was entertained by our banter. He often watched us sitting together at bingo. It made me jumpy. Was he worried that our visits would upset her? She hadn't had one of her episodes since she'd moved here. That fact was the reason I'd been sleeping so well.

Reynaldo finally told me more of the factors that led to their decision to move her here. He'd discovered that Lola had been slipping while he was at work. There was the one night he returned home to find the burner on the stove blazing away and another time the oven had been left on. Then they'd received three identical packages from QVC. She'd ordered the same pair of shoes three times—each time they'd been advertised—because she hadn't remembered placing the order. And then he noticed the scratches on her stomach when she'd walked down the hall in her bra, looking for her bathrobe, an unusual move for her. She couldn't remember where the scratches came from.

I couldn't be mad at them. They'd done the right thing, bringing her here. It was just hard to accept that she was doing so much better at Puesta Del Sol, better than she had when I was living with her and doing my best to take care of her. But then, she had her sisters and her friends...and her damn nurse.

She sang the song beautifully, her voice clear and stronger than I'd heard in a long time. Creed sang with her, and then he stood from the piano and took her by the hand. They danced in a big circle and he twirled her in his arms and dipped her. She squealed happily, but Rey stiffened next to me.

"Tita Frances, you be careful."

She wrinkled her nose at him. "Why? You think I'm going to make these men fall in love with me?"

"More like you'll break a hip," he muttered, but she kept laughing, and Creed spun her again. They danced a few more steps and then took a bow. The other folks laughed and clapped for the pair.

My gaze was transfixed on Creed. Scrubs or not, he was incredibly graceful, and so gentle with Lola. So strong.

"All right, guys, gals and nonbinary pals," Creed said, clapping his hands together. "The piano bar must close for the night."

There was some pouting and boos but the residents began to clear out of the room.

"Boys, I'm going to Stella and Phyllis's room to play cards. You two should go home."

"Really?" I asked her, only partially kidding. "Just going to kick us out like that?"

"I gotta take off anyway," Reynaldo said, giving me a quick bro handshake. We'd come here separately, so he gave her a hug and said goodnight. I watched him stop to chat up Lexi at the front desk on his way out.

Frances smiled demurely at Creed as she moved to my side and kissed me on the cheek. She looked between Creed and me.

"Go out and find some fun, my grandson. Don't you remember fun?"

I stretched my back in the chair. "Not really. Must have lost it somewhere between college and grad school." I stood and shrugged. "Guess I'll just have to go home and record over some more of the family movies."

This time she smacked me hard on the shoulder, and I flinched. *Man*, she was strong. How was it that a month ago, she supposedly kept having to sit down because she felt faint?

"You ladies keep the noise down in there," Creed said as Frances and her sisters moved toward the hallway leading to their rooms. "I'll be in to check on you in a bit, and I better not find you gambling with real money. That's why I brought you the chips."

"Oh, but it's more fun with pennies, Creed."

This time it was Stella flirting with the nurse. She had a hip kicked out and her hands on her waist, a pose I recalled seeing in her old modeling photos. The sisters had been known for their beauty and charm back in the Philippines. They'd had no problem nabbing successful white men for husbands. Lolo hadn't had a chance once Frances decided they were to be married.

"Told you those three would be trouble together," I said to Creed, who had joined me by the entrance to the library.

He leaned against the opposite wall. "But they're happy. They've earned a little trouble."

We watched them all giggling together as they turned the corner. I took the last swig on my Monster Energy drink as they carried on the whole way down the hall, loud enough for us to hear them.

"I guess they're *your* trouble now, then." I tossed the can into a recycling bin. I picked up my green bomber jacket from the chair where I'd been sitting and slid it onto my shoulders.

"No trouble at all," Creed said. He smiled at me like a guy keeping secrets. I don't know why I thought that, but he gave me that impression.

"You wouldn't think this place was for people who needed assistance after these singalong sessions."

He tilted his head to the side. "How do you mean?"

"They're...I don't know. My lola and aunties haven't been this spry since...well, for years. They get here and they're dancing and singing? And the other folks?"

Creed pushed away from the wall and moved closer. "What did you expect when she moved here?"

I shrugged. Loud voices erupted from the library. I leaned around the corner to see a bunch of old guys playing a game of darts in the corner, and another group playing pool.

"Not this." I gestured to the men. "I expected more wheelchairs and walkers—"

"Old folks drooling, staring into space, pajamas in the daytime. Is that what you thought?"

"Yeah, I guess I did." Why the hell was this guy fucking with me?

7

———————

CHAPTER SEVEN

C reed

"MAYBE IT'S MAGIC," I said, my eyes flaring. I wiggled my fingers at Roman and then laughed.

"Or good drugs. You guys legit here?"

I blinked and tried to hold back a smartass reply. Of course Roman would question things. One of the reasons I'd had to move frequently was the appearance of folks like Roman, who had that extra sense about them. Usually it was law enforcement, like his uncle. Sometimes it was a person who had a touch of the Sight or intuition that let them know things weren't as they seemed. I'd learned enough about Roman to know he was gifted in that area.

"Tell me, Professor. What type of drugs would have that kind of effect on geriatric patients? Please, enlighten me."

I crossed my arms over my chest and grinned. I loved that Roman couldn't figure me out. I couldn't afford any attachments, but it sure was fun to play. We'd been pussyfooting around each other for the past month that his grandmother had been here. His cop uncle was more laid back than he was, surprisingly. Roman was standoffish at first, but once I picked up on the way he joked with his grandmother, I took a chance with my teasing...and it was reciprocated. Although Roman didn't trust me, that much was certain.

Roman frowned and then pushed away from the archway where he'd been leaning. "As long as she's happy, it's probably better I don't know."

The emptiness and sorrow bleeding out of Roman's psyche nearly bowled me over. I physically reacted to the pain and swayed on my feet.

"Hey, you okay?"

Roman grabbed me by the biceps, and it hit me that I was overdue for a little nourishment. And the sexy-as-hell man standing before me had most certainly not given his permission.

"Would you excuse me?"

"You look like you're going to faint. You should sit down."

I smiled at him and sighed. Over the past few weeks, I'd become quite fond of Roman San Angelo, even though he was too young for me. Not physically. In fact, we'd make a great pair physically. But though my body was that of a man in his early twenties, I was as old as the folks I cared for. Older in some cases.

"Thank you, Professor. I'm fine. Just a little low blood sugar. I'll grab something to eat and then it's time for me to make my rounds." I couldn't resist one more little dig. "You sure you don't want to check on your family? Maybe if you threaten to report them to Officer Cabral, they'll quit gambling with real money."

Roman chuckled. "Sorry about that. I told my cousin Ronnie not to bring Tita Stella any more pennies from the bank."

I stood to my full height, which was about three inches taller than Roman, but Roman's physique made him seem much larger. He obviously put in a lot of time at the gym. Lord, did he look amazing in that loose tank top and tight black joggers. His smooth golden-brown skin looked like velvet, and I imagined it would feel as soft against my lips.

Shit. I'd licked my lips. And caught Roman watching.

"I should—"

"Yeah, I should go," he said, backing away with a smirk. "I'll be back tomorrow."

I took a long look at Roman. "Can I ask you a question?"

Roman busied himself checking his pockets for his keys and phone. "Yeah, sure," he said without making eye contact.

"Who do you have? I know you have family in town, and the three vixens upstairs. But who do you have for *you*? I wonder about you when you leave."

I hadn't meant to do it, but there it was. I released the pheromone that allowed me to lure people close in order to perform the Exchange. The scent triggered a hormonal response within my prey that relaxed their fight-or-flight reflex and made them...curious, open.

It was wrong, but I couldn't take it back. It was out there and Roman was affected.

His body swayed toward me slightly and his pupils dilated. "I'm alone," he murmured, but then he caught himself and frowned. "What do you mean? I'm fine. I cook for myself, I'm not helpless."

"That's not what I meant."

There was a moment where Roman seemed to ponder just how open he really wanted to be.

Come on. Open for me. But I didn't dare push any further.

"It's weird...with her gone." He barked out a laugh, but not before I noticed him blink back tears. "I know it sounds lame, but I've never lived alone." He rubbed his hand over his freshly cut hair. After that first night, when he'd apparently just gotten off a plane, Roman had appeared with a fresh haircut about every other week. It was still long in the front, though. I loved it. And he was always clean shaven. I noticed these things.

"That's not a bad thing," I said gently. "It takes an adjustment. I've had a long time to practice."

Roman shook his head. "How? What are you, like twenty-five?"

The need grew stronger, and I knew I had to break away from this enticing conversation.

"Ever gets too much, you know where I am. We can grab a beer or something." That sounded bromance-y enough, I hoped. I had to be cautious.

Roman held out a hand to shake. I didn't totally trust myself to accept it, but I did anyway.

"Thanks man," he said as we shook. "I appreciate you taking care of the ladies. I'll see you."

Bromance, gratitude, whatever it was, my soul fed on that little bit of give from Roman. It would have to be enough.

I waved and headed toward the nurses' station. Lexi had been watching me interact with Roman. She sighed loudly as he exited the front doors.

"Yes, Lexi?"

"That family has great genes is all I'm saying."

"Yeah? You asked out Officer Cabral yet? You know you want to." My coworker was attracted to the cop. I didn't blame her. Reynaldo was definitely a handsome guy—and I was pretty sure he was bi—but something about Roman called to me...

She wrinkled her nose at me. "I do."

"You should." *And I shouldn't take my own advice, nope I shouldn't.* "Anything going on?"

"Nothing much. Oh, Mr. Fletcher wanted you to come by before you went on rounds. I think he needs help with his email again."

Relief flowed through me. *The solution to my current need.* "No problem. I'll be back in a bit and after my rounds, I'll walk you to your car."

"Thanks, Creed."

I gave her a salute and made my way to Mr. Fletcher's room. I danced a little jig down the hall from the nurses' station and then to the left and to the room at the end of the hall. I knocked twice and opened the door.

"Good evening, Mr. Fletcher." I took a quick look through Mr. Fletcher's chart and thankfully saw what I was looking for.

Bloodwork was normal. *Perfect.*

The elderly Black man sat at his desk frowning at the computer screen. He was a little more tech savvy than some of the other residents, but they all needed help now and again.

"Creed, you remember my password for my email? I need to send a letter to the VA about my hearing aids."

"Sure." I leaned over past the man and typed in the password from memory. "But next time, if I'm not here, remember it's written down in your little black book in the drawer."

I pulled out Mr. Fletcher's top drawer of his desk and patted the book. Sometimes it helped to remind my patients. Not always, but sometimes.

"Oh, fine, thank you. I sent them a message a week ago and I haven't heard back. I need to get these damn things fixed." Staff Sergeant Robert Fletcher had served in the Marines during Vietnam and was awarded a Medal of Honor for his actions in the battle of Hue City. He received an honorable discharge, came home, opened a garage and worked for the next fifty years until his sons took over and moved him to Puesta Del Sol. The transition to senior living had been difficult, but we'd bonded over music and then developed a deeper relationship, one of reciprocation.

"If you need me to call for you, I'm happy to." It wasn't outside my purview necessarily, but typically the social worker took care of calls like that.

"Maybe," Mr. Fletcher said, and then he turned the chair to face me. His words were imploring, but proud. He didn't like to ask. "I need to feel better tonight," he said softly.

"You got it. What ails you?"

I took his hand and led him over to the loveseat. Mr. Fletcher did seem to be in pain tonight. His gait was slow and cautious, as though he worried his bad hip would go out on the five steps or so across the room. We sat together and I continued to hold his hand.

"Hey, Creed? You remember what you promised me, don't you?"

When I allowed select patients to learn what I was, what I could do, they often had this same request. It broke my heart, but I believed in a person's right to choose how they wanted to end their life when their condition was terminal.

"I do. But that's a long way off, don't you think?"

I concentrated on the pressure point I used to relax my patient and released the pheromone. Mr. Fletcher leaned back against the couch and closed his eyes.

"I'm just tired tonight. Scotty called today."

Ah. He missed his sons and his grandkids. The shop was in Salinas and it just wasn't feasible for the family to pop on over during the week, and then the beach traffic on the weekend didn't help either.

"I hope everyone is doing well."

Mr. Fletcher sighed and his head lolled on his neck. "Yeah, they are. Said my granddaughter got accepted to college up at UC. Isn't that something?"

I smiled and rubbed the inside of Mr. Fletcher's wrist. "It sure is. I'm going to take care of you, okay?"

Mr. Fletcher nodded and his bottom lip hung open. He was so relaxed he couldn't keep his head up. His strong heart, made that way by my healing energy over the past few months, pumped forcefully, the rhythm like an irresistible drug.

Give unto them what they require.

Take from them only what is necessary to survive.

"Blessed be."

I placed my lips over Mr. Fletcher's wrist and my canines pierced the old man's thin skin. He exhaled with a sound like *ahhhhhhh.*

Contrary to popular lore, the bite from, well, someone like me, is not necessarily an orgasmic experience. In fact, if it weren't for the chemical I released before I even approached Mr. Fletcher and the use of acupressure, it could even be painful. Without those steps, Mr. Fletcher would have tensed up and he wouldn't have received the healing benefits from our Exchange. His blood for my healing energy.

I took a few short pulls of Mr. Fletcher's rich blood, made healthier from the time spent in my care, and then I focused my concentration on knitting the cells back together and erasing any signs that I'd punctured the skin. I sat up and felt a rush flood my body with strength and power.

"There. Not even a bruise. Feeling better?"

Mr. Fletcher snored soundly, and I chuckled. I picked him up easily, despite the fact he had about sixty pounds on me, and I carried him to his bed. I stripped him down to his boxers and undershirt and tucked him in. He wouldn't remember this in the morning, but he'd wake up with a little pep in his step and be feeling frisky by the time I arrived for my shift at six tomorrow evening.

It was important that I be there when dinner was over. That was when I was needed most. And while I couldn't work seven days a week, I could be there for my patients five days a week, to keep them happy and as healthy as possible.

It was the least I could give them for sharing their excess energy and, sometimes, their blood. It was all about the Exchange and the manipulation of matter. There was no fairy tale or magic involved. Vampirism could be explained by science. Once exposed to The Source's energy and exceptional blood, those who trained as I had took the blood we were freely given—taking without permission was a violation—and offered our healing energy in return. In the early days of our practice, that violation carried a penalty of death.

We learned to pull from blood the energy required to heal and sustain life, and for some, we were able to extend their lives. Elderly folks at the end of their existence sometimes experienced a breakdown of their mental capacity that was due to an overproduction of negative energy. I learned early on that when it came to sustaining my own existence, the negative energy elderly people let off was even more potent than the blood. I was able to absorb it and draw strength from it. In return, the elderly in my care found a peace that was otherwise unavailable to them.

Sundowner's syndrome was a real problem for those suffering from Alzheimer's. Confusion and forgetfulness were part of the disease, but for some victims, a terror that came on with the waning light and played out in harmful behaviors was a very real experience that I wouldn't wish on a single soul. Just by being with them, I could take in that excess harmful energy produced by the Sundowning and act as something like a processor, sending out warmth and calm instead. Basically, followers of The Way were human-sized energy filters that only required a little blood for longevity.

I was grateful I'd found The Source back in my youth, had been accepted into their ranks and received their teachings, even if I'd been misled. If I would have known what it would cost me... Well, I tried not to dwell on that. Things happened for a reason, that was part of my education, and without the tragedy that befell my cohort of trainees, I never would have had the wide array of experiences I'd had, and I never would have discovered how my abilities were particularly helpful to the elderly. I would be eternally grateful for the people I'd come across on my long journey, even though I'd lost so much...

"Creed?"

I'd been so preoccupied with my thoughts I hadn't realized I was back at the nurses' station where Lexi was waiting for me to walk her outside.

"Sorry. Let me just grab my coat."

Lexi smiled then she sucked in a breath. "Oh! I almost forgot to ask! I got tickets to see Barns Courtney at The Catalyst tomorrow night. It's your night off, right? Please say you'll come with me?"

"What's the matter? None of your girlfriends will go with you?"

She rolled her eyes. "None of them have good taste in music like you do. Please?"

"Sure. I'd like that."

And I would. All that frenetic energy in one place? The psychic high would be delicious.

8

CHAPTER EIGHT

R oman

"THANK YOU, OFFICER."

Reynaldo nodded at the young mother as he walked back to the patrol car. I was on a ridealong with him, doing unofficial research on these bizarre attacks that continued to confound the police.

I'd stood by while he'd taken a report, listening to the details and making my own notes. We'd responded to a call at the municipal lot across from Hula Grill, and found a young mother with a half dozen kids and a busted car window. Nothing had been taken. Her registration and insurance papers were strewn about the passenger seat, but she'd been smart and taken all valuables out of the car. She had her hands full with all of the kids, and so the report she needed for her insurance had taken a bit longer than usual to fill out.

A familiar laugh caught my attention.

"Oh! Officer Cabral. Everything okay?"

I whipped my head around at the voice and couldn't immediately place the man and woman walking towards us.

"Hey," Reynaldo said, immediately relaxing his posture, his hand slipping from his holster's snap. "I didn't recognize the two of you out of your scrubs."

It was Lexi...and Creed? They were dressed as if they'd been out for the evening. *Huh.*

Maybe I'd had it wrong. I could have sworn Creed was gay, and I usually wasn't wrong about these things.

"Everything okay, officer?"

"Yeah, just a busted window," Reynaldo said, smiling at Lexi. He looked between the two of them, probably checking to see if they were both sober, since they were headed towards a car. "You coming from The Catalyst?"

Creed grinned. "Yeah. We saw Barns Courtney." He turned and smiled at me specifically. "You listen to alternative rock?"

I fumbled over my words. It was a miracle I had any words left. Creed had a protective arm around Lexi, who was shivering in the chilly night air, but his smile was for me.

Thought so.

Why that pleased me, I had no idea, other than I'd accepted the idea of him as potentially more than Lola's night nurse. Though I wasn't sure whether I was ready to make a move. His smile was infectious, his sense of humor totally fit with mine, and he was oh so easy on the eyes. Made me forget about my summer fling. *¿Quién es Basajuan?*

I hadn't read the situation wrong. Creed was most definitely gay. I'd had a hard time forgetting that ever since he'd casually asked me to grab a beer. I'd never be able to unsee the alarmingly hot sight of Creed as he was dressed tonight—in a pair of tight black jeans that were tapered at the ankle, which was bare above his checkerboard Vans, and a long-sleeved t-shirt. The guy had the Santa Cruz look down, but it wasn't natural to him. No, I could tell Creed wasn't originally from California by the ever-so-faint Southern accent he let slip occasionally.

"Sometimes. I don't really pay attention to what I'm listening to. I was just doing a ridealong with my uncle." *Shut up! You don't have to explain yourself.*

"We've had a few break-ins around Puesta lately, too," Lexi was saying. "Do you think they're connected?"

"Hard to say," Reynaldo said. "Whoever did this probably got scared off. This parking lot is busy this time of night. Probably surveillance cameras picked something up."

Creed frowned as he scanned the parking lot and pulled Lexi closer. The cold didn't seem to be affecting him, which surprised me. The guy was only wearing a thin shirt, while I felt the chill through my hoodie and a thermal. And I was staring.

"You guys didn't see anyone hanging around on your walk over, did you?" Reynaldo asked, interrupting the staring contest I had going on with Creed.

Creed shook his head. "Anything in particular?"

"Any groups of young men wreaking havoc? Anyone checking out cars? Anyone biting anyone? I'm at a loss. There's way too much weird shit going on lately."

Creed nodded. "I'd say Mercury was in retrograde, but somehow I don't think that's the case." His smile fell a bit and he looked around the parking lot. As I watched him, Creed's boisterous fun-guy attitude morphed into something...darker.

"Is your car parked near here?" Reynaldo asked Lexi.

"I'm over there," Lexi said, pointing to an old Honda Civic parked next to the street and under a light. She looked between us as Creed and I gazed awkwardly at each other.

"Well," I said, trying to smile in a friendly way and succeeding at a smirk. "We better let you guys get back to your date."

"It's not a—"

"Professor San Angelo knows this is not a date." Creed smiled knowingly. "I'm just going to walk Lexi to her car. Goodnight, Officer Cabral. Roman."

"Bye! See you on your next visit to Puesta," Lexi said as she waved.

"See you for bingo," Reynaldo said, then he turned and elbowed me. "What's your problem? Say goodbye."

"See you," I said, my overpriced education aiding and abetting my vocabulary.

Creed had turned around and walked backwards with a sly smile directed at me. Once he'd made his point, he turned around and bent down to conspire with Lexi. She let out a laugh and hip bumped him. Creed led the tiny woman to her car and held her door open for her as she took off her puffy jacket and tossed it in the backseat. Good. I liked that Creed was protective. He hugged her, and then watched as she drove away before heading back toward where I stood waiting for my uncle, who was finishing up his report.

At five foot eight, I was used to guys being taller than me. Creed had at least two or three inches on me, and while he looked fit—he had to be to do the more physical parts of his job—I wondered if Creed could handle any trouble that might find him. Whoever broke into the woman's minivan could still be out there looking for an easy target for his next fix.

"I think I'm done here," Reynaldo said as Creed approached us once more.

"You have a good rest of your shift," he said. He paused briefly, as though he had something else to say, and then he walked toward the darkness in the opposite direction.

"Hey," I called out, unsure if I really wanted to stop him from leaving. "You need a lift?" *What the hell am I doing?*

Creed laughed. "I think it's sweet that you're worried about my safety. Trust me," he said, turning around. "I'll be just fine."

Reynaldo cleared his throat. I turned to look at him and he raised his eyebrows. "It's time for my lunch. You know, if you need a minute."

I rolled my eyes at him. "Why would I need a minute?"

"Really? Mr. Bedroom Eyes over there? You should go talk to him. Lola's not around to make trouble. I'll just go grab a slice over at Kianti's. I'll meet you there. Or not. In case you want to call it a night." He wiggled his eyebrows at me.

I groaned. "Everyone's a matchmaker."

"You telling me you're not into him? No problem. Then you won't mind if I get his number."

"Wait. I thought you were into Lexi?"

Reynaldo looked around me to where Creed was walking, a knowing grin on his face and rocking on his feet. "I mean, they're both pretty."

"Fine." I walked toward Creed, feeling like a loser. "Hey," I called out to him. I turned back to my uncle. "I'll text you."

"You do that, Junior."

I flipped him off.

Creed stopped walking and turned to face me with that smug smile of his. "Good evening, Professor. Are we going to try this again?"

I huffed out a breath. "Where are you headed? You live around here?"

"Why? Are you going to walk me home?"

This man liked to play. "I could. Or we could go get that beer you mentioned."

"That what you want? What about your uncle?"

I turned to look back at Rey's patrol car. He was nowhere to be seen. There were only a few stragglers in the parking lot, the majority of folks finishing up their downtown fun for the night.

"It's his lunch. I usually only ride with him for half a shift anyway."

Creed slid his hands into his back pockets. "I could go for a drink."

I sucked in a breath and with it a whiff of...him. Everything in me wanted to grab a handful of his tousled curls, the natural red high-lights gleaming in the streetlight, and hold his head still while I kissed that smart mouth of his, which was always right there with a remark that walked the fine line of flirting.

"Or I could take you home," I heard myself saying.

Creed's smile faded a bit and his eyes penetrated me, making my body feel all loose and breathy.

"Be careful, Roman."

"Careful?"

"Mmm. Be careful what you offer. Thirsty guy like me might take you up on it."

Is that what I want? The guy drove me nuts, I couldn't get him out of my mind when I was away from him, but did I want to take him home?

Casual sex wasn't really my bag. I didn't want that life.

I stepped back, and he sighed.

"*Might* take me up on it? I think you would."

"And you're feeling ambiguous about that."

I hated that he read me so clearly. So what if I was tired of being alone? I was over the sting of Basajuan's rejection, so therefore it wasn't out of character for me to want some company. But something about Creed...being alone with him wasn't going to be simply scratching an itch. We'd been dancing around each other for nearly two months now. I appreciated the excellent care he gave my lola and titas. I appreciated him and the way he filled out those fucking jeans right now even more.

"Big ego you've got there, Nurse Creed. Maybe I offered to take you home because I don't want my uncle to be called back to clean you up off the street when you get jumped. Maybe I don't want to have to tell my lola and aunties that their favorite nurse won't be back. Maybe...maybe I don't want to see that pretty face messed up."

I kept my thumbs hooked on my belt and knew I should step back, but I wasn't about to give an inch to this confounding man.

Creed moved farther into my personal space. We were standing outside the ring of light from a streetlamp but not completely in the darkness. When he spoke, his breath ghosted over my lips.

"Oh, I'm so much more than a pretty face, Roman. Maybe you'd like to find out how much more." Creed placed his hands on my waist and pulled me close enough that our fronts connected below the belt.

I let out a sound that could have easily been mistaken for a moan.

I wanted to believe it sounded more like a frustrated grunt, but Creed had implored me to be honest.

"Take what you want, Roman. Take it, so I can, too."

His taunts drove me to action. I grabbed Creed by the back of the neck, causing him to make a surprised sound, followed by a soft laugh. But I didn't give in, not yet.

"Only if you admit you want this as much as I do."

Creed chuckled and slid his hand around my back, letting his fingers move under the waistband of my jeans. When they connected with my skin, I sucked in a breath, and he brushed his lips against mine.

"You have been tempting me for weeks now, Professor. I want to know how you taste."

As much as I wanted to give him that taste, as much as I wanted to see if our connection was more than just flirting, alarm bells rang in my head like tinnitus. No, it was tinnitus. The shifting of pressure in my ear was enough to make me step back.

"Hey, are you feeling okay?"

I nodded and rubbed at my ear. "Yeah. Tinnitus. Plagues me occasionally."

Creed frowned, and then he reached for my biceps. "Hey, let's not force this, okay? What if...how about we spend some time together? No pressure. Like a date, or not. Like two dudes out for a good time... that sounds weird," he said, and his drawly accent soothed my unease.

"I'd...yeah. Wow. I...I think I'd like some company."

My insides had that feeling you get when the elevator drops faster than you'd expected, like the ground has gone out from under you, and I listed to the side.

"Why don't I get you back to your uncle?"

"Probably a good idea. I'm sorry," I said, and then I laughed. "Helluva way to ask for a date, huh?"

He swung an arm around me and we walked back toward where Reynaldo had parked his patrol car, which was in view of the pizza joint he liked. How that man ate pizza nearly every lunch and still looked fantastic at his age was beyond me.

"I'm sure you'll be an excellent date, and as a show of faith, I'm asking you out. Officially. We can make it as intimate or laid-back as you want. You pick the place."

I leaned against him as my ears unplugged with a pop, making me a little dizzy. "Oh, you're brave. What if you hate it?"

Creed shook his head and gave my shoulder a squeeze. We crossed the street and Reynaldo was just coming out of the restaurant.

"I won't hate it if I'm with you," Creed said close to my ear. "Now, go get some sleep. I'll call you tomorrow."

I turned to argue that he didn't have my number and—

"Officer Cabral, your nephew doesn't seem to be feeling well."

Rey frowned and spun me to face him. He got all cop-like on me and I batted at his hands.

"I'm fine, I—"

"Call you tomorrow, Professor," Creed said. He waved and disappeared around the corner before I could get a word out.

"Well, that's one way to make an impression," Rey said, his eyebrows up high on his damn forehead.

"Fuck you," I said, pushing his hands off me. I listed to the side again and leaned against the patrol car.

"Hey, what the fuck?"

"It's just my ear. I got dizzy."

"I didn't think that was bothering you anymore," Rey said, placing a hand on my back and guiding me into the passenger seat of his patrol car. "Let me get you home."

"I'm fine," I muttered as he shut the door on me.

I rubbed at my head. The tinnitus subsided into a low-frequency headache that wasn't helped by the slamming of Rey's door.

"I'll take you home, and I want you to call the doctor tomorrow."

"I'm not a child."

"You know, the only time you say that is when you're being a child. Now let someone fucking take care of you, you little shit."

I snorted, he lost it, and then we were both laughing until I held my head and moaned.

"Man, I haven't had one like this in a long time."

"You've been under a lot of stress, Roman. You need to rest. Stay home this weekend. Get some sleep."

"Yeah, maybe." I sat back in the seat and sighed. Then I frowned. "Nurse Creed asked me out."

Reynaldo had his hand on the back of my headrest, watching traffic as he backed up. "You serious? Damn."

"What?"

"Shit, I was gonna call up Lexi. Can't have us both dating nurses at that place."

"What does it matter?" I asked, frowning at him. He pulled out into traffic and drove the few blocks to our family home. My lola's home. My home. He stopped the car outside and finished an exchange on his radio.

"I'm just messing with you. You like the guy?"

I shrugged. "I don't know."

"Are you being a child again or—"

I elbowed him, and he held up his hands in surrender. "No," I said, laughing. "I'm just...there's something about him."

"I'll say. Guy's a charmer."

"It's not that. Yeah, he's hot, but I don't know. He puts me on edge, and I'm not sure if that's a good thing."

Reynaldo lost his smile. "If there's something off about him—"

"No. I mean, I don't think it's *off*, so much as I feel out of control around him. Is that weird?"

"Yeah, but then you're weird."

"God, fuck off," I said, opening the door. "I don't know. Should I go out with him? It would be awkward if it didn't go well and then I ran into him at Puesta."

"Yeah, but you don't have to interact with him if you don't want to. Besides, he seems like a solid guy. They have to pass background checks for that place. He doesn't set off my shitbag radar, so there's that. Why not? Do something safe, you know? Something where you guys aren't tempted to get horizontal right away."

"Whatever. Thanks, Dr. Phil."

"Don't mention it. I'll wait til you're in. Light on, okay?"

We always had a code. I'd turn the light on in the kitchen to let him know I was okay. We'd done it since I was a kid, when I'd be alone in the house while Lola was at work. That was a long time ago.

"See ya."

Thankfully the dizziness had passed by that time and I got into the house with no issues. I stripped off my clothes and fell into bed.

My phone dinged and it was Rey.

Light, **dickhead.**

I went and turned the light on and fell back on the bed. I'd kept the downstairs bedroom, for which I was grateful at that moment. I didn't like to navigate the stairs when I was dizzy.

Sorry. **I'm half asleep already.**

I saw the lights from his patrol car pass across the front of the house and heard the crunch of gravel from his tires on the driveway. Our house was an old Craftsman that needed a lot of work. At one point my grandparents, their niece and nephew, and grandchild all lived there. Vanessa moved out first. Reynaldo still had one foot in the house and also kept a room at Vanessa's. And then it was Lola and me. Now just me. Alone.

I'll check **on you tomorrow**

. . .

I WISHED him a good night and a safe shift and then I tossed the phone on the nightstand. The phone dinged again, and I almost ignored it, but since I was now wide awake, headache and all, I figured I'd check.

The first notification was an email from the library. The materials I'd asked for were available and when would I like to come down?

Excellent! I planned to look at religious organizations with large landholdings along the northern California coastal communities to see if I could find ties to the group I'd located in Spain. Apparently they were fond of seaside communes. That determined where I'd be for most of the day tomorrow.

And the next notification was a text. From Creed.

YOUR GRANDMOTHER INSISTED **I take your phone number. Probably I am violating ordinances and procedures by contacting you to ask you out.**

THIS GUY DIDN'T QUIT. And I liked it. I'd been the pursuer in the last couple of relationships I'd attempted. It was nice to be pursued for once. Especially by someone as attractive and intelligent as Creed Lowell. Nurse Creed.

PRETTY SURE YOU'RE **using the digits as she'd intended. What did you have in mind?**

I CURSED. I should have set the parameters, I should have—

MINI GOLF. **Arcade. Boardwalk food. Tourist observing. Sunset walk on the beach, unless that's pushing my luck.**

. . .

GOD, that sounded like the perfect date. A chance to flex my competitive side, an opportunity to gorge myself on all the crap food I'd missed while over in Spain. People watching was my favorite—I was a psychology major...

WE'LL SEE **how good you are at mini golf. If you can beat me, the sunset walk is yours.**

UPPING the stakes could work in my favor. Letting him know he had to work for it...priceless.

I PROBABLY SHOULD TELL **you I caddied a few summers in my youth.**

"HA. AS IF."

THAT HAS **no bearing on mini golf. No indication of success whatsoever.**

HIS RESPONSE TOOK TEN MINUTES, and I had one eye closed by that time, thinking maybe I'd gone a little too far.

COCKY MUCH? **I like it. You're on. Where and what time?**

I TEXTED him Neptune's Kingdom, the front entrance, and then tried to remember what time the library closed...

9

———

CHAPTER NINE

C reed

I WAITED for Roman's response, the three dots floating for an hour before I finally gave up.

He probably fell asleep. And it was my fault.

I'd lost control in the parking lot with Roman and hit him with a pheromone bomb. And I must have *really* hit him, because it had serious physiological effects, which wasn't fair. If I couldn't keep my biological needs under control around him, it would threaten my status here, and it was too soon to leave.

Because my enemies were here, and they were growing bolder.

A news article on the *Santa Cruz Patch*—the sham of a local news source—turned out to be promising. There had been a few bizarre attacks downtown recently involving groups of young men circling young professionals on their way to or from work, harassment ensued, and two of the victims had actually been bitten. On the neck.

Sure, I'd run across fake vampire nonsense in the past. New York

City in the late '70s, any American city in the '80s after *Lost Boys* came out. LA after *Blade*...Oregon after the first *Twilight* movie. But the group dynamic, the description the victims gave of bullying type behavior...it took me back...

1970

"THAT GUY STEPHEN gives me the creeps, Creed. I don't like him."

"You stick close to me," I said, frowning. "I don't trust the whole group of them."

Muse and I sat at our usual table in the gathering room for our morning meal and kept our heads down. The commune was way different than we'd thought it would be. Instead of a bunch of hippies talking peace and love while tripping on LSD, we'd wound up at something that was a cross between an ashram and a coven.

By day, we learned meditation techniques, practiced yoga, and worked on repairing our chakras, and by night we studied botany, physics, biology and anatomy. We were moved from station to station, kept busy every hour of daylight, with the exception of two small meals a day and four hours of sleep at night. There were no drugs, but enough chemical compounds to build an entire pharmaceutical empire. There was no fraternizing with each other except for a few exchanged words over meals or during discussions in class.

Some small groups had formed, however. In a typical school setting, they would be considered bullies, but there was nothing that set them apart otherwise. We all dressed in matching white clothes, we all had our heads shaved, we were all kept in check. No one received favoritism or encouragement from the Leaders, who dressed in pale pink clothing, and no one interacted with The Source, who wore blood red.

The Source was the center of everything, they were taught. And though the being never spoke or interacted with others in front of the Learners, as we were called, they were an imposing presence. You felt them whenever they entered a space; you sensed it as if there was a shift in the atmosphere, the barometric pressure. We were told that if we passed the first set of evaluations, we would be allowed more knowledge of The Source.

After the orientation with the Leaders, I'd been ready to split. No thanks. I'd had my share of religious indoctrination as a kid. I wasn't about to volunteer for the shit. But then I'd heard someone ask about The Source.

"So is he like a god?" a woman had asked.

"*They* are not a deity, and they are not like you and me. They are a being that has evolved beyond human comprehension. The Source is above the basic elements humans must have to survive. They require only energy. And we will teach you to exist on a similar plane, above the pain and anguish that comes with wondering where your next meal will come from."

That had intrigued me. I'd always loved science. I'd had a high school teacher who talked about how humans only use a small fraction of their mental capacity. Mr. Frazier had taught us about mind over matter, how people walked on coals and slept on nails...real Ripley's Believe it or Not stuff, and I'd eaten it up. It was refreshing to not hear "the Bible says, that's why" whenever I asked questions.

Of course, Mr. Frazier had been fired and run out of town at the end of that school year. Figured.

So I'd been interested, and Muse was just happy to feel safe and clean again. Living on the streets of San Francisco, we hadn't had access to showers with any regularity, and the lack of a safe place to rest at night had taken a toll on both of us.

There were baths at the commune. Sort of ritualistic, done in groups, the water provided by the San Lorenzo River that ran through the Santa Cruz mountains. Muse loved them.

We ate our meal between whispers so as not to draw attention to ourselves.

A bowl crashed to the floor, the sound of ceramic breaking on wood reverberated through the room's glass walls and vaulted ceilings.

Our heads snapped around to look in the direction of the commotion, and we saw an older woman surrounded by Stephen and his cronies. They'd boxed her in by the window and were crowding her, using their bodies to block her. They didn't touch her with their hands. Not once. But their sadistic laughter made the hair stand up on the back of my neck.

They didn't use their hands in the way soccer players didn't touch the ball. Didn't mean they didn't have control over it. They used their thighs, hips, and shoulders to maneuver the woman. Her eyes were wide as they darted between the men, looking for a way to escape.

"I hate this shit," I said as I stood from the table, but as I was getting ready to intervene, I felt a hand on my shoulder.

"There is no need for your involvement," a gentle voice said. "Leader Bryce will diffuse the situation."

"Leader Bree, I don't mean to speak out of turn—"

"Then don't speak, Learner Creed. Listen." The tall, willowy woman clasped her hands in front of her. "There are times when Learners must discover for themselves the limits they will go to in the search for an energy exchange. We do our best to guide all Learners to have clear boundaries and to not cause harm."

"And what happens if the Learners don't learn?" I asked, astounded that they would allow this behavior to go on.

Leader Bree smiled at me in a cool way that raised even more hair on the back of my neck, and also sent an icy-cold feeling of dread throughout my body.

"Learners who insist upon taking the knowledge we freely give and doing harm are shown the error of their ways and are dealt with accordingly."

Her gaze traveled over to the group of offenders, and mine followed. The four of them were being led out by four of the Guardians, which were Leaders who were tasked with providing security for the compound. They were all incredibly strong and obviously had some sort of training in restraint and discipline. Their clothing was a light gray color, only slightly off from the Learner's color.

"Learner Creed, you have an admirable sense of honor that serves our community well. When it is time to choose your position, I would not be surprised if Destiny leads you down the Guardian path."

"Thank you, Leader Bree, but I came to learn healing. I believe that is the best use of my skills."

"And it could be that you are too close to the decision to choose for yourself. Trust in your Leaders to guide you, Learner Creed, and in The Source. And thank you."

Leader Bree walked away; the flowing layered material of her clothing seemed to float along behind her.

"Be careful, Creed," Muse whispered. "I don't know if I trust these people. It's you and me, remember? If things get weirder, promise me we'll leave together?"

I turned to face her. "I thought you were happy. You say the word. I'll leave at any time with you."

She smiled. "Thank you. That makes me feel better."

I squeezed her hand and then everyone stood, announcing it was time to go to our first station of the day. We had energy exchanges together, which seemed appropriate after this strange conversation. If the leader allowed questions, I had a bunch ready to go.

I ONLY RESTED a short time before taking Rhonda for a walk. She was not happy to be walking before dawn in the chilly gray light. Fog hugged the coastline like a big puffy parka. I loved mornings like this. The moisture in the air cooled my lungs and woke me up from the inside out. We jogged a good five miles before she just stopped. Her way of saying, "Enough, pretty boy. We're both geriatric, but only one of us feels it."

It was true. I felt as good as I had in my twenties. Even stronger now. Especially after last night's moment with Roman.

Which shouldn't make me feel giddy. That man was a ball of energy just waiting to be siphoned. He carried around so much anger and guilt that it leeched off of him like water vapor. It was potent. But it wasn't just about the energy for me. I was coming to truly empathize with him.

When I got back to the house, I showered and then picked up my phone, hoping to hear from Roman.

How does 3 sound? I'm at the library downtown so I can walk over when they close.

No, Creed, that was not an invitation. Still, I was curious what Roman would need with the local library when he had access to the university's collection.

Research, Professor? I've got connections at that library, you know, if you need anything.

I had time to make a sandwich and eat half of it before he responded.

Yeah. Local real estate holdings. Boring stuff.

"Au contrere. What might the professor be studying that involves real estate?" I'd looked him up on the university website and found him in the psych research department.

I want to hear about your work tonight. I'm always intrigued by academia.

. . .

I DIDN'T WANT to seem too pushy, but I was curious about every aspect of Roman. He seemed like a pretty driven guy. Which made him hotter, and even more irresistible in my mind.

UP TO YOU. **See you at 3.**

DEFINITELY. I figured I'd do some reading of my own, and what better topic than Professor San Angelo's paper on a religious organization in San Sebastián, Spain?

However, the contents of said paper floored me.

How could this be?

The similarities between the La Mente in Spain and Gateway of the Sun were eerie. The emphasis on learning geared toward improving the quality of life, and giving back to the community. I hadn't thought that the usurpers would have been bold enough to cross an ocean with The Source, but perhaps they had. What if all this time I'd been crisscrossing the United States, looking for clues, and instead they'd been hiding out in Europe?

I COULDN'T WAIT for the arcade and instead, waited on the steps of the library for Roman. By 3:15, I worried I'd missed him, but then the head librarian opened the door and ushered the subject of my concern out into the sunlight. Roman winced, but continued talking to her.

"So you'll call the supervisor and let them know I'm coming?"

"Yes, Mr. San Angelo, I'll call her first thing Monday morning. Nothing I can do until then. Enjoy the rest of your weekend."

Chelsea Beckett saw me sitting there, and her irritation left her.

"Mr. Lowell. Did I miss you inside? I apologize, I was away from my desk helping Mr. San Angelo."

The head librarian pursed her lips, tossed her hair and her eyebrows raised in a quick come-hither move she'd used on me many times. Only once did I succumb, and that's because I was particularly needy and it was too cold outside to linger and wait for a less-invasive opportunity for an energy exchange.

Roman's brow furrowed as he looked between us.

"No, ma'am," I said, pouring on all the Georgia sunshine I could muster. "I was waiting for Professor San Angelo."

"You know, technically," he said as he descended the steps, "I'm not a full professor until I complete and defend my dissertation. Your use of the title could be considered bad luck."

Chelsea gave me a finger wave and let down her hair from the large clip at the back of her head. "Goodbye, Creed."

"Until we meet again," I said, bending low in a formal bow. *Again meaning only if I'm on my last breath and require sustenance.*

"How do you know her? And why does it look like you've had carnal knowledge of the sweet and stuffy librarian?"

I sighed as I turned to face Roman. He remained two steps above where I stood, probably to feel he had a height advantage.

"Chelsea is sixty years old by my calculations, and is much more willing to assist with research if you treat her like the beautiful, irresistible woman she once was and wishes she still could be."

"How do you—"

"Roman, do I not work with elderly women for a living?"

"Well yeah. I better never see you act like that around my lola."

I smirked at him. "Why not? If it makes her feel better? If it gives her a thrill to have the attention of a much younger—"

"Gay man. One might consider your behavior opportunistic. Do you use this act to get them to rewrite their wills, maybe?"

"Not intentionally, but it's happened."

Roman squared off with him. "What? They've changed their wills? To leave you piles of money?"

Oh, yes, Professor. Your anger is delectable. "Professor San Angelo, are you accusing me of impropriety?"

"If the scrubs fit."

We stared at each other, and I had to fight not to moan at the rush I was getting from his aggressive behavior.

"Roman, I won't lie and say I've never received a gift. But every item, every penny, was documented by my superiors, and then donated to the Alzheimer's Society." I shifted my weight and rested a foot on the step below him, keeping my hands at my side.

He frowned for a moment, and then stepped down so we were eye to eye.

"That was out of line. I'm sorry. You've done nothing but be nice to me and take great care of my grandmother and her sisters. I don't know where that came from."

I stepped closer to him, tugging on the front of his track jacket, which hung open over a tight knit shirt. "You have every right to be concerned. And I'm afraid I've been pushing your buttons. It's me who owes the apology." Just because he didn't know exactly *how* I'd been getting under his skin didn't mean I owed him any less.

Roman looked down at my hand and smiled, the aggression running out of him like an untied balloon. "You *do* push my buttons. What's that about? I find myself wondering why it is that I let you get to me."

I pulled him closer, running my knuckles over his tight abs. "Because I'm charming?"

I wanted to kiss him. I wanted to finish what we'd started last night. He wanted it too. And we were standing in the overcast afternoon sky in front of the now-deserted library with no one around.

"Or because I'm a masochist."

Roman reached up and grazed my jaw with his thumbs, his dark brown eyes searching mine. His black hair fell in his eyes and his jaw twitched, hollowing out his cheeks and presenting me with a visual cue to his thoughts.

He wanted this too.

But I wanted him to want it *and* take it, and damn if that didn't make me a master manipulator.

"No. I think you're a man who often gets in his own way when it comes to what he wants. A man who worries about everyone else." I nipped at his bottom lip. "Get out of your head, Roman. Take what you want."

His eyes darted around, as if he was concerned about an audience, and when they refocused on me, I felt a surge of his lust as it made up his mind for him.

He came at me with no pretenses of a sweet brush of the lips. His kiss was like a push to the chest. A challenge. And then another. And then he held my head in his hand and dove tongue-first at me, a moan coming from his chest, the sound equivalent to a warning that said, "This dam of self-control is about to burst."

As he leaned into me more, I grabbed his hips, bracing for impact.

Yes, Roman. Give me more.

He dropped his hands to my shoulders and continued to assault me with his tongue, and I wanted it all. His anger, his confusion, his desire. He'd been holding a lot of frustration in, and though I didn't know everything he'd been through, I had an inkling of the source of his feelings.

Roman San Angelo had suffered a loss, and then returned home to experience abandonment. I'd heard enough of his conversations to know that it hadn't been his choice to have Frances moved to Puesta Del Sol, and that he held resentment against his uncle and an auntie, who I'd yet to meet since she came in during the day.

"Goddamn you for tasting so good," he said against my lips.

"Mmm, I could say the same for you."

He pulled back but only enough to take a few breaths. "I'm not usually a big kisser, but you make me want to start the subscription, sign up for the lessons, and fuck, buy the set of steak knives."

"I do come with a guarantee," I teased. "I can make you forget your own name." I licked at his lips once, twice, enough to let him know I wasn't done playing with him. "But I also promised you a proper date. So what do you say we quit giving those guys a show and get on with it?"

I hadn't been able to move, I was so enthralled with Roman, but I'd noticed that we'd attracted the attention of some displaced gentlemen who had a tent complex on one side of the library that provided them shelter. And right on cue, two of them began making kissing noises at us and whistling. I laughed, but Roman stiffened.

"It's all right," I said, smoothing his hair back. "I'd be whistling too if I saw two hot guys making out in my living room." I hooked arms with him. "Come on. I believe you planned to try to destroy me at mini golf?"

That got a laugh out of him. We descended the stairs, and I found I enjoyed walking and talking with him nearly as much as kissing him. Nearly.

"So did you find what you needed today for your research? I'd love to hear more about your project."

"Be careful what you ask for," Roman said with a humorless laugh. "There's a reason I'm single."

"Now I *really* want to know."

Roman exhaled and looked at where our arms were connected. "I'm researching a religious organization with ties to Spain, South Africa, Monaco, and here. All wealthy parishioners, some very influential members. It's very much like a Scientology vibe, but instead of celebrities, they've got ties to biotech and venture capital."

"How does a psychology research fellow get involved with religious organizations?"

"You looked me up, huh?"

"I was curious."

"Uh-huh," he said. "The connection is that my dissertation is on cults and criminal behavior."

Something shifted in me at his words and their implication. He was treading into waters that could have benefits...or that could cause real problems for me. "Interesting. You'll have to tell me more after I win."

We'd made it to the arcade at the opposite end of the Santa Cruz Boardwalk from the rides.

"I love how you think you have a chance," Roman said, holding the door open for me. "You know I grew up here, right? And you did not."

"How do you know that?" I asked him.

"Your accent. You slip into it sometimes. And you're, like, a little too wholesome to be from Santa Cruz."

My head fell back as I barked out a laugh. "Preposterous. I've been around."

"Fair enough," he said, leading me to the counter, where he proceeded to pay for both of us to play two rounds of golf.

"You didn't have to do that," I said as he handed me my club.

"Seems only right since I have the advantage." Roman led me to the first of the 18 holes of the Buccaneer Bay course, which spanned two floors and advertised a black-light cave.

He did play very well. It was obvious he was familiar with the place, which may have had more to do with it than actual putting skill.

I hadn't been fibbing. I actually spent summers in high school caddying at a local golf club in Georgia. My experiences were part of the reason I'd run off after high school, eschewing the wealthy country club life for the draw out West of "flower power" and LSD.

"The first round goes to you," I said, noting it was after five o'clock. "So how about you buy me dinner before we play round two?"

We gorged ourselves on corn dogs and French fries, and Roman moaned every few minutes.

"I missed this so much," he said. "They definitely eat differently in Spain."

"I've never been," I told him. "What's it like?"

He dangled a fry as he prepared his answer. "Lots of ham and cheese with bread, but in the north they have these absolutely amazing finger sandwiches called pintxos, and I fell in love with them. Whenever I could, I'd go from bar to bar, just chowing. A lot of seafood in the north as well. I lived in Bilbao most of the time I was there."

"Sounds incredible. You said there was a religious organization you were studying there, too?"

"Yes. The Order of Mind, or La Mente, as they call it. I had a couple of interviews with their representatives, but they only gave me their public face. Most of my information came from a couple of sources and police reports. I need to dig deeper."

I leaned my chin on my hand. For such a young guy, he'd accomplished a lot. It was sexy as hell. "How did you even decide on such a topic?" I longed to reach across the table and take his hand. I wanted to keep a physical connection to him...for selfish reasons, of course. The more he talked, the more that bittersweet energy seeped out. I knew rationally that it was helping him, releasing those built-up toxins, kind of like a massage releases the nasties from your muscles. But the fact that I was benefiting from his pain—getting fucking high off it—well, wasn't that just pure evil?

Roman took a long sip from his Coke and stared at me, wide-eyed. "My great-aunt and uncle were victims of the Jonestown massacre. My uncle Reynaldo? His parents."

"Oh. God, Roman. I'm so sorry. That was a terrible tragedy."

There had been talk at our commune of leaving the country around the time Jones took his people to Guyana. Some of the Leaders had even been sent to scout locations abroad, but The Source insisted that they were most powerful along the fault lines in the Santa Cruz mountains, and so they'd remained. That part of the "science" behind the teachings had not made a lot of sense to me.

"Thank you. My aunt and uncle went into law enforcement, and I went into academia looking for answers." He finished off his Coke. "Anyway, Lola's brother and his wife struggled, so she ended up raising Reynaldo and Vanessa, alongside my mother."

"What about your parents?"

"Killed in a home invasion. I was fourteen. I was out with my friends when it happened. Fucked me up for a long time. Lola kept me in line, threatened me with bodily harm if I didn't graduate high school. I owe her everything for that."

So much tragedy. "And I know she's proud of you. Of all of you. She shows me your pictures on her computer every time I come in to check on her."

Roman rolled his eyes. "Her and those pictures. She's obsessed."

"It's how she keeps you close, how she holds a piece of you all even when she can't be there."

Roman frowned at me, and then smiled. "Something like that. Hey, you're, what, twenty-four? Five? Why does it seem like you're so much older? You have like this old soul thing going on."

I had a canned response to this question, but I didn't feel like using it with him. "I'm older than I look, but yeah. Something like that." I echoed his words, and he nodded.

"Right. Okay, you ready to get beat again? You get enough to eat?"

"I see where your priorities are. Thanks, the food was good. And I plan a full comeback this time. I still say you won because you have the course memorized. How can I compete with your years of experience?" I winked at him as I stood up and tossed our trash.

"We'll see about that," he said, falling in behind me. "You are pretty distracting," he spoke in my ear. "Kind of hard to focus on strokes when—"

"Are you watching my ass, Professor?" I turned around and walked backwards and caught him in the act. Yeah, he was watching me. God, could I make it through 18 holes so I could get my hands on all he had going on?

"Merely observing your skills, Nurse Lowell." He rubbed at his chin as though he had a goatee.

"Watch and learn," I said. However, he had me so distracted between his smart-assed comments and his smart ass...Roman was definitely winning.

And if we'd been able to finish our games, he definitely would have come out the victor. But a ruckus at the exit doors leading to the Boardwalk caught our attention.

Roman heard the scream first, but I sensed the fear.

Without speaking, we both fisted our golf clubs and made our way over to see what was going on.

10

CHAPTER TEN

R oman

CREED MOVED with a speed and grace that probably came from years of working with fragile folks who frequently needed medical attention. He leaped over a table and around two groups of spectators while I tried to keep up with him.

The scene we found brought on some serious déjà vu.

I pulled out my phone and shot a quick text to my aunt and uncle with our code for an unsafe situation, knowing if they were local they'd use Find My Phone to get my location. I knew Rey was on duty today.

Four frat-boy-looking dudes had an Indian man backed against the glass of the display case outside the door. The man looked out of place at the Boardwalk, wearing a dress shirt, slacks, and sporting a nice watch...but then I saw a group of young kids holding balloons and a woman in a dress who could have been his wife. The kids were crying and huddled against their mom.

The tallest one of the group of frat boys had a sickening smile on his face as he pressed his chest against the victim's. His teeth were blinding white and really big for his mouth, or maybe it was just the way he was grinning.

"Please," the man pleaded in a lightly accented voice. "We just came to take our children on the bumper cars."

The three other frat boys laughed like that was the most ridiculous thing they'd ever heard, but Smiley kept up his grin, all teeth, his lips pulled back for effect.

"Yeah? Just the bumper cars, huh? You think they want to see their father beg?"

The man's knees buckled and sweat dripped down his neck. "Please, take my wallet, whatever, just leave us—"

"I like birthday parties. Can't I come to your child's birthday party? What kind of cake are you having?"

The other three howled with laughter as they moved in closer—and that was enough.

"Hey, why don't you back off?" I shouted. I had the golf club. I wasn't going to fuck around with Biff and the Bro Hoes.

He turned slowly to face me with that eerie-as-fuck grin plastered on his face. "I don't recall asking you for advice, friend."

The guy's eyes were...electric. He was practically vibrating with excitement.

"Call 9-1-1," I heard Creed say to the worker at the counter. "Let them know they may need EMS on scene."

I glanced at him out of the corner of my eye and saw him drop into a defensive position with the golf club at the ready.

"Let the family go and enjoy their day," I said, calling on my experience volunteering with the S.W.A.T. training program. I'd spent time interviewing the trainers for my master's level thesis on hostage negotiation strategies with different personality types, and how officers can quickly assess which tools would be most effective. These four young men appeared to be after the thrill rather than any gain, as they hadn't tried to rob the guy and there were no weapons evident, so I wasn't sure if humanizing them would make any difference. They weren't even touching him with their hands, just using their bodies to trap him against the window. Odd.

"We have committed no assault, the man is free to go," the ringleader said in a calm voice. His eyes zeroed in on the man, almost like the alpha wolf making his intention clear to his pack.

"I'll believe that when you step away from him."

"You want to play, why not level the playing field?" Creed stood to his full height and relaxed his stance.

"How is this scenario level if you're holding a weapon, Outsider?"

Creed blanched, but didn't ease up the pressure. He tossed the golf club behind him and moved closer to the men, who closed ranks around their leader. The cornered father ran for his family and ushered them away.

"Creed," I warned. "Stay back."

The leader of the group tilted his head and his creepy grin was gone. He now assessed Creed to be a threat, as did his accomplices.

I moved toward Creed but he shook his head.

"It's all right, Professor. They're done having fun now. Aren't you?"

Heavy footfalls sounded behind me.

"Roman, stand down."

Uncle Rey approached, his weapon in hand but pointed at the ground.

"We were just leaving," the frat boys said. Then they turned and walked away as a unit.

"Stay right there. Raise your hands above your head and don't move."

Rey's partner went after them and he checked with me, never taking his eyes off of me. "You hurt?"

"No. They cornered that man over there," I said, pointing to the family, who were trying to fade into the crowd. "Creed and I intervened..." My words trailed off as I looked at the nurse. He remained in the same position, staring at the group as if he'd seen a ghost, but knowing he couldn't let on that he was spooked. He remained at attention.

The leader turned with his hands up and glared right back at him. A wordless exchange passed between them until Rey's partner shouted for the leader's attention and their eye contact was broken.

"Do you know those men, Creed?" Rey must have noticed Creed's bizarre behavior.

Creed shook his head but didn't break eye contact. "No. But their methods are familiar."

"What do you mean?" I asked him, placing a hand on his shoulder. He was rock solid, his entire body poised for action. I was pretty strong, I could deadlift 225 pounds, and even though Creed was a bit taller than me, I didn't think he was much stronger...until now. "Creed?"

"You two stay put," Rey said. "I'm going to go interview the family."

Rey walked off as another unit approached, and he sent them to his partner to deal with the young men.

Creed bent and picked up the golf club. "Can you return these? There's something I need to—"

"Creed! My uncle needs to interview you."

"I know. I swear, I'll talk to him, I just need to check something out."

"But—"

"Roman, I would never hinder a police investigation. Do you trust me?"

I'm not sure. "Yes."

His gaze was steady, his breathing calm, he didn't appear to be exhibiting any threat. "Thank you."

He turned and walked into the arcade, and as I watched him, my heart started pounding. *He can't be leaving the scene. I can't just let him go! But I'm not a cop. I—*

"Where did he go?" Rey said as he approached.

"I don't know. He said he needed to see something. What's up?"

"The dude said it was a misunderstanding, that he wasn't attacked, but Jesus, he was scared to death, and his kids... We had to let those guys go with instructions to leave the Boardwalk."

"*What?* If we wouldn't have intervened—"

"They didn't have weapons. They claimed they were asking the man directions. There's nothing we can do."

I laced my fingers together on top of my head and exhaled. "What about security cameras? Wouldn't they show what happened?"

"There were no visible injuries and the other party won't file a complaint, so there's nothing."

"Rey. It was like the woman downtown. They didn't bite this guy, but if Creed and I had been a few minutes later..."

"Look, you two shouldn't have gotten involved. The fucktards claimed you two came at them with golf clubs and they feared for their safety. The only reason we're not having a convo with you in the back of my squad car right now is that neither of you raised those clubs or took a swing. You've got to be more careful than that, dammit."

"I know, asshole," I muttered, getting pissed that he'd question my behavior. "You didn't see it, man. It was gonna be bad. That man was *terrified*."

Rey frowned at me, and then stepped away to answer his radio.

Creed came trotting back from the arcade.

"Where the hell did you go?" I pressed him.

He held up his hands. "I went out front to see if they kept walking down the boardwalk to the exit or if they were sticking around. I knew they would be let go with a warning. I wanted to make sure they actually left and weren't a threat to that family."

I wanted to smack him. "Creed! You can't just do shit like that."

"Did my partner get your statement?" my uncle asked, stepping back over.

"Yes, I met them out front."

"Good." Rey looked between us and smiled. "Was this a date?" He flicked a finger back and forth.

I rolled my eyes but Creed smiled.

"Yes, Officer Cabral. I let your nephew beat me at mini golf."

"Let? There was no letting. Are you for real?"

Rey laughed and tilted his ear to his radio and listened. "Shit.

Gotta roll. You two have fun and stay out of trouble. Oh, and no rides for you, Junior. You call the doctor?"

I wish he was not in uniform right now. "Don't you have someplace to be, Officer Dicknaldo?"

Creed snorted and raised his hand to cover his laughter.

Rey waved as he strolled off to meet up with his partner.

"Doctor? Is something wrong?" Creed turned to face me and got, well, *nursey*.

"Fucking asshole. No, not you. Him. Nothing's wrong. Nothing new, anyway. My tinnitus was just acting up."

"The dizziness last night?" he asked, and he stepped closer. "Are you experiencing it now? Any blurred vision? Headache?"

I batted away his hands when he went to take a peek at my pupils. "Not you too. I'm fine. Old surfing injury. Undertow is brutal here. Smacked my head, hit a rock right here," I said, placing a hand on my right ear. "Partial hearing loss from a ruptured eardrum. Had tinnitus off and on since. Part of why I didn't go the law enforcement route like my uncle and aunt. Wouldn't pass the physical. Figured maybe I could still be of some use in a research capacity."

"Hey," Creed said, placing his hands on my arms. "Roman, you are doing great things. You were amazing, by the way, the way you de-escalated the situation. You kept those kids from seeing their father get seriously injured."

I shook my head and suddenly needed some air. "I'm so pissed though. They're just going to walk away and do it to someone else."

"They'll have a reckoning. I have no doubt. Bullies always do."

"I hate bullies," I grumbled. But then I noticed the vivid colors of the sunset, and it did wonders to calm me. I took a deep, cleansing breath and instantly felt better.

Creed followed my gaze up to the sky and smiled. "It's going to be a beautiful night."

"Yeah," I said, pressing my shoulder to his. Standing next to him seemed to make the anger and stress dissipate. I'd noticed it before. I wouldn't say he had a calming effect on me, not at all. But there was an effect, and I wanted more. "The sky looks painted."

"Indeed." Creed wasn't looking at the sky anymore. He smiled at me. "I believe a walk on the beach at sunset was mentioned."

The guy was definitely a romantic. He held out his arm all old-school like, but I reached for his hand instead. I linked my fingers with his, feeling as if it were the natural thing to do, although I usually wasn't touchy-feely on dates. My hands seemed to have a mind of their own, and they were of a mind to keep touching him. We took the steps down to the sand and, once we got there, we took our shoes off and linked hands once again.

"You were pretty impressive back there, wielding that club like you knew how to handle yourself," I said as we took off towards the water. "You always work with old folks?"

"No," Creed said, his gaze someplace off in the distance. "I prefer working with the elderly, but no. I've worked in juvenile placements before. And psych wards." That would explain his cool demeanor.

"So you learned how to handle tense situations, huh?"

He gave a wry smile. "You learn all you can after a three-hundred-pound man doesn't want to take his meds, that's for sure."

"I bet. That's tough. You can't appeal to their reasonable side."

"Nope. You just have to know how to subdue them, hopefully without hurting them or yourself in the process." He glanced at me. "You seem to have experience as well?"

I shrugged. "I work out with my uncle. We've taken Kajukenbo for years. I've also volunteered as tribute for his department's S.W.A.T. Training."

"Wow. What's that like?" he asked, his brow furrowed as if that didn't sit well with him.

"Mostly they make me a victim needing to be rescued, or if I'm lucky, I get to be the bad guy. Although if Rey's there, he hates it when I do that."

"Why?" Creed asked with a chuckle.

"He doesn't like seeing me at the business end of a gun." I ducked my head a little. "Maybe it reminds him too much of what I could have been if it weren't for Lola taking me in. He prefers if I stay with the hostage negotiators, which actually is where I've learned the most."

"That's interesting," he said, squeezing my hand. "Aren't you afraid?"

"Not at all. They don't use live ammunition. They've trained extensively. The worst part is the flash bangs. Makes my tinnitus worse for a few days after."

His smile slipped. "Does it bother you? The militarization of the police? I can tell you, I've squared off with riot cops in the past. They can be brutal."

"At, like, a demonstration?"

Creed nodded and lifted his chin higher as if he were reliving a difficult memory.

"That's different, but you're right. I've spent many hours arguing with my aunt and uncle about the need for mental health services rather than tanks and riot gear. A Youth and Family Services program with licensed therapists on staff is critical to any police department. I wrote up a proposal for a mental health crisis response team. I want to present it to the city council and the department, but it still needs work. That's why I started doing ridealongs with Reynaldo and Vanessa."

Creed whistled low.

"What?"

"You continue to dazzle me, Professor. Is there anything unattractive about you?"

I barked out a laugh. "Depends on who you ask. My ex would say I'm too involved with my work, my uncle and aunties would tell you I'm immature, and my lola would tell you I'm shit at cleaning house."

Creed laughed. "I think your work is fascinating. I think you have your whole life to grow into who you are meant to be. And cleaning house is an art. You're a scientist. Makes sense you'd be shit at it."

I bumped him with my shoulder. "What about you? You work at the home and what else? What should I know about the extraordinary Nurse Creed?"

Creed's smile slipped a little. "Depends."

"Depends? See, there you go with the mysterious shit again."

Creed stopped walking and tugged on my hand to bring me to a halt. "It depends on why you're asking, Professor. If you're trying to find out whether I'm safe to be caring for your grandmother, that will determine how I answer—"

"Creed—"

"Let me finish," he said, turning to face me, brushing against me. The contact of our hips made my skin hyper aware of him once more, and I had that static electricity thing going on.

"If you're asking to make just enough small talk to gauge whether I'd be a good hookup, that *definitely* will determine how I answer you."

He shifted once more, bringing our pelvises into contact.

"What if I'm asking because I genuinely want to get to know you, *and* I'm interested in hooking up?" I couldn't help the cocky grin that covered for my uncertainty. What *did* I want with him? And did he want me too?

"That's my favorite of the possibilities. Okay, Professor. I've lived a lot of places, traveled around for a long time, and I want to stay here. In Santa Cruz, at Puesta Del Sol. I love the residents, love my coworkers, and I don't want to do anything to interfere with that, including but not limited to having a disastrous fling with a resident's grandson. So while I'm into you, I'm not interested in a random hookup."

I sucked in a breath at his admission. "You never cease to throw me off with your statements."

"How's that?"

This face-to-face discussion was a little too...close. I needed to keep moving. I tugged his hand and started walking again, hoping he'd get the clue.

The sky was awash with pinks and purples and silvery blue, as though an artist had squeezed the colors out onto a palette and ran his fingers through them in big swirls. It was hard to believe it hadn't been created on purpose, that it had just sort of happened that way.

"You come on strong, and just when I think I'll call your bluff, you take a step back."

11

———

CHAPTER ELEVEN

C reed

HE READ ME SO WELL.

"Maybe I'm testing you. I'm sorry, Roman, but I'm very careful about letting people get close to me. There's a reason why bullying is such a trigger for me. I believe you mean well, but at some point I became invested in whether or not you would be like the others, or if you'd be different."

"I'm a good listener, or so I've been told," Roman said. "You've been there for me. Maybe let me return the favor?"

I shoved my hands in my pockets to keep from touching him and shrugged. Either he'd trust me or not, and that would tell me a lot about him.

I sighed and plopped down in the sand. "This okay?"

"Yeah, sure." He lowered himself down beside me and we sat with our knees up, toes dug into the cool sand, watching the waves embattle the shore relentlessly, as if it was their mission to keep something down. To drown it. That made me wonder about his accident.

"Did you lose consciousness when you had your accident?"

Roman nodded, his face hidden by shadows now, even though he sat inches away. "Thankfully a beachgoer knew CPR or I might not be here talking to you."

And what a travesty that would be. To never have been in Roman's orbit? Never have felt his unique energy signature that I felt under my skin hours after being in his presence. I was so drawn to him. We sat side by side and I couldn't help but press my shoulder against his. I craved all the heady emotions coming off of him, the fear, the anger, the anguish, and repeat.

"You were fortunate, no doubt about that. And now you're here, ready for me to seduce you?"

He wrinkled his nose at me and laughed, leaning away just a bit. "Always with the push and pull."

"Mmm. Like the ocean. Do you still surf?"

He sighed. "I thought you were going to tell me about you." He rubbed his hands together and fell quiet, his gaze intensely directed toward the water.

"Okay, fine. I'll give you a little peek." I leaned back on my hands and rolled my head on my neck. I caught sight of the spiritualists at the other end of the beach, arriving with the evening tide for their session of meditation. "Part of what I love about my job is being around families like yours. Sure, not all of the residents have tight-knit clans, but the ones that do...it does a lot. Gives me hope, you know? I didn't have that."

It shouldn't hurt this much to talk about it after all these years. Well, wasn't that nice, to think I could control how I felt. I might be able to keep a lot of my emotions in check, but not all.

"What was your family like?" he asked me. He'd turned his head toward me and rested his chin on his arms. I lost my focus tracing the curve of his biceps with my eyes, wishing I could take a more hands-on approach.

I let out a big breath and groaned, which made him laugh.

"That bad, huh?"

"Old news is more like it. Put it this way, I left home like I had the hounds of hell chasing me the minute I turned eighteen." I'd been sure to take care of everything. Applied for conscientious objector status, which I got because of my work for the church...the church I hated with all of my essence. As soon as my draft card came, I was out of there. Worked out my thumb hitchhiking cross country, San Francisco in my sights. Peace and love, baby. That's what I was after. I was going to change the world, or at least get laid trying.

"You left? Your home—wait, where were you from?"

"Macon County, Georgia." It wouldn't hurt to tell the truth. Not anymore. I'd changed my name several times since leaving home. It would be difficult to find the origins of Creed Lowell before he received his driver's license in Nebraska eight years ago. I'd been setting up a new identity every ten years since I fled Boulder Creek in 1973. Christopher Creed Lowry, however, died in a car accident shortly after leaving home in 1969. At least that's what I'd eventually had my death certificate say. I knew I needed one after the cohort was destroyed. I couldn't have the usurpers track me back home and attack my family trying to get to me. No, I made sure there was no link.

"Creed?"

"Hmm? Sorry," I said when he chuckled.

"You drifted off for a moment. I said I knew it was the south. Every once in a while I hear your accent slip out. Mostly when you're dealing with the folks at the home."

I laughed. "There's something about that good old Southern comfort that seems to soothe folks. Makes you seem like you're not a threat, like you're trustworthy." I turned on the accent thick, laughing at the way it felt on my tongue.

Roman's nostrils flared. "That's...God, I never thought I'd find a Southern dude sexy."

I barked out a laugh. "Well yeah, because you California boys think we Southern men are all slow and simple."

"There's nothing simple about you. But tell me, Creed, are you a threat? Or are you trustworthy?"

His lids were heavy and I realized that I'd gotten so relaxed talking to him that I hadn't kept myself in check. I'd allowed my pheromones free rein and they'd hit him hard. I was about to suggest we get up and walk when he turned toward me, leaning in, licking his lips.

Yes. You want this. We both wanted this, and I wasn't sure which one of us wanted it more. I sat up, bringing our chests into contact and I brushed my nose against his.

"I'm only a threat if you don't want me to kiss you right now."

He whimpered and reached for me, but his need hit me first. Oh, sweet Jesus, he needed this, and *his* need made *me* need.

Roman spent so much of his time trying to keep his anger in check that when he let go, gave in to his baser wants, he *slayed* me. It took very little effort for him to push me onto my back on the cool sand. He stretched out next to me and slid his knee in between mine as his tongue and lips did incredible things. The abrasiveness of the sand against the exposed flesh of my lower back was the reminder I needed not to let our exploration of each other go beyond the fiery kisses that threatened to melt all of my self-control. Like his name, he was a firework ready to ignite, ready to explode, and God, I wanted to be on the receiving end of that pent-up passion.

"I could suck on your lip for hours," I finally said, needing to catch my breath. "The way it curves down in the front, that ridge, so delicious. *You're* delicious, Roman." And I wasn't just talking about his lip, although I could pontificate about its pillowy softness, its greediness as he used it to seek entrance into my mouth. How when he was busy exploring the secrets of my mouth with his tongue, I was content to run my tongue over that curve.

When he pulled back, it was even puffier, swollen from my attentions.

"I could do this for hours," I drawled, loving the way that little trick with my voice made his eyes cloudy with lust, heady with desire.

"Then let's do it. Come home with me," he said, pressing his thigh against my very, *very* hard dick. "I'll kiss you all night. I'll kiss you wherever you want. I'm very good with this lip you seem to like so much."

I brushed his hair back from his face and was so, so tempted. But sweet Roman had no idea what he was getting into, and I owed it to him to not suck him further into my world...

Creed, you're fooling yourself. You're already deep into this, and so is he.

I pressed our foreheads together and fought to catch my breath.

"Soon, Professor. I promise. For now, let's get you home." I couldn't give in. I cared about him too much. I knew he didn't fully trust me, and I knew he *shouldn't* trust me. I couldn't do that to him.

He pulled back.

"You keep putting the brakes on and I'm going to think this is just a game to you." He pushed himself up to his feet. "Thanks for the golf game." He started to walk away and I scrambled to catch up with him.

"Roman, wait."

He stopped but didn't turn to face me.

"I'm not playing games here. I'm trying to do what's right."

He turned to face me and his anger hit me hard, nearly knocking the wind out of me.

"What's right? Look, if you don't want this to happen, just say it. If you've got some fucking secret, fine. But make up your fucking mind. I've got too much going on in my damn life to play games."

"Roman, that was not my intention. I apologize if I made you uncomfortable. It's been a really long time since I've been close with anyone and there are things you don't know—"

"Then fucking tell me! Or don't. But don't treat me like I can't handle stuff. I hate that. My family does that shit to me all the time and I can't stand it." He started to walk away again, and I blurted out the last thing I ever thought I'd tell him.

"I was in a cult."

He stopped and spun around to face me. "You...what?"

What are you doing, Creed?

"Yeah. Ran away from home and ended up in a commune like some sort of cliché." I laughed and it came out a little hysterical.

Roman approached, concern on his face. "Creed, I'd never think that. That you were a cliché."

"I'm not ready to talk about it, but I know what you're working on, and I can't pretend like I have only a passing interest in what you're researching." It was true, but not the real reason I was hesitant to take things further with him. I didn't trust myself. I couldn't keep myself in check enough with him to let go. It wasn't fair to him. So I guessed I was putting up another barrier to hold him at arm's length. Which was real mature.

"All right." He glanced around at the dark creeping in around us. "Let's go get some coffee or something. We can *not* talk about it, or talk about it."

He held out a hand, and I gratefully accepted. He was pissed, I could feel it rolling off his shoulders, but he wasn't going to walk away. At least not tonight.

12

CHAPTER TWELVE

R oman

I WAS STILL REPLAYING the scene on the beach in my head the next day after teaching my online Criminal Behavior and Psychology course.

Creed had me tied in knots, and I hated being in this position, but when he'd dropped that bomb about the cult after I'd been ready to write him off as a cock-tease, what else could I do?

Of all people, I understood more than most the toll spending any amount of time in a manipulative religious order could take on one's psyche. He'd opted not to tell me more than he'd lived with them for a couple of years after running away to California, and he'd left after a bad situation, still not feeling like he was totally safe. That was it, though. Something held him back from talking, and I couldn't figure out what it was. I got the sense he hadn't planned on telling me for a long time, but I was glad he had.

It made his bizarre behavior more understandable.

My cell buzzed in my trousers and I pulled it out.

"Tita? Everything okay?"

"Yeah, everything's okay. Why?"

"You're the one that called me. No one calls me unless there's a problem. You only text me."

She exhaled. "I'm calling on behalf of the department."

That had my back straightening. "Okay."

"Captain Rojas would like to hire you to consult on the case."

"Hire me?"

"Yeah."

"Like a paid gig? Not just me talking cases with you over beers?"

"Yeah, Junior. Now when can you get here? We have a lead to discuss with you, so the sooner the better."

I looked at the time. "I've got office hours until four and then I can come."

"Good. Be here then. We're ordering in dinner and we'll get you out of here in time to go see Lola."

"Thanks."

By the time I made it to the PD, it was near five and my dress shirt was choking me. This was exactly the kind of work I wanted to do, the kind of help I wanted to provide, but imposter syndrome was strong. My family had always done such a good job of treating me like the fragile kid that it was a shock to be going in on this as my tita's peer.

"Sup, Junior," I heard from behind me as I climbed the steps.

I turned to find Rey in street clothes.

"What are you doing here? I thought you were off today?"

"I'm part of the plainclothes detail. I hear we've got some hotshot professor coming in to consult on the case." He pulled on my tie and I smacked his hand away while he laughed his ass off.

"Can you at least pretend you're not an asshole for five minutes?"

He reached around and held the door open for me and then showed his ID to get us buzzed in.

I'd been in the department countless times, but this time everything seemed stark, grim. I was used to coming in as the wonder kid and having the officers make a fuss over me, not dressed in a suit and being led through the desks to the conference room rather than around the outside of the main room to the break room or roll call before a ridealong. This was serious, and I hoped I could deliver what they were hoping I would.

"Roman," Tita Vanessa said as she greeted us. She gave me a side hug and then showed me over to the table where there were stacks of folders next to a laptop. "This is Ross Sterling, the other detective working the case with me. You know Grant and Tompkins," she said, gesturing to two other patrol officers I'd met over the years. They looked up from files and waved, and then all eyes looked expectantly toward me.

"Hi," I said lamely. When no one spoke, I turned to Vanessa. "You said you had a lead?"

"Yeah," she said, clicking on the laptop and projector. "We ran the names of the four men from the Boardwalk and while nothing showed up on first look, we dug a little deeper and found that two of them had Spanish passports and one of them is from Monaco. They're here on work visas."

She flashed through their info and pics on the screen, and I rested a hand on the back of a chair.

"You shared with us that you researched an organization called La Mente in Spain?" Sterling asked me. I hadn't met him before, but Vanessa had spoken highly of him.

"Right. The Order of the Mind, it's a religious organization. They have a series of learning centers throughout Europe, and I found stories of their existence in South Africa and Monaco. Their literature states 'we educate our members to better themselves through mindfulness and learning to serve a greater good, and we use our tithes to support improvements in medical science.'

"They're very secretive, so I was only able to read a few articles about them, read some police reports, and I spoke to several families and members of the Catholic church who claimed there were multiple children that had been seduced by the group and then disappeared. Eventually I'll try to go to South Africa and Monaco as well, definitely before writing my book, but in the meantime, I want to finish my dissertation and degree."

"I can't see where there would be a link between something like that and this type of bullying behavior," Sterling said. He crossed his arms and his legs in front of him and leaned back in the chair.

"La Mente studied the effects of fear on health and they allegedly put their recruits through months of psychological torture, teaching their initiated members how to use fear to control and manipulate new recruits, who in turn would learn their methods. It was all part of biological research they were conducting through their biotech company."

"One of the suspects is employed by a biotech firm in Santa Clara." Sterling shrugged. "Maybe there's something there."

I took a seat. "Vanessa, will you put up their information again?"

"Please," she muttered.

"Please?" I gave her a smirk, and she laughed. Guess she'd always be tita, even if we were at work.

They all had shaved heads and they were all wearing white t-shirts in the pictures, but these were definitely the four men from the Boardwalk.

"Can we get more information on them? Where they've lived the past five years, whether they've gone to school? How old are they?"

"Jonathan Aldridge, Dominique LeMonde, Sacha Bernard, and Federico Diego. They're all between twenty and twenty-five, according to their passports."

"Perfect age for recruitment. If they've got markers like behavior problems, home schooling, isolation, mental health concerns, substance abuse...you may be looking at prime indicators of vulnerability."

Four hours and four slices of pizza later, we had written up profiles for the four men and we'd found employment records showing the four of them were employed by the firm BioBourne. This was too much of a coincidence. They had to be connected somehow to La Mente. The bioresearch firm was too close of a link to ignore.

Rey and the other two patrol officers were going to be hanging out downtown and at the Boardwalk in the evenings for the next few nights, and Vanessa and Sterling were going to visit BioBourne tomorrow and then see if they could interview the four men, although there was talk of putting that off, to let them feel the pressure and see whether they would act again.

As I was packing up my computer and cleaning up my pizza mess, Vanessa walked over and placed a hand between my shoulder blades.

"You did good, Ju—Roman. Thank you."

"I hope it helps," I said, shoving my hands in my pockets. I appreciated her not using my nickname. "I'll keep digging, but La Mente is locked up tight. I'll go back through my notes and see if there are any other connections."

She cocked her head. "If I can get in touch with my contacts at INTERPOL, maybe you could talk with them. They'd likely have some information, especially if this group was involved in a criminal investigation in the past." She shrugged. "It could help both of us."

"Thank you. That would be huge. It was difficult to get Policía Nacional to share much information with an American grad student. I'd appreciate the connection."

"How's it going in here?"

I turned to find an older bald guy dressed in a suit that fit him like a glove. He was incredibly fit, about my height with light brown skin, and he wore a big smile.

"Captain Rojas, this is my nephew, Roman San Angelo. Roman, this is Captain Jaime Rojas."

We shook hands, and he looked me up and down. Then he spoke to me in Spanish. He asked whether we'd found any connection between the attacks and the group I'd studied in Spain, and I explained, also in Spanish, that there were a few common details that were not likely to be coincidence. He pounded on my shoulder.

"Excellent work, son. Glad to have you on board." He turned to Vanessa. "You have him sign the paperwork?"

"Oh, here, Roman." She slid a packet of papers toward me and smiled. "Your contract for consultant work with the Santa Cruz Police Department. You've already passed the thorough background check as part of your volunteer work and the study for the Youth and Family Services project. Read it over and sign, please."

"Let's see how this goes and then we'll talk about whether or not you're interested in collaborating further." Captain Rojas nodded at the other officers, told Rey and the others on plainclothes duty to be careful, and then he left.

My tinnitus flared to life as he shut the door. Thankfully I didn't get dizzy, but I couldn't hear much over the buzz as I looked down at the paperwork.

All of my hard work was paying off. Not only was I the first person in my family to receive a graduate degree, but I was on track to earn my doctorate in the next year, and now I was officially consulting on my first police case. I was kind of making something of myself, thanks to Lola, Rey, and Vanessa.

"Hey, you have any questions?" Vanessa placed a hand on my shoulder and it startled me.

"Hmm?"

"You okay? I asked if you had any questions?"

"No, no. I'm just about through here."

"Good. I gotta take off. Bernadette has been texting me for the past hour. Just leave the paperwork with Ross, and then Rey will take you up to get your ID."

I blinked. "ID?"

"Yeah. You're legit now. You don't need an escort anymore. I'll call you tomorrow after Ross and I go to the biotech firm and we'll schedule our next meeting. Sound good?"

"Sure. Great."

I could barely make out that there were actual English letters on the papers, but I signed it anyway. Rey took me up front, they took my picture, gave me a copy of the contract and some employment paperwork to fill out and return, and when I finally left, it was nearing nine-thirty and the sky was dark.

"It happens," Rey said as I stood there, dazed. "You go in and it's bright and sunny and when you leave it feels like doom has descended."

I turned to frown at him and he started to make "dun dun dunnnh" sounds.

"You are disturbed."

"Thank you. Give Lola a hug for me, would you?"

Rey hugged me and started to walk away.

"Hey," I said, keeping him close. "Be safe, okay?"

He pulled back and laughed at me. "Right. Because vampires are real and someone might give me a hickey." He pounded on my back. "Good one." He waved as he walked toward the other two officers who were going to be downtown that night.

I shook my head and walked toward the visitors' parking lot. Lolo's Honda Accord continued to serve me well, but at some point I was going to need to buy a new car.

I thought about how I was going to manage all the things I needed to take care of as I drove over to Puesta Del Sol. I hoped the car would at least make it until I finished my degree in Clinical Forensic Psychology and was either hired on full time by the university or picked up elsewhere. Or I finished my book, landed an agent, and received a decent contract. Or, worse case, I'd go back to bartending. Cousin Ronnie could always use some extra help. I'd been able to pay for my grad school tuition that way.

But then I got to thinking about all the work that Lola's house needed, about how we were going to afford to keep paying for her to stay at Puesta Del Sol...how I'd pay the property taxes—

A knock on my window made me jump and I cursed.

13

CHAPTER THIRTEEN

C reed

"Jesus," Roman said as he opened the car door, and I stumbled back. It was as if he was hotboxing anguish in his car. "You scared the shit out of me."

"Hey," I said, crouching down next to him. "Hey, what's wrong?"

He was dressed as if he'd come from an interview or something. He wore gray slacks and a black dress shirt with a maroon tie. His hair had been styled and off his face but it was coming down around his eyes now, probably because he'd been sitting in his car stewing.

"Nothing, I... What are you doing out here?"

"Oh, Lexi had to leave early tonight so I walked her out to her car. She gets nervous out here."

Roman looked around the darkened parking lot and frowned. "You guys need better security. And more light. It's so dark."

"It *is* dark. Your lola is already asleep. She and her sisters are taking the sunrise yoga class tomorrow so they turned in early."

"Oh," he said, and he seemed to melt into the seat. "Damn. I didn't mean to be so late. Was she upset?"

"I don't know what the right answer is here," I said, placing a hand on his thigh. "I could tell you she asked about you, but honestly, she and her sisters cleaned up at our poker tournament, and then they went to Stella's room to watch *CSI*. So yeah, I think you're in the clear."

The pain coming from him was feeding my soul, but I *hated* it. I hated how helpless I felt. I wanted to take all of his pain and replace it with...well, something that wouldn't hurt him anymore.

"I'm glad," he said. "I want her to be happy."

"But *you're* not happy. What would make you happy, Roman?"

He laughed and wiped at an eye. "Honestly? Can you rewind time, or maybe fast forward? Like, I know I was happy at some point, and I know things will be better once I finish my degree, but right now...I'm, like, caught in the middle. It's like the undertow all over again."

He looked down at my hand and paused briefly before taking hold of it as if it were a lifeline.

"I don't know about time-travel, but I think I could make you forget about things for a while?" I couldn't help it. It was probably a terrible thing to say after our last date, and the moment his smile slipped, I cursed my mistake. "I'm sorry—"

"No, *I'm* sorry," he said. We'd talked after our argument at the beach over coffee and agreed to just hang out, give it some time, not rush into anything, but it was obvious that neither of us were happy about it. "Look, I know I carry a big chip on my shoulder, Creed, but I'm kinda lost right now."

Screw the distance, screw my personal rules. I knelt next to the car and took him into my arms. He came willingly, and blessed be, he let me hold him. I absorbed all of his pain I could take. I hated for him to be carrying all of this weight, and I knew I could heal him. Him coming willingly to me for comfort was as much consent as I needed.

"God, Creed, why does it hurt less when I'm with you?"

I pulled him tighter and inhaled against his neck. His scent made my mouth water and my canines ache with desire.

"There are several reasons I could offer, but let's go with…because I want you to feel better."

He sniffled. "That's it, huh? You want it and it happens?"

"You have no idea."

The moment grew awkward though, and I had a rock digging into my knee so I released him.

"What time are you off?" he asked me with a hopeful smile.

"Six. Why?"

"If you want to come over, I'll make you breakfast?"

No one had offered to cook for me in so long. Roman was going to break through all of the barriers I'd so carefully constructed to keep others from getting too close. The fact was, I didn't want to keep him out.

"That sounds heavenly. I've gotta go home first, but I could be over around eight?"

He grinned. "I don't have class until one. Sounds like a do-over date to me."

"I like that," I said.

Several hours of uninterrupted Roman time, just the two of us…

"Oh, do you mind if I bring a friend?" I asked, knowing it would throw him off.

"A friend? Uh—"

"Of the non-human variety."

"Oh, uh, sure. Do you or your friend have any dietary restriction?"

We both laughed, and the stiffness in his body subsided a bit.

"I mean, you can ask her, but I haven't found any. Let me get back to work so it'll be morning sooner. I can't wait to have breakfast with you."

He pulled me in for a kiss, just a tender gesture to seal our plans, but it was enough contact to have me trembling.

What is this? I don't tremble.

One kiss from this man and I was ready to surrender, to forget everything and dive in with no safety rope.

There was no being careful with Roman. It was too late for that.

"I'll text you the address. See you soon," he said as I stood up and closed his door.

Goddess help me.

He waved and drove off, leaving me alone in the darkness to try and catch my breath.

Or so I thought.

"Finally I get you alone."

I spun around, but all I could make out were shapes in the shadows. "What do you—"

"I have a message. Leave Santa Cruz and never come back."

"And if I don't?" I pulled all of the static electricity and energy I could gather from my surroundings into my being and readied myself for attack. There were four of them, and they were itching to get physical, but something held them back.

"We know who you are, *Learner* Creed. You are no longer welcome here."

Hearing that title broke something loose inside me and the energy I'd collected was pulled from me. Anyone who knew I'd become a Guardian no longer existed, so who could it be?

"Show yourself. If you know who I am, then you know of The Way. This is not how we behave."

"We know why you're here, and you will not succeed. Leave at once."

I felt their signatures leave and I was alone once again, my heart pounding with the adrenaline rush, excess energy seeping out of my body, out of my control. I stumbled, the loss affecting me profoundly.

The attacks. It was them. Somehow these men had been trained in The Way, but they used their power unscrupulously. Draining someone's energy as a threat was such a violation, it went against everything we were taught in the Gateway of the Sun.

1970

. . .

"THE STRONGEST OF Learners will master the ability of manipulating the energy around them for not only healing, but also for protection. This ability is a gift that we must always respect. We are never to manipulate energy to harm another. Now, you will be paired up to practice. You will attempt to form a deep connection with your partner and find the root of any pain or discomfort they may be experiencing. Our goal is only to identify the pain, do not go any further."

Leader Lauren paired Muse with Stephen, and I felt her concern. I made sure to position myself where I could see her.

"Learner Creed, you shall work with Learner Mack."

Mack and I nodded at each other. He was a quiet guy, older. Didn't talk much, but I never got a negative vibe from him like I did from Stephen. We sat cross-legged in front of each other, our knees touching, and I turned my body so I could sense any discomfort from Muse.

"You may begin," Leader Lauren directed.

Mack and I made eye contact and then closed our eyes as we'd been taught. I opened my inside eye and watched the colors inside of Mack shift and swirl. Apparently it was different for all of us, but I would often see redness where there was inflammation, as if I were looking at some sort of infrared image.

"Learner Creed, what do you see?" Leader Lauren asked.

"Mack, your left knee is bothering you. You injured it recently?"

I heard him clear his throat. "Uh, yes. I fell on the steps last night."

"Learner Mack, did you not report this injury to a Guardian?"

"No, Leader Lauren. I didn't consider it to be serious—"

"But Learner Mack, there is never a need to experience pain as long as we are a community. Now, Learner Creed, would you like to try to heal the injury?"

I was startled. I knew I could do it. I'd been practicing with a tree, and even with Muse a bit when we had an ounce of free time. I didn't know if this was a test, however.

I opened my eyes. "Yes, Leader Lauren." I looked to Mack. "Do I have your permission, Learner Mack?"

His lip twitched as if he wanted to smile, and I felt a rush of heat from him.

Oh.

"Yes. Please."

I did smile as I closed my eyes. He made it very clear that I had permission to do more than heal him.

But for now, I focused on his left knee. First I collected as much energy from my surroundings as I could, and then I directed it toward those red swaths of pulsing light. I saw my infusion of healing energy in a warm golden hue as it worked its way in to surround the red, and eventually the red was displaced until it was no more.

I heard Mack suck in a breath. Worried I'd hurt him, I opened my eyes but he was smiling. He ran his hand over his knee and laughed.

"You did it," he whispered to me, and then he reached out and squeezed my hand. "Thank you."

"Blessed be," I murmured. His joy and lust combined to give me a helluva rush. *I could do this all day.* When he didn't shy away with those feelings, I began to wonder if he planned to do anything about it—

"Stop it!"

Muse's voice rang out through the grove of redwoods, and I saw her scramble away from Stephen.

"Learner Muse?"

Muse gazed around and her cheeks reddened under the scrutiny of our cohort.

"My apologies, Leader Lauren. May I be excused?"

Leader Lauren gave Stephen a hard look and nodded at Muse. "Learners, you are dismissed. Except Learner Stephen."

We all stood and walked toward the path in a single line. I took Muse's hand and pulled her close to me. As soon as we were out of sight of the clearing, I pulled her with me into the bushes.

"What happened?"

Muse's eyes were wide and her whole body shook.

"He...he can *show you* things. He made me...he made me see what he wanted to do. I tried not to show him I was afraid, but what he did, what he wants... Oh my God, Creed. He's awful."

I pulled her into my arms and held her. I wanted to tear the guy apart for scaring my friend.

"And the more afraid I got," she continued, speaking into my shoulder, "the stronger the images, the more intense. It's like he was feeding off my fear."

Leader Caleb had talked to us about absorbing negative energy to heal, but this sounded like creating negative energy in a continuous loop, one that would drain the person and continue to feed the creator until they were gorged with it.

That motherfucker.

I started to go after him, but she grabbed my arm.

"Creed, you can't."

"But we have to. If he's allowed to continue this way, he's a threat to anyone around him."

A tear rolled down her cheek and that was the last straw for me. After all the shit we'd been through in San Francisco, I'd never seen her cry. She'd been beat up, taken advantage of, hungry, and sick, and I'd never seen her cry.

I took her hands in mine. "Muse, darlin', I can't let this pass. We are being given too much responsibility here." It was true. We'd learned so much from our teachers over the past year, and as we progressed, we were promised more and more training, one-on-one sessions, and eventually, an audience with The Source, who we'd only been exposed to in passing a few times.

"Okay, but let's go to Leader Bree. I feel like she's the most likely to listen to us."

"Okay, but until then, you stay away from him. Stay close to me. I won't let him hurt you, okay?"

She hugged me to her tightly, and I tried to use some of the healing energy I'd learned how to express.

"You're so strong, Creed. I really think we were meant to be here. You're going to be a great healer."

I kissed the top of her head. "Let's join the others before they come looking for us."

She wiped her face with the bottom of her tunic and took a few deep breaths. I admired her strength. And as we joined the others at the baths and Mack gave me an inviting smile, I knew I needed to be more careful. I couldn't let anything happen to Muse, and now, I was determined that Stephen and his crew—the other three obnoxious twits who were drawn to him for some stupid reason—would not gain any traction. If I really was meant to be here, it was to protect the others from their violations.

I WENT INSIDE to finish my shift, but I was dragging. An event occurred in my favor in the wee hours, however. One of the residents in the B wing, which I usually wasn't assigned to, woke with night terrors, and none of the staff were able to calm her. I volunteered, knowing full well that I could get her right back to sleep.

Sure enough, after fighting two much bigger nurses and scratching the shit out of them, she sank into my embrace and I absorbed all of her fear, her dread, and the agony her body was putting her through as it began the process of shutting down. She began to weep, and we slumped to the floor. I held her until my calming energy put her into a restful state.

"Man, she's strong when she gets like that," Jamal said. He'd been one of the nurses she'd attacked. "She's been doing this at least twice a week for the past month."

"Call me next time," I said as I picked her up and carried her back to bed. The worst part was, I hated that she'd had to suffer in order for me to be at full strength, despite knowing that I wasn't the cause of her misery. I would do anything in my power to ease her until it was her time to leave this plane.

Six o'clock seemed to take forever to arrive. I couldn't wait to see Roman, and Rhonda couldn't wait to see me, either. She barked at me when I opened the door and then stood by her food bowl, refusing to look at me until I fed her the gourmet, organically sourced food she loved and gave her a full-body rub down. When it was time to go, she pranced by the front door, ready to greet the day.

"Let's hope you like him as much as I do," I said to her, and she gave me one of her looks I liked to think meant, "whatever, dude. As long as you rub my belly for an hour before your next shift, we're golden."

We walked the three miles to his house and by the time we arrived, she was pulling on the leash as if she knew something I didn't.

"Hey, I hope you like— Oh, your friend is beautiful!"

14

CHAPTER FOURTEEN

R oman

THERE IS nothing better for an ailing soul than cuddling a willing dog. Okay, maybe the kiss I got from Creed last night was pretty good, but when I bent down to introduce myself to his beautiful dog, and she rubbed her face all over my cheek and licked my ear, I was in love.

"Who is this incredible creature?"

Creed sighed. "This is the woman who owns my heart. Rhonda, meet Roman. Roman, this is my Rhonda."

"It's been so long since I've been around a dog. Lola was allergic so when my parents died and I came to live with her, my dog Bunny went to live with my cousin Ronnie, Tita Stella's son—and wow, why am I telling you all of this?

I stood up and Rhonda leaned against my leg, obviously not done with me. Creed stood before me and he smiled.

"Come here," I said, holding my arms out to him, and he didn't hesitate. After I'd left Creed outside the home several hours ago, I made a big decision. I refused to resist him anymore. The whole suffering-in-silence shit was overrated, and being in his arms felt so damned good. He had this way of pulling me in tight, rubbing his nose along my neck as if he were breathing me in.

But Rhonda wasn't having any of it.

"I'm sorry," Creed laughed when she shoved her snout between us and pawed at his thigh. "I might have promised her a morning snack after our walk over here."

"How far away are you? You don't have a car?"

"We're close enough to walk anywhere we need to go," he said with a shrug.

"Even after your shift? I'm sorry, I could have come to get you."

He held up a hand. "We walk every day, don't worry. I'm two blocks from the lighthouse."

"Damn." I closed the door and led Creed and Rhonda into the kitchen, where the bacon was just about finished. "That's a hike. Well, your good girl has earned whatever she wants to eat. Mean old Nurse Creed making you walk all that way."

I swear, the dog shot Creed a dirty look before shoving her nose in my hand again. She was tall with a broad chest, probably one of the biggest Dobermans I'd ever seen, and I'd been around some of the meanest police dogs.

"She can be bought, don't worry. I hear it from her every morning when I get home from work."

"That's a long time for her to be alone, isn't it?" I asked him. "Wait, unless...do you have like a roommate or something?"

"No, it's just the two of us. She sleeps most of the time I'm gone, and on my days off, she sleeps the whole time I would have been at work. We get plenty of play time. Well, plenty of 'whatever Rhonda wants, Rhonda gets' time."

"Have a seat," I said, gesturing to the small two-person table where Lola and I used to take our meals together. The house had a formal dining room that sat twelve tightly when we had family gatherings, but most of the time it was the two of us, and we sat at the cozy nook by the French doors that led to the backyard. It was nice to have someone to eat with again.

"Thanks. It smells good."

"I didn't think to ask if *you* had any dietary restrictions. You're not vegan, are you?"

"No," Creed said, and then he coughed. "Wow, no, I'm, uh, not."

"You want coffee? Juice?"

"Water is fine. Did you get decent sleep last night?"

I noticed him checking out my attire as I pulled down a glass from the cupboard and filled it at the sink. I didn't want to get grease on my work clothes, so I'd put on flannel lounge pants after my shower and wore a fitted long-sleeved thermal.

"I did. I really did." And this was where I walked the walk and talked the talk. "I felt better after I talked to you."

Creed sat back in the chair, his long legs kicked out and his hands resting on his powerful thighs. He wore jeans, which I liked. A lot. They were traditional blue Levi's, 501s, even with a button fly. They must have been vintage. I never saw anyone wear jeans with a cut like that anymore.

"I'm happy to help," he said, his voice slipping into that drawl that did things to me, his lips sliding into a sultry smile.

I brought the water to him and this time, I was the space invader. I stood between his parted thighs to see what he'd do.

"Here," I said, setting the glass down on the table next to his plate. "Food's almost ready. Hope you like your eggs scrambled."

"I'm just honored that you're cooking for me," he said. He kept up the smoldering act, and I was going to eat *him* for breakfast.

"It's...well, it's morning." I laughed at the dumb coming out of my mouth. "Made sense. I'm happy you're here, although when will you sleep? Do you work tonight?"

He reached for the back of my thigh and ran his fingers over the tendons behind my knee. But he didn't take control. He simply stared, his lids heavy.

"I'll be fine," he said. "Feed me and then let's talk."

I had a feeling his words had a double meaning, especially as he let his gaze drift lazily down to the front of my pants. And suddenly I was all blushing and nervous. I stepped away from him, grabbed his plate, and fled to the counter to pile it with food.

"I haven't cooked for anyone since—"

The door crashed open in the living room.

"You here, Junior? Damn, what smells so good? Oh…"

I stood in disbelief with Creed's plate in my hand. Of all the days to decide to crash here…

"Officer Cabral," Creed said, sitting up a little straighter. Rhonda moved swiftly to his side and stood at attention, just short of growling.

"Hey, Creed, how's it going? Am I… Wow, is this your dog?"

"I invited Creed over for breakfast." I didn't want him to go all Dicknaldo on me and start talking shit about overnight guests. He actually for once didn't do that.

"This is Rhonda," Creed said, patting her back to reassure her. "If you hold your hand out and avoid eye contact, that's usually the best way to approach her."

Interesting. Rhonda had been all over me with no sign of threat. Perhaps she could tell how her owner felt about me and that put her at ease.

Rey approached slowly and casually with his hand out and smiled at me. "I was just coming by to let you know last night was a bust, but we'll be out there again tonight."

"I'm sorry and I'm not," I said, scooping some of the eggs and potatoes and bacon onto a plate for my uncle, since it appeared he was hungry, or maybe he just drooled all the time and I hadn't noticed before. "I don't want them out there hurting people, but I want you to catch them in the act, if that makes sense."

"Thanks, man," he said, taking my seat at the table. "Vanessa's going to call you later to see if you can meet up tonight."

"I need to go see Lola. She was asleep by the time I got there last night."

Rey finished his food in like four bites. "I'm going to go by before I report in tonight. I can tell her what you're up to. I'm just going to grab some more street clothes. Man, I need to do laundry, but Emmanuel keeps leaving his clothes in the washer and forgetting about them and I'm not doing that punk's laundry. Anyway, thanks for breakfast. And thanks again for all the info last night." He slipped Rhonda the last of his bacon, which got a tail wag from her, then he stood and went up the stairs to his bedroom.

I sighed as I heard him slam his door.

"He stays here sometimes, but he lives with my auntie Vanessa, his sister. Maybe I'll pack up his shit for him after he leaves so he's not tempted to just pop in."

"Why?" Creed asked. "Afraid you'll be interrupted?"

I froze with a piece of bacon halfway to my lips. "Why? You interested in something interruption-worthy?"

Creed wiped his mouth with a napkin. He'd eaten most of the food I'd served him. Meanwhile, I'd nibbled a bit but was too nervous to eat much. His sultry smile was back and he let his legs fall open a little wider, inviting me to come closer. I was about to say more when Rey's boots pounded down the stairs.

"I hope these fuckers come at me tonight. I'd love an excuse to knock their heads in—sorry, Creed. I'm not usually violent, but seeing the faces on these people they've attacked... It's awful. By the way, Junior, Vanessa said they talked to that doctor at the biotech firm and she seemed really nervous. We were thinking since you know a lot about that Spanish organization, maybe you could talk to her. Maybe she'll talk to you."

I glanced at Creed, who was sipping from his water glass and frowning. "Yeah, whatever you guys need. I'll talk to Vanessa. Later."

Rey looked between the two of us and grinned. "Let me just grab some coffee and then I'll be out of your way so you can enjoy your... breakfast. You teaching today?"

"At one," I said, my eyebrows raised. His attempt at cock-blocking was elaborate and drawn out. My patience was gone.

"Dope. See you later then. Bye, Nurse Creed."

"Have a good day, Officer Cabral."

Their formality was ridiculous.

Rey grinned at me, winked, patted Rhonda once more, and headed for the door with a little dance step, singing to himself.

"Was he just singing the song from *Grease 2*?"

"The bowling scene? 'Score Tonight'?" I asked, and Creed nodded. "Probably. He spends a lot of time watching chick movies with my titas."

Creed laughed out loud and shook his head as I once again moved between his thighs. I brushed his hair out of his face, and he tilted his head up to look at me.

"What was that about the doctor?" he asked. I was surprised he wanted to talk now that we were alone. That didn't necessarily vibe with his hand now running over my ass.

"Oh, the PD hired me to consult on these weird attacks. They found a connection between my research and a local biotech firm."

Creed sat up a little straighter and placed his hands on my waist. "Is it safe? For you to be involved, I mean. I don't want you to get hurt."

I smiled down at him, running my fingers through his hair. It was soft and smelled so good, like sugar cookies. I wanted...

"I'm fine. But I do want to talk to this doctor. Maybe she'll open up to me as a colleague rather than the police."

"If she's involved with a cult, Roman, then you must be careful. Trust me, I know how manipulative those people can be, and if they see you as a threat at all, they have ways of neutralizing that. If they're anything like...well, sometimes they have a far reach, beyond the police."

His fingers were digging into my waist. I reached for his hands to relax his grip, and he stood suddenly. Rhonda sprang up and whimpered, pressing close to his leg.

"Please, Roman."

"Hey," I said, pulling him into an embrace, and once more he nuzzled my neck in that way he seemed to love. "Hey, I'm going to be okay, but you're not. What happened, Creed? What happened to you?"

He pulled away a little and his smile was back. "I'm fine, it was a long time ago."

It was my turn to frown. "But it's obviously still affecting you. Maybe it would help if you told me about it? I'm not going to push, but I told you, I'm a good listener. I kind of get paid to teach people how to be good listeners, you know."

He ran his hands up and down my back and stared at my chest as if he wasn't sure how much or what to even tell me.

"Okay. I'll tell you, but you're probably going to think I'm—"

"Stop," I said, pressing a finger to his lips. "Creed, I'm not going to judge you on something from your past. I've had my share of dustups and fuckups. I was a shithead as a teenager, for real. I can tell you stories... But I want to hear yours, and you won't get judgment from me, okay?"

He slouched a little, which made him seem not as larger-than-life. Nurse Creed was gone and in his place was a troubled young man.

"Alright. I'll talk, but I'm also fully aware you might not want to see me anymore when I'm done."

I pressed a kiss to his bottom lip, and then another, and he moaned a second before he had me pulled up against him, his fingers digging into my ass as if there was no such thing as close enough. Somehow he maneuvered us over to the couch and lay on his back, pulling me down on top of him. Rhonda wandered over and lay on a rug next to the heater vent on the floor. Right where my Bunny used to lay.

A twinge in my chest nearly pulled me out of the moment, but Creed held me tightly, overwhelming me, and I *wanted* him. His kisses were so drugging I could have easily forgotten we were supposed to be talking, especially when he ran his hands under my lounge pants and his fingers grazed my crack. I shuddered and ground against him, so fucking turned on I was ready to throw all caution to the wind.

"Roman," he breathed, and then his hands were gone.

I opened my eyes to see he'd placed a hand over his own and was struggling to breathe.

"Hey," I said, scrambling off of him to kneel beside the couch. "What's wrong?"

He smiled for me and reached for my hand. "Nothing is wrong, not even in the slightest. We just...we were talking today, right? Not fucking."

I laughed and ran a hand over his chest. "But we *could* be fucking."

He let his head fall back and chuckled. "We *could* be. And I'd *like* to be. But I won't feel right going there with you if you don't know even the basics about me."

"I know that you're a fantastic nurse, that my grandmother and aunties love you. I know you're quick on your feet and have a good heart. I know you like to do this whole mysterious shit, but I don't know what that's all about."

"And that's why we need to talk. Here, come here," he said, and he rolled onto his side to make room for me next to him on the couch. "I like you close like this."

"Okay," I said, sliding my knee between his. "You talk, and then *we'll* talk about how much I hope you like to bottom."

Creed laughed again and pulled me close. "I could be persuaded, especially if you let me eat you first."

"Deal," I said, surprised at how easygoing he was about all this. "Now, tell me...Georgia, then you came here?"

15

CHAPTER FIFTEEN

C reed

THE TRICK WAS to tell Roman the true story of my involvement with Gateway of the Sun without the time element...and to do that while we were both pressed together, our dicks aching for each other. *No sweat.*

"I hitchhiked my way to San Francisco first. Always wanted to go."

"Oh wow," he said. "Like a little hippie boy, huh?"

"Right...but this was, like—" *Shit, how old am I supposed to be?* I was always so careful, but Roman had me unsettled.

"Yeah, how old *are* you? I'm almost twenty-six. I guess I thought you were younger, but then you say shit that has me thinking—"

"We're about the same age then," I said, smoothing right over that discussion. "So this was like eight years ago."

"Still some hippies there I bet. Just, with different drugs?"

"Sure," I said, rolling my eyes. "It wasn't about the drugs for me, man. I wanted to be where people were trying to change the world. Isn't that what San Francisco is supposed to be all about?"

"Eh, maybe. I think some people in the city still are, but it's mostly tech bros there now."

"Right, well, after a year of living on the streets basically, I ended up meeting some folks who were going to a commune in the Santa Cruz mountains, and my friend Muse and I—" Oh, fuck, it hurt to say her name. It came so easily because I wanted to be open with Roman, but part of me wished I could tell the tale without her in it. Maybe then it would be as if tragedy had never struck.

"Muse?"

"I, um, met her in the city, and we kind of looked out for each other. We went with these people up to the commune. It was such a change. Really beautiful. A safe place to sleep and enough food to keep us comfortable, if not full."

"Oh, wow, what was that like? It's strange to think there're places like that still around, but I see folks like that sometimes down at the beach. There's something timeless about this area, I think."

Roman's intuition was so strong, I wondered if he had any clue how in tune he actually was. "Yeah, I've met them. Different group, same M.O., I think. It was just what you'd think a spiritualist community was like; lots of meditating, terrible food, and a whole lot of roughing it."

His smile faded a bit and he ran his thumb over my cheekbone. "Sounds like it was challenging. Was it..."

"It was a shock at first, especially after coming from the streets where there was no schedule, no routine. This was like boot camp but without the weapons and violence. We had classes in herbs and manipulating good and bad energy—"

"You mean like chakras and chi?"

I relaxed a little. I should have expected that Roman would get it. He was a psychologist. Damn near had his doctorate degree in a field that was often treated like hocus-pocus. I was relieved that he didn't ridicule me.

"Yeah, something like that. The Leaders at the commune, they taught us how to heal people by helping them purge the negative energy and replace it with the good stuff."

"Hmm," he said, still running his thumb over my cheekbone. The more he pondered what I was saying, the more rhythmic his movement became. I wondered if he realized what he was doing, that his attempt to soothe me was working. "Kind of like recycling then, huh?"

"It's subtle," I said. *For you maybe. Not so much for me.* "But it helps a lot, especially over time."

He sat up a little and stared at me. "That's...you do that with the old folks. At the home. That's...that's why they're so—"

"Happy?" I interjected, laughing nervously. This was make-or-break time. Either he would start laughing and tell me it was bullshit or maybe...just maybe...

"Yeah," he said, his face lighting up. "Wow. So you really are magic," he said, snuggling a little closer.

"I've got a few tricks up my sleeve," I said, leaning forward to kiss his neck. *Oh, Goddess, to have a taste of him while he's glowing like this...*

"I like your tricks, Nurse Creed. I do." He pulled away. "And I want more of that, but let's get to the part where you seem so sad."

I had that sensation like when you've just recently fallen asleep and you feel like you're walking along all fine and dandy and you miss a step. My whole body jerked as I fell.

"Hey, you okay?"

I sighed. That moment of bliss that had been so close was now dangling from a precipice.

"Yeah, I am. Things were good, hard but good, until they weren't. Some of the other Learners at the commune didn't agree with the way the Leaders ran things, and they staged a little mutiny, I guess you'd call it." *Muse, I'm so sorry.* "People got...hurt. Those of us who could, fled."

"That's awful," he said, his hand cupping my cheek now. "Were the police involved? I don't remember hearing anything—"

"No, I don't think anyone reported anything. It never made the news."

I had to tread carefully here because knowing Roman, he'd be curious and he'd go look, but back then the Santa Cruz mountains were wild and there was a lot of unincorporated territory. A lot of shit went on and the hippies who'd moved out there wanted away from The Man. They'd had enough of the police throughout the years of protests and the Summer of Love.

"We were all a bunch of runaways, throwaways from society. No one was looking for us and the Leaders kept things really under wraps. The two years I was there, no one new started, and we didn't have any contact with outsiders. I had another year to go before I could have tested to become a Leader, and I thought that was what I wanted, but then I noticed that they often let some bad behavior slip, said it would be worked out naturally—"

"What, like karma?"

"Hmm. Something like that. I think if they would have acted, maybe expelled the bad apples, then maybe the uprising wouldn't have happened, but it's over now. I never heard from anyone after that, so I don't know. The group isn't there anymore, I know that much. It's a church campground now, so someone must have bought the place or maybe the commune was renting it. Beats me. I went by when I came back to the area and no one I knew was still there."

"Where did you go?"

I laughed. "Where *didn't* I go? I traveled around, worked for a bit. Finished my nursing degree, got my license, and that's what I do. I take care of people."

Roman observed me for a long time, perhaps taking it all in. His dark eyes were so kind, not judgmental like those of some of the other people I'd tried to talk to over the past fifty years, and the sorrow I usually felt pouring from him was gone. In its place was empathy. Admiration, maybe. And he still wanted me, that was clear, and not just from the bulge in his pants that pressed into my thigh.

"And you're good at it. But who takes care of *you*?" he asked, and then he smiled. "You asked *me* that once."

"I did." Instead of me using my pheromones to ease him, his were doing a powerful number on me. He was broadcasting clearly what he wanted to happen. And while I hadn't told him everything, I'd told him enough for me to not feel like an evil man for taking what he so desperately wanted to give.

"Let me. Let me be the one for you," he said, sliding his hand from my face, down over my chest that was barely keeping my pounding heart contained, over the front of my jeans... He hooked his fingers in my fly and yanked the buttons open, one at a time. "Fuck, these are hot. No one wears button flys anymore. It's a shame."

"Shame, yes." I sucked in a breath. "I—"

"Yes?" he asked, sliding his hand inside my boxers.

His touch was too good to deny, and who was I fooling? I'd known that if I ever got him alone, we'd end up horizontal, pheromones or no.

We were horizontal now, and alone, and it had been *so* long...

"Yes, Roman. All the yes."

He paused with his hand wrapped around my dick. "Here or the bed?"

"Bed, please." If I was going to be weak, why not enjoy it to the fullest?

He stood quickly and then held out a hand to pull me up. Rhonda lifted her head, stood, and then hopped onto the couch where we'd just been.

"She okay on the furniture?"

"She's yours. She can do whatever she wants."

He led me down a short hallway past a bathroom and into a dark bedroom.

"I kind of like it dungeon dark when I sleep," he laughed. He pulled off his shirt and crawled into bed, waiting for me.

"You'll get no complaints from me." I yanked off my Harvard hoodie and slid my jeans down my legs, but I left on my boxers in case...well, in case Roman got cold feet.

Speaking of cold...I ran to the bed and slid in, pulling the covers over both of us. "Other than it's so cold."

Roman laughed. "Santa Cruz weather. Don't worry, I'll keep you warm."

We kissed for a long time, and it was enough to sate me, the taste of him, his scent, his lust, all of it fed me. I was drunk on him, the buzz so good. And yet, I wanted more.

"I was being a pushy bastard earlier," he said. "We don't have to do anything—"

I rolled him over onto his stomach and covered him with my body. He gasped and squirmed a bit, but then I pressed gentle kisses along his spine and he melted into the mattress.

"I heard what you said," I murmured against his velvety skin. "Let me taste you first."

He moaned as I made my way down his delectable back, kissing and licking until he was writhing beneath me. I straddled his thighs and gently pulled his flannel pants over the swell of his gorgeous ass, praising it as I removed his clothing.

"So fine. You never cease to amaze me, Roman. I hope you don't mind," I said, pouring on my drawl. "But I'm going to be here for a while."

"You...you don't have to. I'm on PrEP, but you don't have to—"

"Unless you don't like this," I said, not worried at all about his health status. I would have known if he was ill. "I want to."

"No, it's fine."

"Good. Because it's just about my favorite thing in the world." I ran my hands over his ass again and again, waiting for him to sink into my touch. He sighed as I ran my nose and lips over his sensitive flesh until he moaned, and then I ran my tongue over his hole.

"Oh God, Creed," he cried out, looking back at me over his shoulder.

The fact that he was watching me, or attempting to watch, made it all the more intense. I wasn't kidding, rimming a lover was probably my favorite thing in the world, but for him to watch me was almost more than I could take.

But then Roman started to get twitchy, and he pulled away. "I want...it's my turn."

And, blessed be, he loved rimming just as much as I did. Maybe even more so by the sounds coming from him as he rolled me onto my back, pushed my knees up to my shoulders, and had a feast, licking until I was leaking...and then he took my dick into his mouth and sucked until I could resist him no more. I gave him warning, he grunted his decline to pull off, and he took all I had to give, working me until the shudders got to be too much.

"Roman, oh...oh *sweet Georgia peaches*, was that so good!"

"You better be ready to do that again soon, because I want more."

He got to his knees and stroked himself, making such a luscious picture, I wanted to remember it always. I slid around on the mattress to take him into my mouth, and he laughed and lay down the opposite direction. I'd truly, *truly* never known another man to taste as good, to *feel* as good, and damn if I wanted to do anything else for the rest of my existence.

We lay like that for what felt like hours, each teasing and tasting the other in between laughing and talking until one of us would get a little more enthusiastic.

"You have to stop," he said after he'd come for the third time. "I might die."

I cleaned him up with my tongue, loving the closeness we were developing, enjoying the haze of sheer pleasure we'd experienced together.

"I wouldn't let that happen," I said, finally rolling over onto my back. "But you might not see straight for a day or two."

"That would be a problem— Shit! I have class in thirty minutes." He rubbed his hands over his face.

"Oh...well, Rhonda and I will get out of your hair then."

He placed a hand on my thigh. "No. Please. Stay. It's an online lecture. Only an hour. Then I can take my clothes back off and crawl in here with you."

I laughed. "You're serious? What about the police department?"

He frowned and reached for his phone. "I'll text Vanessa and see what's up, but she said she'd get in touch with me when she needed me. We didn't make a firm plan for today. Don't make me have to make adult decisions. I want more Creed time." He grew serious, turning around on the bed to face me. "Not just sex. I want to talk. I want to know more. I want…"

"Yeah. I want, too. Let me take Rhonda out for a bit, and then I'll come back. When you're done with class, let's want together."

Roman beamed. "*Let's.*"

16

CHAPTER SIXTEEN

R oman

I WAS STILL FLOATING that night. After class, which Creed watched with interest, we walked Rhonda, and then fell back into bed for more kissing and touching...and sucking. God, I couldn't get enough of him. I fed the two of them dinner and then I dropped him and Rhonda off at the lighthouse so they could go for a run. I was invited, but I really wanted to catch Lola awake tonight. Vanessa and Rey hadn't answered my texts, so I figured I wasn't needed at the PD.

I still couldn't believe that I legit had a consulting gig—my first—with a law enforcement agency. If you would have told teenaged Roman that he would be working with The Man, he would have run over your foot with his skateboard, flipped you off and probably grabbed his crotch or something equally vulgar and disgusting.

No. I'd turned into a highly educated, upstanding citizen and was a police consultant on a case that potentially involved an organization that I was investigating as part of my doctoral research.

What is this life?

And I'd had an incredibly kind and generous and *sexy* man in my bed all day, who gave the best blow jobs on the planet and who loved to eat ass. Life was just fucking awesome.

I practically skipped into the doors of Puesta Del Sol, I was flying so high. I snuck up behind Lola as she stood with Stella in the doorway to the library and I spun her around in a big hug.

"Roman! What's gotten into you? You're going to give me whiplash acting like this. What is wrong with you?"

I couldn't have wiped the smile off my face to save my life. I felt like the damn Joker. I did some excuse for a dance step, tried one of the ones she used to try to teach me when I was little and would let her boss me around.

"Roman," she said, pulling me into a corner away from her sister. "You're going to get fired at that college if they find out you are on drugs. What are you thinking?"

I burst out laughing and wrapped my arms around my beloved grandmother. "There were no drugs involved in the making of this mood, Lola. This is pure, unadulterated bliss you're witnessing."

"Now you're an adulterer? That's it. I'm calling Vanessa. You need to be checked out. Maybe one of the nurses here—"

"Lola, I promise, I'm just in a good mood. Guess what?" I asked her, rather than saying *it's because of one of the nurses here that I'm in such a good mood.*

"What is it?"

I took her hands in mine and bent down to her level. "I signed a contract yesterday to consult with the police on a case. I'm working with Tita and Tito."

Her eyes widened and she pulled me in for a hug. "I didn't need another reason to be proud of you, my sweet boy, but you give me more reasons every day." She kissed my head, patted my back, and then backed away, straightening herself. "But you were almost late for Bingo, and since your aunt and uncle are working, you have to sit with me."

"It would be my honor."

Bingo was a blast. Lola and Stella were neck and neck with their wins, but Lola grew tired earlier than normal and I had to take her up to her room before the session was over. I tucked her in and she asked me to get Nurse Creed for her.

"Lola, he's off tonight."

She sighed. "Okay, I'll just go to sleep then. Good night, Roman."

"I love you, Lola Frances."

She patted my hand and then rolled over to go to sleep. I figured it was all the excitement, but in that moment, I realized just how attached she'd gotten to Creed. What would she think if I told her we were seeing each other? I wouldn't tell her until I talked to him, though, and we ascertained that we were, in fact, doing more than... having a freaking fantastic time together.

I climbed into my car and got goose bumps thinking about how much I couldn't wait to get him back in my bed. But it was more than that. We'd had a real breakthrough that afternoon, and I wanted to see where this could go, me being all grown up and shit with a legit job, and him being—for once—a really good guy for me.

I was pumped when it was time for me to meet back up with Creed at a local club. He'd asked if I wanted to check out a new band he'd heard about from the bartender at The Catalyst, and they were playing at The Blue Lagoon, a dive bar down the street. My taste in music was a little more R&B flavored, but the idea of spending an evening dancing and carousing with him, and then potentially taking him home to bed with me, sounded like heaven.

I parked in the public lot next to the Hula Grill and walked down Pacific to the bar. I was immediately sucked into a crush of bodies, all cheering for the band, Bloody Brilliant. I'd heard of them before, but Creed hadn't seen them so I figured why not? Whatever made him happy after the day we'd had.

The band was legendary in Santa Cruz for taking on the different vampire personas that were pop culture hits. Their music varied from classic and stoner rock to new wave throwbacks, depending on which of the members was singing. They had a few originals but they also took classic songs and changed the lyrics to make them fangy. It was a riot. Folks here loved to poke fun at their vampire history and happily welcomed the tourist dollars that history brought.

Once inside, I spotted Creed at the bar, so I worked my way through the press of bodies to his side.

"Sorry I'm late," I said into his ear, loud enough he could hear me.

He turned and gave me a smile, but it was strained and quick. He turned his attention back to the band with a frown, and my good mood deflated a bit. He did reach for my hand though and gave it a squeeze. A little tighter than an "it's good to see you" squeeze. This almost hurt.

The band finished their song and announced they were taking a break. The room filled with hearty conversation as Creed turned toward me.

"Hey," he said, pulling me in for a hug. "Can I get you a drink?"

"I got it." I asked the bartender for a draft. They always had the best local brews on tap so I knew I couldn't go wrong. "I'm sorry I was late. It was Bingo night."

Creed's attention was elsewhere though, despite the fact that he was still holding my hand under the bar. I got being discreet, but he seemed...distracted.

"Hey, you okay?" Then I realized that he hadn't slept today and figured maybe he was tired. "You want to go?"

"No," he said. "Sorry. I'm okay. I'm glad you got to spend some good time with her tonight. She doing okay?"

"She really is. It's so strange, she's so much better now that she's there. I'm almost wondering if she just needed the reassurance of not being alone, you know? Maybe now that I'm back, she can come home and she'll continue to get better."

Creed's smile slipped and he focused his amber eyes on me. "Roman, she's better *because* she's there. I know you want her to be home, that you want to take care of her, but she's really in the best place for her. You have work and school and the consulting job. You couldn't be with her twenty-four-seven, and she wouldn't want you to."

I knew he was right. I wasn't even sure why I'd brought it up. I'd just been on such a high today, it seemed like anything was possible.

"Yeah, you're right." I tried to shake it off to get back to the vibe we'd had that afternoon, but something was still off about him, too. "Hey, you want to get out of here? You seem tired. Maybe?"

He glanced around the bar and toward the rear stage door. "Yeah, I am a little tired. I'm sorry." He drained the rest of his beer. "I think I should go home."

The mood I was trying desperately to hang onto deflated. "Okay. I'm sorry. Let me give you a ride."

"No, it's fine. It's not far."

I finished my beer and let him lead me out of the bar. Once outside, he took me around the corner to a dark spot and he pulled me close, burying his face in my neck.

"I had a great day with you," he said close to my ear. "I'm sorry it has to end."

"Me too," I admitted, kissing his lower lip. "Why don't you let me drive you home? I could tuck you in." I pulled back and wiggled my eyebrows at him, but he had this strange expression on his face that gave me pause. Was I seriously getting the "this has been fun, but I'm moving on" speech?

"Some other night," he said, answering my tentative kiss with a little more feeling. "When I'm more myself. Let me walk you to your car," he said—and then we heard the shouts.

Creed's head snapped around to the back of the bar, and then he turned to face me. "Go on, get inside."

"Fuck that, Creed."

He cursed and ran for the back of the bar. Fast. Like I couldn't have kept up even if I'd been ready to sprint.

"You picked the wrong fucking bar, you pieces of shit."

I recognized the laughter that followed.

I turned the corner and ran into Creed's back. In front of him were the four assholes from the Boardwalk, and the bass player from the band.

The assholes' laughter stopped when another band member

came outside, the guitar player this time. Then they looked to Creed and their smiles faded further.

"Run along," the guitar player said, giving them a "shoo" gesture. He had a long, thick beard and a head full of dark wavy hair. He wore black eyeliner and an upside-down cross hanging from one ear. He was certainly built strong enough to take on all four of the assholes.

I recognized the leader of the group as the one working for the biotech firm. He looked at Creed and flicked his chin at him. "You should have learned after last time to stay out of things that don't concern you."

Creed held his arms out. "I'm here now. And I don't scare."

The kid's eyes flicked to me, and he laughed. "You sure about that?"

He gathered his fellow assholes and they disappeared into the darkness, laughing all the way.

"You okay?" I said to Creed, but he was locked in a stare with the bearded guy.

"Yeah." He turned to me. "You should call your uncle. Let him know they're headed toward the Boardwalk."

"Let me see if I can get a hold of him." I stepped away and pulled out my phone, but Creed was barely paying attention.

"I'll be back," he said, and at first I thought he was talking to me, but then the bearded guy nodded. He seemed surprised to see Creed. There was a shocked expression of recognition on his face.

"We'll be here."

Creed took me by the arm just as my uncle answered.

"Rey, dude, those guys were just here...The Blue Lagoon...I'm here with Creed...yes, my tetanus shots are up to date. What? Fuck you. Go do your job, they're headed to the Boardwalk. Yeah, bite me, Dicknaldo." I hung up and shoved my phone in my pocket. Creed was pulling me at top speed down the street. "What are you doing?"

"I want to get you to your car and then I want you to go home."

"Creed, whoa. Slow down." We were at the municipal lot already, and I was nearly panting. "Just so you know, I've got a black belt in Kajukenbo. I'm not helpless, okay?"

He stared at me as if there was something he really needed to say…but he remained silent. Which was getting old. I sighed. "Let me take you home. Please. Those guys are still out there."

"There's something I need to do first." His eyes were wide, and he looked as if he'd seen a ghost. Again.

"What? What's wrong, Creed?"

He took my hands and exhaled. "The guy in the band? I know him. From my old life."

His expression implored me not to ask questions, to just trust him, but I asked questions for a living.

"Creed, it's okay, whatever it is—"

"I have to go. Please. Go home so I know you're safe. I'll…I'll call you."

I pulled myself up to my full height, yanked my hands out of his, and glared at him. "I fucking hate being dismissed. If you've got shit going on, fine. I get it. But don't fucking dismiss me as if I can't handle whatever it is. Call me or not, do whatever the fuck you want."

I was pissed now. If I had one character flaw that had caused me more headaches in my life than I could count, it was my fucking temper and the fact that I would snap anytime I felt like people thought I was incompetent. My family, the fucking cops when I was a teenager, even Basajuan. I could handle my business, and my business needed to get the fuck out of here before I said anything I couldn't take back.

"You can handle whatever you put your mind to." Creed stepped back from me and his gaze dropped to the ground. "Forgive me, Roman. I have to go."

And he was gone. Like, really fucking *fast* gone.

I was vibrating as I climbed into my car. It took me a couple of tries to stick my seat belt buckle in. I cursed so loud, I attracted attention from a couple walking past my car. *Oh, it's just me fighting with my seat belt like a little kid.*

What the fuck was wrong with me?

I started the car and put it in reverse, but instead of driving home, I went to the Boardwalk—because I wasn't about to let the guy I was falling for tell me what to do.

17

CHAPTER SEVENTEEN

C reed

BACK INSIDE THE BAR, I found a dark corner and tried to pull myself together.

Cross was here. Alive. And he had another guy with him who I could tell knew The Way.

How had he survived the mutiny? How was it that I hadn't run into him before now? Bloody Brilliant was popular, and people all over town had recommended I go see them, but I hadn't ever caught one of their sets as they mostly played nights I was at work.

As I watched his band play, with him on acoustic guitar, I was taken back to the night it all went wrong.

1971

. . .

IT WAS INITIATION NIGHT, and I was terrified. Only a handful of us from our cohort—a number that did *not* include Muse, unfortunately —had been selected to be initiated by The Source. We'd been told that the initiation was the final step before we were sent into the next phase of our learning.

I'd wanted to turn it down as I didn't want to leave Muse, but she told me no way, she wanted me to continue. She knew how important our training was. She was disappointed that she hadn't come as far as she needed to move forward with the organization, but she was proud of me and ready to move on. By this time, she'd connected with another Learner named Shaw and the two of them had talked about leaving together. She loved learning The Way, but Shaw wasn't feeling it and when the two of them weren't selected, I figured that meant they would be leaving. She hadn't come out and said it, but I could see the signs. I wanted her to be happy and safe, the latter being the most important to me.

I also wanted to move forward with the training, but not necessarily because I was a dedicated convert. Yes, I was a believer. I'd learned how to manipulate the energy of others in tangible ways. According to all of the Leaders, I was a natural. I passed all of the tests they gave me, and I'd even healed Muse's sunburn one day. The two of us had cried over the fucking miracle we'd been given.

I wanted to move forward because I wanted to watch over the defective members of my cohort. Stephen and his followers had continued to grow stronger, just as I had, but they were doing it by focusing on the negative energy. They continued to torment the weaker members, cornering them, terrifying them, and then laughing when they got the desired effect. They'd managed to make an older man named Clark wet himself in front of the group.

That had been the last straw for me. When the announcement was made that The Source had chosen the initiates from our cohort —that I'd been chosen, and not Stephen—I was all in.

I'd do whatever it took to stop Stephen and the others from continuing to terrorize people to make themselves stronger.

"Hey," Muse said, finding me at the baths. There was a group sitting around singing—Cross had been playing the guitar, now that I recalled—and I'd lingered to listen. He played often, sometimes to accompany our healing sessions even. The Leaders said he had a gift, and we all believed it. I was still drying off and had yet to put my special black garment on for the ritual. Muse didn't hide her appreciation for my body. She never did, but she knew that as much as I loved her, sex would never be a part of our relationship.

I wrapped my towel around my waist and hugged her close. "I'm sorry you won't be able to come to the initiation. I guess it's only for the initiates, Leaders, and the Guardians."

"It's okay." She put her lips to my ear. "Shaw and I are taking off. I came to say goodbye."

I pulled back and my eyes burned. We'd been through so much together since we met, and we'd never been apart. This felt like more than goodbye for now. It felt final.

"Oh, Creed," she said, wiping a tear from my cheek. "We'll meet again. You're going to do such great things. You've become so powerful."

I certainly didn't *feel* powerful. I was nauseous, like you might feel right before going on your first trip away from home. Scratch that, I hadn't been afraid of leaving Georgia. I'd been gleeful, giddy, ready to take on the world. I wasn't sure I was ready to take on this new world, but I'd committed myself to the teachings of The Source, and I was dedicated to protecting people, just as Leader Bree had said in the beginning.

I had the heart of a Guardian.

So while I would continue to learn the ways of healing, I would learn to use my power to protect those who couldn't protect themselves. This would be my path, my chosen task for the remainder of my existence, and when my body ceased to function, my essence would return to The Source and be absorbed to be passed on to others, as it had been for thousands of generations.

"How will I... Will I see you again?"

She laughed. "Of course you will, silly. I'll leave word with my granny in Modesto, wherever we end up. Remember how to find her?"

I did. She'd told me her grandmother owned a biker bar in Modesto and her parents had tried to keep her away from it her whole life.

"Tammy's, right?"

"Right. It's where Main Street meets the highway. If you ever need me, just get word to Granny Tammy."

"I will. I love you, Muse."

She winked at me. "Love you, too." She pressed her hands to her chest and she walked away.

The next time I saw her, she was crumpled on the ground outside the hall where we took our meals together. Lifeless. Cold. I couldn't stop for her. I had to run to avoid capture and the torture I'd seen them do to the other initiates.

They'd called me Guardian, but when I was needed, I'd fled.

I would not run this time.

By the time the band finished their last set, I'd had a couple more beers and ignored texts from Roman asking if I'd gotten home safely. I refused to lie to him—it had been hard enough to tell him half-truths earlier—but I couldn't protect him if he got any closer to this mess. I hoped his aunt and uncle could protect him if anything happened to me.

Because it wouldn't be long before he became a target, especially if I continued to see him.

I followed the band out the rear door where they all lit up cigarettes and laughed, toasting to another good show. I waited in the shadows until the one I needed to talk to moved away from the group.

"I know you're here, Creed," he said, his back to me.

"Cross."

He turned to face me with a welcoming smile. "It's been a long time."

I stood before the big man with the beard and thought that he didn't look all that different from that night fifty years ago, with the exception of a lot more hair.

"It's really damn good to see you." His gaze softened and he reached a hand out. I took his peace offering and clasped hands with him, feeling the energy flow between us.

He was strong. Maybe as strong as me, but that remained to be seen.

"I didn't know you were here," I said. "I didn't know…"

"That I made it out? Same here. I thought I was the only one. Then I found Mark and we ran together."

"I couldn't remember his name, but I recognized him."

Cross took a long drag on his cigarette and I laughed. He frowned.

"No more treating the body as a temple?"

Cross blew smoke out his nose and snorted. "Please. That part was all bullshit. Once you were initiated, you didn't need any of that shit, you know."

"What do you mean?"

Cross put out his cigarette butt on the bottom of his boot. "The energy transfers? The rules? The Way? It was all bullshit, Creed. Tell me you realized that."

I stepped back. "I continue to follow The Way. It's served me well. I made an oath."

He rolled his eyes. "An oath. Dude, you're a fucking *vampire*. The only oath that matters is that you take care of your fucking business and you stay out of sight."

It was my turn to scoff. "By pretending to be a vampire in a fucking bar band? How do you figure?"

Cross let out a big belly laugh. "The best way to fool people is to make them believe it's all a fantasy. Mark and I have been doing this for years, first in Hollywood—yeah, hella easy to fool folks there when they assume everything is fake—then in Austin, then in fucking Vegas…and now here. We 'break up' every so often, move, hire new bandmates, and then it's on. Nice work if you can get it, all the pussy or dick you want, and the best fucking blood whenever you need it."

I had no comeback. It was a perversion of everything we'd been taught. It was an abhorrence. It was fucking brilliant.

"So the energy of the clubs and bars…"

"It's…nice," Cross smirked. "Like a handy under the table. But blood is what sustains us, Creed. It always has been. I'm no different than the other vampires I've met. I have needs, I sate them, I take care of my business."

Creed was stuck on the middle part. "The vampires you've met? You mean—"

"The Source wasn't the only one of their kind, Creed." His sarcasm faded a bit. "Come on, you didn't know? The way we were taught? That was one being's chosen path. The Source amassed followers for centuries…millennia…gained and lost members, culled their herd, and then settled in Boulder Creek, founded the commune, and thought they would build an empire."

"Wait…how do you know all this?"

He shrugged. "I've been around, I keep my ear to the ground."

"So you know about the attacks, then? These assholes who were here? They're hurting people. Like Stephen did."

Cross's eyes darkened and his scowl was fierce. I'd always found him to be a bit intimidating, though we never had any issues with each other. He'd been with Muse for a while before we went to the commune, but he was never serious about her. He wasn't ever serious about anything, which is why I'd been surprised he was chosen for the initiation with me.

"That sonofabitch. You know he was the one… They were going to take him out, did you know that?"

I'd wondered. After the incident with Clark, the Leaders couldn't pretend anymore that he would come around. "They didn't move swiftly enough."

"No, they didn't. We have a lot to discuss, my friend. Shall we have a drink?"

I wanted to know more. I wanted to hear everything he knew, but

I'd survived this long on my own, and if I was going to take these fuckers down, I didn't want anyone getting in my way, especially if he was of the c'est la vie school of thought.

"Why should I trust you?"

Cross blinked and his eyebrows shot up, though I wasn't sure why he thought I might not trust him. "Because I have nothing to gain by deceiving you, and everything to lose if these punks out us with their foolish activity." Cross put an arm around me and sighed. "I always liked you, Creed. You didn't put up with bullshit and you were a stand-up guy. But if you've been living like a monk this whole time, we need to have this conversation."

I allowed him to lead me inside and chuckled at his comment.

"Not *totally* a monk…"

He laughed hard at that, grabbed Mark, and we went up to the bar, which was nearly deserted by now. A cute bartender in a halter top and fitted jeans asked us what we wanted.

"You know what I want, baby."

She batted her eyes at him and wiped her hands off on a towel. "And for your friends?"

"I'm good," Mark said with a grin. "I'm the wingman tonight. Creed?"

"No, thank you. I'm fine."

She shrugged and came around the bar to stand in front of Cross with her back to him. Mark blocked them with his body and kept watch, though the few stragglers were either deep in conversation, making out with each other, or on their way out the door.

Cross slid her hair to the side and held my gaze as he kissed the side of her neck. She wiggled in his arms and giggled. "That tickles," she said with a laugh. She ran her hands up and down his thighs and pressed her bottom into his groin.

"You keep that up and we're going to end up giving my friend more of a show."

She looked me up and down. "I wouldn't mind that."

Cross laughed and went back to work on loosening her up. I

recognized his technique. I smelled his pheromones the moment he released them.

Damn, he smelled good. Even from four feet away.

"Relax, baby. I'll take care of you. And if you want more, well, I'll come find you after you close up."

She sighed and tilted her head to the side, closing her eyes.

Cross was so smooth you couldn't tell he was doing anything other than kissing her, and he was done wicked fast. It was obvious he did this...often. He looked at me as he finished with her, then turned her around in his arms and kissed her on the mouth.

"Thank you, Marina. You always taste so good."

She nibbled on his ear. "I'm done at two. You know where I keep my spare key. Come on by." She kissed him once more and they hugged for a long moment before she went back to cleaning up the bar.

"And that's how I've kept myself sated and happy, my friend."

"You just...tell them?"

He laughed. "Not exactly. Marina knows because I've known her a long time. She owns this place and we have an arrangement. Most people, they don't believe it. Sometimes in the heat of the moment, I get sloppy, as you do, but yeah. Baby, you tell most people you're a vampire and they think you're playing a game."

"Yeah, and we don't hurt anyone, Creed. You need to know that. I get a sense you think we're abusing what we've been taught." Mark's solemn look reassured me. It bothered him, thinking I might have a bad opinion of them

I thought about Roman and my gut clenched. If I continued seeing him, spending hours in his bed, eventually I was going to drink from him, and I needed to get his permission, which would mean telling him everything.

But the more time I spent with him, the closer the police got to the attackers, the more likely that they'd go after him. To get to me.

"I'm glad for you. But we've got a problem, and I could sure use your help figuring out what to do about these attacks."

Mark looked between Cross and I. "I'm ready. Let's fuck some shit up."

18

CHAPTER EIGHTEEN

R oman

I MET up with Rey and we hung out for a bit, but things were dead at the Boardwalk. We even drove his unmarked car up and down the streets in the neighborhood to make sure they weren't lurking. At three, his jaw cracking each time he yawned, Rey said we should call it a night. We went back to the station to pick up my car and then went back to the house. Rey mumbled something about things to discuss in the morning, and then trudged up the stairs to go to bed.

I checked my texts, but no response from Creed. I knew he had to work the following night, so I decided that if I hadn't heard from him, I was going to Puesta to confront him.

Like, what the fuck happened?

Something spooked him at the bar, and I had no idea if it had to do with the attacks or if it was the guy he'd run into, but he'd acted so weird.

I was still brooding the next morning over coffee, hating how much I'd let this situation affect my mood. I knew better than to let a man have such sway over me. You'd think I would have learned after Basajuan.

My phone buzzed and I picked it up.

"Hey, Tita."

"Roman, we need you down here this morning, whenever you can come. Wake Reynaldo, too. There's been a development in the case and I need you."

I loved hearing her say those words more than I should. Talk about too much importance placed on other people's opinions of me.

"Let me get cleaned up and I'll be right down." It was Friday and I didn't have class, only office hours. I could reschedule them. *It's good to be the prof.* Okay, the TA. But I was ABD, and would have my degree soon.

She thanked me and hung up just as Rey came groaning down the stairs.

"Fuuuuuu this special-duty shit is fucking with my program."

"Don't worry, there's coffee. Want me to throw on some eggs?"

"You better," he said, scratching his balls at the foot of the stairs. Then he stopped and looked around. "Wait, you don't have company, do you?"

"No."

He laughed. "No? After the way you two lovebirds were acting yesterday morning, I thought for sure—"

"Yeah, you thought wrong."

"Ouch. Trouble already?"

"You know what—" I'd been about to chew him out, but that would have been the immature Roman move he'd expect. "Yeah. Something happened last night before I came and met you and...I don't know...it's like he was all in, and then he pulled back." I told him the entire series of events at the bar while I cooked us breakfast. The night before, I'd only had time to tell him that the assholes had shown up before we went on a wild goose chase trying to find them.

"It's just...he told me some stuff yesterday that I don't feel at liberty to share, but it was like he'd seen a ghost at that bar. Something about these attacks and the guy from the band...it's got him really spooked. He's keeping something from me, and I don't know whether to push it or let him tell me when he's ready."

Rey finished his first cup of coffee and started to pour a second. "You want Tito Rey or Officer Dicknaldo here?"

I chuckled. "That's tough. I don't think I ever want Dicknaldo, but in this case—"

"Yeah, you gotta find out what he's holding back. Especially now that you're officially working with the PD."

I nodded and finished up the eggs. "That's what I was thinking."

Rey took his plate of eggs and we sat at the table. What a difference a day made, huh?

"Do you think he knows more than he's told you about the suspects?"

I shrugged. "I think they're somehow connected to him, but I don't think he knows why or how, although something about last night...I get the sense that he's trying to protect me from something, but I don't need protection." I stabbed a bite of eggs a little hard and my fork scraped the plate.

Rey snorted and made a face as he repeated what I said.

"Fuck off," I said, throwing a piece of toast at him.

"I'm sorry," he said, holding up his hands in surrender. "I have to get this out of my system here so I don't fuck with you at the department."

I rolled my eyes and finished my food with a scowl.

"I'm serious. You're so damned grown up and competent, Junior."

"You better call me Roman at the department."

He kicked me under the table, I kicked him back, and within seconds I had him in a headlock and about to take him down to the ground when he tapped out.

"Fuck, I surrender. Geez. That's some serious aggro you've got going on."

I pushed him away and pulled up my pants, which he'd managed to yank down in his attempt to trip me and get free.

"In all seriousness," he said, catching his breath. "Let's fucking catch these guys so you can get back to your nurse, all right? I like you two together. He's a good guy."

I stood with my hands on my hips. "What about you? Special duty? Is this just about Vanessa, or are you finally thinking about taking the sergeant's exam?"

"I guess. What, are you going to ride me, too?"

"No, I swear," I said. "You just don't usually volunteer for this kind of assignment. The only extra thing I've ever seen you do is SWAT. I know Vanessa razzes you, but I don't know why you haven't done more. I just know it's a thing."

"It *is* a thing, and frankly, you're not the only one in this family with a mouth on them. I don't like the politics."

I raised my eyebrows. "Really? That's why?"

He shrugged. "You tell me if you like having people up your ass."

"Actually," I said, grinning. "I don't give a shit when it's not my family." Okay, I was sort of lying. After how I'd treated Creed the night before... "What do you think academia is like?"

He grumbled something about being left alone and stomped up the stairs, and I couldn't contain my laughter.

WE DROVE TOGETHER to the department an hour later; me in my suit and Rey in his "regular joe" clothes in case they were sent out on the streets again. It was the first time I used my own ID to get in, not as a guest, and I tried to be all cool about it, but it got stuck in my wallet and I held up the line trying to pull it out. Rey laughed at me, and I had to control the urge to put him in a headlock again.

The conference room was full of people when we arrived, and Vanessa immediately grabbed us.

"There's been a development. The woman we talked to at the biotech firm? She was brought into the ER late last night. Single car accident on Highway 17. She's terrified, asked the nurses to not let anyone know she was there except for me. I'm heading over there to talk to her, and Roman, I want you to come with me."

"Yeah, sure."

Rey stayed to meet with the other detective, Sterling, and the officers who'd gone out in plainclothes to make a plan, and I followed Vanessa back out to the lot.

"This woman was on top of her game, really slick when we met, but obviously our visit shook something up. I talked to the CHP and they said she was frantic, said she was being chased."

"Is she seriously injured?"

She shook her head. She hit the key fob and let us into her Explorer. "No, and she never lost consciousness. They kept her overnight to observe her because she got knocked on the head. She's at the hospital in Scott's Valley. Do you need coffee or anything?"

"No, I'm good."

She nodded and pulled out of the lot in a hurry. She filled me in on her conversation with the woman as we drove.

"She's working on some cutting-edge project involving replicating blood."

"Like, synthetic blood?"

"Yeah, something about the gene sequence for certain types and how to replicate it. Supposed to be the answer to the blood shortage. Her company is worth billions."

"It's not like Theranos, right?"

Vanessa shrugged. "I don't think so. Everything we've found out about the company seems legit." She shared with me as much information as she had on Donna Hicks, and it was mind-boggling. This did not sound like the kind of woman who would run away from anything.

"Sterling is still digging through their financials and we've got warrants out for the four men. I heard you saw them last night?"

"Yeah. I was out with… They showed up at the bar I was at."

"Don't worry, Roman. I already know you were out with that nurse. Unlike my brother, I wasn't planning on giving you shit about it."

"Thanks," I said. "Although Rey gave me some good advice this morning, believe it or not."

"He is capable of maturity sometimes. What does he think about the nurse?"

"I told him I think he's keeping something from me, but that I don't think he's involved. He said I need to find out."

"Sounds fair. Does the nurse make you happy?"

That was the thing. He made me ridiculously happy. I didn't have to try with him, didn't have to put on a front. I had to let myself *relax* with him, and then when I did...it was phenomenal. Then it was weird. Could we get back to that phenomenal?

"We're here. Now, I'm going to ask her questions if she's awake and alert. The doctors think she's going to be fine with no lasting damage."

Vanessa on a mission meant you had to hustle to keep up with her short legs. She carried herself with so much confidence in uniform, but now? In a suit, she was fire. She was power. I was descended from some fierce women, and I would never forget that.

She showed her credentials at the nurses' station and we were led down a series of hallways. The doctor was just coming out of the woman's room.

"I'm Detective Cabral, Santa Cruz PD, we spoke on the phone?"

"Yes, Ms. Hicks is recovering nicely, although she still seems agitated. Her husband called, and she asked that we not give him any information. I'm not sure what that's about, but if he shows up here, I'm directing him to the social worker."

"Good, thank you. I appreciate it."

He nodded to us, and then entered information into a computer in the hall outside the patient's room.

Vanessa raised her eyebrows and I followed her inside.

"Mrs. Hicks? I'm Detective Cabral, we met yesterday?"

The woman I recalled seeing in a picture in Vanessa's report looked very different from the frightened woman with the big eyes lying in the hospital bed.

"Detective, can you protect me? I'll tell you anything, but you have to get me out of here before my husband and the organization find me."

"The organization?"

"Yes, it's called… Wait, please. I don't want to withhold relevant information, but I need to know you can get me out of here. If he finds me, he'll turn me over to them. He's brainwashed, and they have ways of…" She looked at me and her eyes widened. "Who is he?"

"This is Roman San Angelo, he's a research fellow at UCSC and a police consultant working with us on the case."

I took a moment to preen about the additions to my CV and then I stepped forward and tried to remove my perma-scowl. "How do you do, Mrs. Hicks?"

"What is your area of research, Dr. San Angelo?"

"I'm completing my dissertation this year. I'm doing work in the area of psychology and criminal behavior, specifically cults. I believe my au—Detective Cabral explained that we were interested in the men who work with you because of some assaults in the community?"

"Yes, yes, I remember. Did you talk to any of them?"

Vanessa shook her head. "No, they didn't return to work, and the addresses your company gave us were incorrect."

Mrs. Hicks sank into the pillow as if she wished the bed would swallow her up. "They're protected. The Leaders, they send them out. They're looking for someone, but they're also gathering energy. I know it sounds weird."

"What do you mean, energy? Like solar, wind?" I asked her, something tickling the back of my mind.

Her frightened gaze landed on me, and she clutched at the hospital sheet, pulling it up to her chin. "They believe human-created energy can sustain us, could even cure hunger, if it's harnessed properly. They're doing research on the most powerful and reliable sources."

"How do they mean…harnessed?"

She shook her head. "I'm not involved in that work. I'm kept in the department working on the blood synthesis project."

She's kept? The report I read said she was the director of research at her company. How is she kept anywhere? "Tell us about that."

Her eyes darted to the door, and Vanessa picked up on it. She closed the door and came back to the bed.

"They have the blood of this...person...and they're trying to copy it. They are saying it's because their blood contains properties that will eliminate the need for human donors—"

"I thought they were doing that already with plasma?" I asked.

"They are, and they say it's for mass production, but I've overheard them talking about creating this blood only for particular people, ones they would select if they were worthy. Look, my husband and I were invited to join this elite group of executives...I thought it was going to be like a way to rub shoulders with the highest echelons of society here in the Bay Area, but it's something... else.

"Once you're accepted, you have to turn over every aspect of your life to them for approval, and when they learned what I did for a living, they forced me to introduce them to the board members and officers of my company. Next thing I know, one of these men—they call each other Leader—Stephen...he's the new CEO of my company. The board was replaced with members of the organization, and they're throwing all of the company's focus into this blood program and the energy shit, which I think is bullshit, but I don't dare say anything. Stephen and his cronies are...they're manipulative, and I don't feel comfortable around them."

"So what were you running away from?" Vanessa asked her. "You told the CHP officer that you were trying to escape."

She looked down at her hands and let out a shaky breath. "They initiated my husband. He promised me he wouldn't do anything unless we both agreed, but then he did...and he was so...*different* when he came home. He scared me. So I left."

"What do you mean by initiated?" I asked her, my neck getting tighter as I waited for her answer. If there was any way that Creed was even remotely tied to this...

"I don't know," she said, shaking her head as if she could shake the negative thoughts right out. "I don't. You only get to know if you are chosen, and I haven't been. The other people I've met in the organization are all like Stepford Wives-ish. There was no one I could go to, so I tried to leave, but someone followed me."

"Were you leaving from your home?"

"Yes. We live in Aptos. I figured if I could get out of the mountains, get to San Jose, I could catch a flight, I could go far away. But as soon as I got on seventeen, someone was following me in a gray Mercedes SUV. They ran me off the road."

Vanessa had been jotting down notes the whole time. She read through everything and she looked up at me. "Ms. Hicks? Is there anything else you can tell us?"

She gazed out the window, still hiding behind her sheet. Her fear was tangible. Whoever these people were, they had a successful woman terrified of repercussions.

"The organization has some powerful members. Local politicians, police, CEOs of tech companies...I even saw a state senator at one of the meetings."

"What is the name of this organization, Ms. Hicks?" I asked her.

"EVE. It stands for Elite Ventures Enterprises. There's not a lot of information about them on the internet. I looked before we joined. It's a word-of-mouth kind of thing. They have a house off of Highway Seventeen. I don't know the address, but I could tell you where it is."

"Thank you, that will be helpful. Now," Vanessa asked, "is there someone you'd like us to contact? Someplace you'll be safe?"

She was quiet for a long time. She really had to think hard of a possibility.

"I suppose my sister. She lives in Colorado. We don't talk much. We had a falling out after Timothy and I were married. I was kind of awful to her. Timothy would never expect me to go to her, and her husband is a correctional officer."

"Good. That's good," Vanessa said, placing a hand on her arm. "We can have the hospital social worker help make arrangements for you. If you need a police escort to your home to pick up your things, we can arrange that as well."

"Thank you," she whispered. "Perhaps tonight. I think they're releasing me today, and there's an EVE meeting tonight, their monthly gathering. It's when they bring in new members, usually only one or two couples each time."

"How many members do you think they have?"

"Maybe a hundred? It's tough to tell, tough to get in. You have to be invited, and sometimes it takes up to a year of conversations before they finally bring you to a meeting."

Vanessa and I looked at each other, and I could tell what she was thinking.

"No," I said to her. "You can't."

She sighed. "You're right. But maybe we could have someone go out and take a look, get some license plates. It would help if we knew who we were dealing with."

"If it helps, I know the gate password. They must have some sort of security, but I don't think it's sophisticated. I've never seen anyone outside, never seen any cameras. They are kind of...arrogant. They think no one can get to them."

Vanessa spent a bit more time talking to her, had her draw a map as best she could of where the house was, what the layout was like, and as many of the names as she could recall. Meanwhile, I checked my texts. Still nothing from Creed. I was going to confront him tonight when I went to see Lola. He couldn't just spend a wonderful day with me and open up about his life, and then ghost me. I wouldn't allow it.

19

CHAPTER NINETEEN

C reed

FOR THE FIRST TIME, I was not looking forward to going to work. This business with the attackers had me tied up in knots. Cross, Mark, and I had talked into the night and brainstormed what to do about them. We determined we needed to find out who was behind them and agreed that we needed to intervene, although Cross had been hesitant about it.

"I'd say I'm of a mind to let them be, but you're right. They're punks, and they're going to out us with this stupid behavior. And if Stephen's behind this, I want to punish that motherfucker."

"And it's personal now, for me," I said. "I can't take the chance of Roman or his family getting hurt."

Cross raised his thick eyebrows. "Are you going to initiate him?"

I'd frowned. "What do you mean? No. It's always been my plan to find those who killed The Source and the members of my cohort, take care of them, and then stop. Settle down someplace and live out the rest of my natural life. Do no harm, just as we were taught."

"What do you mean, stop?" Mark asked. "No more exchanges? Creed, you can't."

"Sure I can. They taught us that if we chose to no longer use the tools we'd been taught, to live by The Way, we would live out the rest of our natural lives and then be reabsorbed into The Source."

Mark snorted and shook his head. "You mean—"

"Creed," Cross said. "If you stop drinking blood, you stop existing."

"But I rarely ever drink now. Maybe once a month?" How long had it been since I'd last had an Exchange? Now I was nervous. "I can mostly get by just on energy."

The two of them looked at each other gravely. "We had another with us, Creed. Lourdes, do you remember her?"

I shook my head, but then I thought about it. "Guardian Lourdes? She escaped, too?"

"She did. But she was distraught over failing The Source. She never drank again. She aged rapidly, grew weak, and within a couple of months...she didn't wake up one morning, and that was it."

I sat down hard on a bench. We'd been talking outside the bar on the back patio for a long while. I could tell the two of them weren't ready to invite me back to wherever they were staying, and I didn't want them to find Rhonda. I didn't want to hear it from them when they discovered that I'd kept my only companion alive for thirty years.

At first I'd been so lonely that I couldn't give her up, and I figured out I could travel around with her under the right circumstances. Then she tore her ACL while we were out running, and I'd been devastated, thinking that I could lose her like I'd lost everything else. I had no idea if The Source's power could be transferred at all, much less to a less-intelligent species, but then I realized how much of my healing energy came from her, her presence, that I thought...maybe. It had been reckless, but I thought perhaps it would just lead to nothing.

Year after year, she continued to live a healthy life. I took her to the vet when she would have been fifteen and fibbed. I told them she was a rescue, and I didn't know how old she was. They figured her to be between seven and nine, which was how old she was when I first gave her my blood.

It may have been cruel, but she was my one weakness. I didn't hurt people. I gave everything I had to heal the people I cared for through my work...that was how I justified it. I didn't even know if it would work, to be honest. And whenever I moved, I had her examined at a vet. Never did they say there was anything wrong with her than was normal for a middle-aged dog.

"So you're saying that if I stop, I'll die." *And so will Rhonda.*

"Yeah, man. And it's not a nice way to go, to be honest," Mark said with a shudder.

I sighed. "Fine. So what's the plan?"

"Next sighting, we follow them. We find them, we end them. The end."

I'd told myself all along that's what I would do, but the idea of killing another being went against everything I'd been taught, everything my life meant.

"It's really the only way, isn't it?" I asked rhetorically.

"Unless you lock them in a room with no access to energy exchanges or blood, yeah. I don't know about you, but I ain't got them kind of resources. Contrary to popular belief, bar bands don't bring in a lot of dough these days."

"Yeah," Mark said. "And our internet streams are down. Money is tight, man."

"You guys have recorded albums?"

Cross flicked his hair back. "They don't call 'em that really anymore, sadly. I miss those days. Although vinyl seems to be popular again. We're kinda between managers right now so our recording schedule is on hiatus."

Neither of them seemed too upset about it. In fact, nothing really bothered them much at all, except for the attacks. I sensed we were all furious about what happened, and that somehow these ignorant twits had corrupted what we'd been taught and were putting us at risk.

"Okay. You have a plan as to how we dispose of the individuals?"

Mark and Cross shared a look. "Better you don't know the details. We've had to take care of similar situations before."

"Yeah, other jackasses causing chaos. Put it this way, we should have our own murder mystery podcast where we talk about all the killers we've taken out of business."

My eyes widened. "You're kidding! That's...well, you were going to be a Guardian, Cross. It makes sense."

"You and me both, kid. Mark, too. If you ever decide to follow your true calling and want to join us... Hey, can you play? We could always add you to the lineup of Bloody Brilliant."

I burst out laughing and patted him on the shoulder. "I play piano, man, but no thanks. I've got my own gig."

Cross's smile faded. "You should tell us how to find you, Creed. You know, if we're going to be sharing territory for a while."

Fuck, I wanted to trust them, but then I thought of the folks at Puesta Del Sol, the residents and Lexi and Jamal.

"I'll think about it. I—"

"I get it," Cross said, holding up a hand. "You've got people."

"I'm sorry—"

He placed his hands on my shoulders, and I felt a wave of reassurance from him. I closed my eyes and tried to answer it with honesty.

"Let's get through this mess. If you decide to have an alliance of sorts with us afterward, we would be glad. It gets lonely. We have each other, and we have a few friends in other cities that we can call on in times of need. We'd be opening our network to you as well. Take your time."

I thanked them both, we exchanged hugs and phone numbers, and then I went for a long, roundabout walk to make sure I wasn't being followed. By the time I got home, Rhonda was scratching at the door. We spent the day on the beach walking and getting some Vitamin D while I pondered my situation.

I wouldn't be able to stay here permanently. In fact, there would be no permanence in my life. Ever.

So what did that mean for a future with Roman?

I couldn't drag him into this world. I didn't want to stay away from him. Would he become another weakness like Rhonda? Would I be led to a selfish act because of loneliness?

It was with these heavy thoughts weighing on me that I dragged myself to work that evening, dreading what might occur. I should probably quit. If I was going to have to leave anyway, why not now? It would hurt worse the longer I stayed. I could quit, take care of Stephen's minions, and then hit the road. Maybe I'd find another community on the coast to start over. Maybe—

"Creed, thank goodness." Lexi met me at the employee entrance. "I'm so glad you're here. Mr. Fletcher had a rough day and asked for you. Mrs. San Angelo is having an episode, and Jamal called in sick, so—"

"Frances?" I dropped my bag and pulled off my hoodie and started walking toward her room.

"Yes, she didn't recognize her niece this afternoon, and then she fought with the afternoon-shift staff when they tried to give her a sedative—"

"You should have called me," I said, running now. Poor Frances, and poor Roman if he arrived and she was upset.

"Creed?" Lexi stopped at the end of the hall and frowned at me as I ran off.

I turned the corner and was about to enter Frances's room when a wave of negative energy almost knocked me to my knees. It was a combination of her sundowning, Vanessa's sorrow, and Roman's helplessness.

"Tita Frances, the medicine will make you feel better."

"Roman, my son...but you were dead!"

Oh, no.

Roman had his grandmother by the shoulders as she pulled on his shirt. She was crying, and his face was red from exertion. The afternoon nurse stood by helplessly as Frances had a breakdown the likes of which I hadn't seen since she'd arrived.

Roman and Frances stood in the middle of the room.

"Frances, it's Nurse Creed. Can I help?"

She pulled away from Roman and fell into my arms. I focused all the healing energy I had on her as I picked her up and carried her to her bed.

"I'll take care of this," I said to the nurse.

"You want me to leave the sedative?"

"No, that won't be necessary," I said as I lay Frances down and sat next to her. I brushed her hair out of her eyes and watched as the haze lifted and her gaze came back into focus.

"Nurse Creed, I'm so glad you're here! I had such a terrible dream." She held onto my arms, her grip strengthening the more energy I gave her.

"Tell me what happened," I said, never taking my eyes from hers. Roman pulled his aunt into a hug as she cried, but I didn't have enough to send them any calming energy. That let me know I was seriously depleted. I needed an Exchange. As soon as I had Frances calm.

"My son was here with some strange woman, and then they were trying to give me a shot of something. My son is dead, Creed. How could he be here?"

"Lola," I heard Roman say, but she remained focused on me, pleading, tears streaming from her eyes. Her blood pressure was high, her blood sugar *way* too high.

"Roman, please get Lexi and tell her Mrs. San Angelo may need another dose of insulin?" I kept my focus on Frances and was relieved her color was coming back and that the fruity smell was dissipating.

"Creed, where were you?" Frances asked. "Where is my grandson? You will take care of him, won't you? He needs a nice man like you to take care of him."

"I will if he'll let me," I whispered. Something broke in my chest, and it was as if I lost control of the energy currently flowing through my body. Everything I had went into Frances, and she gasped before passing out.

"Oh my God, Tita!" Vanessa cried.

"She's okay," I said. "I'm going to have Lexi give her some insulin just in case." Lexi came in then and started to hand me the syringe, but I held up my hand. "Can you give it to her? And see that her blood pressure is back to normal. I'll be right back."

I brushed past Roman, who called my name, but I needed a moment.

He followed me into the hallway. "Creed, what's wrong?"

I turned to him and felt my strength waning fast. "I have another patient to see, and then I'll be right back."

"Hey," he reached for me, a confused expression on his face, but I turned away from him, wishing desperately that I could fall into his arms and allow him to be my healing.

No. That wasn't possible. And it would serve me well to remember. But I couldn't leave, not yet. Frances needed me, and I couldn't stand for Roman to lose her now.

"I'll be back," I said, and made a beeline for Mr. Fletcher's room. I knocked on the partially closed door, and he called out for me to enter.

"Creed," he said, alarm in his voice. "You don't look so good."

I closed the door behind me. "I'm sorry, Mr. Fletcher, you asked to see me?"

He took me by the hand and led me to the loveseat at the foot of his bed. "Looks like you and me both could use this."

"I'm sorry to come to you like this, sir," I said, barely able to get the words out. "There are some extenuating circumstances I'm not at liberty to share."

"Fair enough. I was just looking for a little kick tonight, so you take whatever you need, son."

"Blessed be."

I barely remembered to release the pheromones before I sank my teeth into the thin skin of his wrist. He sucked in a breath, and I worried I'd hurt him, but I couldn't help myself. It took all of my will to stop after three pulls.

"You need more, you take more," he murmured, placing his hand on the back of my neck as I started to lift my head.

I glanced up at him. "I don't want to hurt you."

He shook his head and smoothed my hair down. "You won't, son. Besides, you've given me more peace than any human on this planet." He began to hum and gently pressed my head back down to his wrist. I released plenty of pheromone this time and took three more long pulls, sensing that this time he was receiving as much healing energy as he was giving me.

This was truly a gift. I would never regret that I'd made this choice with my life, and I knew I'd helped countless people, relieved their suffering, and only took what I needed from them in order to survive. I hadn't hurt anyone.

I grew livid thinking those men were out there, taking what didn't belong to them, torturing their fellow humans and misusing the gift we'd been given.

I would end their reign of terror. One way or another.

"Thank you, Creed." Mr. Fletcher let his head rest against the back of the couch. "And forget what I asked you to do awhile back. This life of mine is too precious. I'm going to live it 'til the end, come what may."

I leaned back next to him, my body thrumming with his healing blood, recharging my cells, giving me that essence that kept me strong, made me what I am, allowed me to do what I must.

"What changed your mind?" I asked, curious.

"I realized I was just tired and maybe feeling a little sorry for myself. I owe it to myself and my family to be around as long as I'm meant to be. My granddaughter came to see me, and we had a real nice talk. She told me that knowing what I've been through and survived in my life gives her strength and motivation in her own life. Kickin' around this life is the least I can do for a smart kid like her."

"You've got your purpose, huh? Your marching orders?"

"Yes, sir," he said. "Thank you, Creed. You've kept me going when I didn't think I had any reason."

He held out his hand, and I shook it.

"Same here. Need some help getting to bed?"

"No, thanks," he said, pushing himself up from the loveseat with more ease than usual. "I'm floating a bit. I think I might write for a while before trying to sleep."

He usually went right to sleep after I fed from him. I felt a little less guilty about taking extra, seeing him bounce back so well tonight.

"Thank you, Mr. Fletcher. I'm sorry—"

"Don't apologize, Creed. You need, I'm here."

I bowed to him and headed for the door as he sat at his desk, humming a little tune. I cursed as I reached for the door handle and realized I hadn't locked it behind me. I was so out of sorts...I was never careless like that. I couldn't afford to be. Thankfully, no one had come in.

I stepped into the hall and ran smack into Roman.

"What are you doing here?" I asked, a little out of breath.

"Creed, what is going on? And don't you dare send me away with some bullshit answer—"

I grabbed him by the hand and pulled him into a darkened corridor with a set of rooms that weren't currently being used. I had half a mind—and a buildup of energy urging me on—to pull him into my arms and kiss him until we were both breathless, but his posture was stiff and definitely not inviting.

"I'm sorry, Roman. Is your grandmother resting?"

"She is, but what the fuck *was* all that? Were you...was that what you meant? Were you healing her?"

I nodded slowly, trying to gauge his reaction. "Are you angry?"

"No!" he said, and he reached for me finally, placing his hands on my shoulders and guiding me back to the wall, out of the light from the hallway. "I was *worried*. It took so much out of you. But you're... you're okay now. What... I'm so confused, Creed."

I rested my head on his shoulder and he moved closer, wrapping his arms around me.

"I know. I'm sorry. I have things to tell you, and I'm torn because I don't know what will happen—"

"Then don't tell me yet. Just fucking kiss me. I'm going out of my mind right now; I was so worried."

I gazed into his dark eyes and took in his worry and his fear. I ate it all up, and then I kissed him with all the pent-up energy I had from the Exchange.

"Oh, fuck, Creed, I want..."

I moaned as he pulled my hips into his and he ground against me. I gasped as he pulled away from my kiss and worked the column of my throat with his tongue and his teeth, the pressure against my groin punishing.

"I want to fuck you right here, Creed, you make me so goddamn crazy."

I wrapped my arms around him and held him still, wishing I could let him do what he most desired, knowing I'd love it too.

"But you don't want me to lose my job, do you?" I went with the simplest reason why I couldn't let him fuck me in a dark hallway not quite out of sight at my workplace, despite the fact that I wanted exactly that.

"Fuck," he said, biting my neck one last time. Harder this time. His chest heaved with his attempts to calm down, and he reached a hand into his pants to adjust himself. "What the fuck? What is it you do to me, Creed? I'm not like this. I'm *not*."

"I'm certainly not complaining," I said, "except for the fact that we can't continue on this course right now. But I owe you information—"

"I have things to tell you, too," he said, pushing his hair out of his face. "I wanted to update you on the case. There's a warrant out for the four men, we ID'd them, and I got information from a person involved in the case that I think is going to help—"

"Roman." I placed my hands on the sides of his face. "You need to let your aunt and uncle handle this. You need to stay away from these people."

He put his hands on top of mine. "See, I *knew* you knew something else. What do you know, Creed? How are you involved? I can protect you."

"No, you can't. And I'm not involved with them, I swear. You're going to have to trust me."

Roman pulled away. "Creed, if you know anything that can help us find them—"

"If I did, I swear, I would tell your aunt or uncle."

His scowl made my hair stand on end. "But not me."

I sighed. "Roman, I don't want you to get hurt. These people are dangerous."

"Right, and I can't take care of myself. You know, I'm sick of hearing that. I get it enough from my family. I thought you respected me enough to give me credit for knowing what I can handle and what I can't." He turned away from me and swore under his breath.

"Roman, I'm sorry. I think you're incredible...but this situation is not what you think, and I can't have you getting hurt—"

"Yeah? Well, I can't have my aunt and uncle getting hurt, or anyone else, because I'm not doing everything in my power to help. So I'll ask you again, Creed. What do you know that can help us stop these guys?"

My heart pounded in my chest. This was a precipice that I created, that I allowed to form between us. I had the choice to step across and fall into a situation where I had no control of the outcome.

The safe choice would be to remain on my side, where at least I couldn't make things worse.

"I've told you all I can, Roman. I'm sorry."

He stiffened. "So that's it? You're just going to... You know what? Forget it. You're not who I thought you were. If you don't want to help, fine. See you around."

His name was on the tip of my tongue. My lips yearned to call him back, to confess, to express how much I desperately wanted him, wanted to help, wanted the same things he did. But I fought the urge. I let him walk away.

Let him think I was less than. Let him think I wasn't worth his time.

It was easier to let go that way.

I straightened my scrubs and went to the nearest bathroom to inspect the damage. I flicked on the light and ducked my head to splash cold water on my face, figuring at least it would cool the redness. I looked up...and gasped.

He'd bitten me so hard he'd left teeth marks.

I never left teeth marks when I drank.

That dichotomy made me burst out laughing, but it was hollow.

I never thought it was possible to be in love and to feel more alone than ever at the same time, but there you have it. My chance at love walked away from me, or I drove him away. Either way, it was time to get my head on straight.

I needed to get through my shift. I needed to go home and tend to Rhonda. I needed to have a good cry. And then I needed to find Cross and Mark and do what we'd agreed to do.

20

CHAPTER TWENTY

R oman

I LEFT Puesta Del Sol in a state. I had the urge to go out and break shit, do something totally destructive, but I also had a keen focus.

I needed answers, right? And if Creed wasn't going to give them to me, I had two choices. Either say the hell with all of this and go about my business, or I could find the answers myself.

So I went home and I started digging. Deep. I cross-checked everything Donna Hicks had given us with everything I'd researched about La Mente. There were a lot of things that seemed coincidental between the situations, and that made bells go off when I thought about Creed.

The attacks. Here, four men were cornering people on the street, scaring them, and then biting them. In Spain, the two people I spoke to who'd "escaped" from La Mente's headquarters talked about mental torture, that they were put through hours of torment in order to gauge their body's reactions to it. And Creed, talking about his cohort, how they learned how to manipulate energy, and some had chosen to misuse what they learned.

What if they really were all connected? What if these people Donna mentioned, EVE, were what Creed's group had been about?

I called Sterling and we talked. He urged me to bring everything I had down to the police department, so I shoved a sandwich in my face, threw on a sweatshirt and headed out into the night.

Once I arrived at the PD, I used my ID to get in and didn't freak out this time. I joined him in the same conference room. Sterling walked me through the financial trail and a few things became clear: EVE had its fingers into research facilities in the US, Spain, Monaco, Germany, and South Africa. We found records dating back to 1975. We had a web of names and organizations, all of them with huge gaps as they tried to cover as much of their tracks as possible.

Sterling decided it was time to bring in the FBI, and when Vanessa and Rey came in, she agreed.

"There were about forty cars at that house tonight, none of them worth less than eighty grand, and we got license plates for all of them."

"Yeah, we found a good vantage spot off the property where we could use the zoom camera. Easy-peasy," Rey said, and he high-fived his sister, who looked at him like he was nuts.

We caught them up on our information and, with the captain's approval, Sterling called the FBI field office.

It was after midnight and I had class in the morning. I stood to stretch and was about to tell Vanessa and Rey I was heading out, when everyone started rushing around, grabbing coats and keys.

"What's happening?"

"There's been another attack. Come on."

I followed Rey and Vanessa and climbed into the back of her Explorer. I knew it was serious when they didn't even argue about who was driving.

"Where was it?" I asked.

Rey turned around. "Roman. It's Creed."

My breath caught in my chest.

All of the shitty things I'd said earlier that evening came back to me and sucked all of the oxygen from my body.

"Hey," Rey said, putting a hand on my knee. "He's okay, there were no serious injuries, but he was sent home.. work."

I pulled out my phone and texted him, my hands shaking. "Please," I pleaded.

Tell me you're okay. **Please, Creed. I'm sorry.**

We pulled up to Puesta Del Sol, and I realized he probably wasn't going to answer me. I stayed behind Rey as he talked to the other cops there, and out of the corner of my eye, I spotted Lexi. If anyone knew where Creed was, she might. I told Rey where I was going, and he nodded, still in mid-conversation.

"Hey, Lexi," I said as I approached. It was obvious she'd been crying.

"Roman," she said, wiping at her eyes and trying to smile. "Hi."

"What happened?" I asked her.

"God, it was awful! Creed was walking me to my car—he always does when we work together because I'm chicken." She barked out a laugh. "Anyway, these four guys came out of the shadows and surrounded my car. Creed pushed me inside and told me to lock the doors, and then they just all swooped in on him. I called the police and started honking the horn so someone would come out, some of the other guys or something. Then they were gone, and Creed was on the ground. He got up, though, and he seemed okay, but when the cops came, he talked to them real quick and before I was even done giving my statement, he told me he was going home."

I glanced around. "Do you know where he lives?" I asked her.

She frowned at me. "Um, no, actually. Somewhere near the light-house I guess? I've never been to his place."

I sighed. "Look, Lexi, he and I...we kind of had a falling out earlier, and now he won't answer my texts. I just want to be sure he's okay."

She raised an eyebrow at me. "Give me your number, and I'll try to get in touch with him."

"Thank you. That would mean a lot." We traded addresses and phone numbers, and she got into her car and drove off.

"Let's get you home, Junior," Rey said.

"Wait." I'd spent all evening researching Creed's potential link to EVE, but I'd forgotten about one more loose end. "I think I know where we might get some more information."

Rey raised his eyebrows, and then he trotted over to Vanessa. He got her keys and she waved us off.

"Okay, where to, Mr. San Angelo?"

I rolled my eyes at him and we took off for the Explorer.

"The Blue Lagoon. If the attackers came here, they may go there next. They knew the guys in the band, too. There's some link between Creed, the attackers, and the guys in the band, I just know it. Creed wouldn't tell me, or maybe he *couldn't* tell me—"

"But we can get these guys to talk, is what you're thinking? Okay, let's go."

Rey drove faster than was legal but stayed off the main roads as much as possible. There were a lot of folks out even though it was after midnight. Downtown was still hopping on the block between The Catalyst, which was just letting out its big show of the night, and the dive bar. Rey made a bunch of comments about typhoid and salmonella poisoning, basically any weird diseases we could get going into a bar like this, but he shut up and was all business once we got out of the car.

Bloody Brilliant was playing, thankfully, and we stood in the doorway looking around. I didn't see Creed, but the place was packed. He could have been anywhere. The band ended their last set of the night, and I pulled Rey through the bar. We followed them out the back door to the patio.

"Excuse me," Rey said, pulling out his badge. "I'm Officer Cabral, and this is—"

"Roman San Angelo. Pleasure to see you again."

Rey and I both frowned. The guy with the big beard gave us a smirk and the bass player stood at his side, ready to assist, although we weren't throwing off any aggro vibes so I had no idea what that was about.

"We're looking for Creed Lowell. Have you seen him?"

The bearded guy gave Rey an appraising look, and then he turned his attention on me. "Whatever you think you know about him, know that Creed would do *anything* to protect you—even disappear. If he doesn't want to be found, you're not going to find him."

Rey looked at me. "Look, he's not in any trouble—"

"Oh, but he is. He's trying to get out of it, and take care of this problem once and for all."

Rey stepped closer to the guy, not giving two shits that he was about six inches shorter. "And that's not for him to take care of, so if you would be so kind as to tell us where we can find him, you'd be doing Creed a big favor. If he takes matters into his own hands, he's going to make it worse for himself."

The sidekick stepped forward but Bearded Guy put a hand out. "It's okay. Officer Cabral is right to be concerned."

"Please," I said, not wanting to deal with this posturing bullshit anymore. "I care about him, okay?"

Bearded Guy cocked his head to the side. "Do you, now? And how far does that go for you?" He stepped toward me, and part of me wanted to flee, or at least step back, but I held my ground.

"I want him safe. I—"

"Do you care enough to accept all that he is?"

I opened my mouth to speak, but I froze. The guy was...I felt something, something pulling at my chest, like taking the steam out of my anger, taking the indignation out of my stance.

"I do," I whispered, then I shuddered, trying to clear my head from the euphoric feeling coming over me. "I need to find him. I need to make things right."

"Yes, you do," the guy said, and then he backed up and looked at Rey, who was thoroughly perplexed by this situation. "Tell you what,

I see Creed, I'll tell him you came by. I see him, I'll tell him what you said."

"Thank you," I answered, and I meant it. I needed Creed to know. I had this sick feeling that something would happen, and I'd never get the chance to tell him myself.

"You okay?" Rey whispered to me, elbowing me when I didn't answer him right away.

I nodded. "Let's go."

Rey gave the guy his card, which he looked at carefully and made a show of tucking into his chest pocket. He winked at Rey as we backed up.

"Nice to meet you, Officer Cabral. Be seeing you."

Rey grabbed my arm and started speed-walking toward the Explorer, muttering, "Weird weird weird. I'm tired of fucking weird. Wasn't that weird?"

"What's not weird in this town lately?" I asked, thinking that ever since I'd returned from Spain, my life had been one strange scenario after another. Then I chuckled. "I do think he was hitting on you, though."

"See? I knew it. Weird, though, right? I mean, I don't usually go for the big burly, bearded type, but fuck, that guy was throwing off some heat."

I burst out laughing as Rey adjusted the waistband of his pants.

"What's the matter, Tito? You having a little trouble with your sidearm?"

He punched me in the stomach and then ran for the car as I cursed him out.

I don't know why I felt better admitting all that to a guy that was basically a stranger, but I had an idea that somehow, it made a difference.

CHAPTER TWENTY-ONE

C reed

"You hear all that, buttercup?"

I was still rubbing my chest. "Yeah, I did."

He came after me. The damn kid came after me. He was breaking my heart and making me the happiest man on earth. Well, vampire. Hippie, whatever.

"You need to hit that, I swear to the Goddess," Mark said. "And that uncle of his."

"Yeah, I wouldn't mind a little handcuff action with Officer Cabral." Cross and Mark slapped hands together.

"You two are awful."

"Come on, Creed. You can't tell me that cop's not fine, man."

I shook my head. "Reynaldo is an upstanding guy and he's protective of his family. That's what I know." And I couldn't see anyone past Roman anyway.

I was in love with a goddamned grad student.

"All right, whatcha got for us?"

I grinned. "An address. Those fools. Coming for me at work was a bold and foolish enterprise. I caught up to them and followed them to a house off of East Cliff. The place was empty except for the four of them and a damn TV and video game console. The nitwits are drinking beer and playing first-person-shooter games when they're not out terrorizing the neighborhood."

"Sounds good. Let's roll."

Mark had a truck they used to haul a trailer around with their equipment, and we drove it the few minutes it took to get to the house. We parked down the street and from two houses away, we could hear them shouting and carrying on.

We approached the house on foot, and I was about to direct them to the separate entrances when Cross pulled me to a stop.

"You need to say goodnight, Creed."

"What the—"

"Guardian or not, Creed, your soul is innocent," Mark said, placing a hand on my shoulder. "You need to let us handle this."

"Is this the kind of scenario where I'm going to be expected to return the favor?"

Cross rolled his eyes. "I'm not the damn Godfather. Just get lost, all right? We'll be in touch when it's all done."

It felt wrong leaving it to them, but more than that, I was struggling with the idea of actually taking a life. "What if they're *not* like us? What if they're not...vampires, they're just bullies? Can we just let the police handle it?"

"You can't deny they're vampires. You felt their energy just as we did. Besides, would you really want to take the chance that Roman's uncle is the one to arrest them?"

"I—"

A black SUV rolled up to the house and parked in the driveway. Mark pulled us back into the bushes where we were out of sight but could still see what was going on in the living room.

Four people dressed in suits climbed out of the vehicle, and my stomach churned as I watched Stephen hold out a hand to someone inside.

"Dear goddess," I murmured. The attacks, the negative energy...it all made sense now. Stephen was here.

All three of us gasped as a figure draped in red gauzy material stepped down from the tall vehicle. A wave of power came barreling across the street and nearly knocked us off our feet. Streetlights popped and the lights in the house went off, followed by shouts from the four men inside.

"You guys feel that?"

Mark squeezed my biceps. "I haven't felt that in fifty years," he whispered.

The figure's head turned toward where we were hiding, and we sank back and held our breath.

"If we felt that, do you think..."

Stephen led them forward, and the other men walked into the house. The last man let the others in before him, squeezed Stephen's shoulder as they passed, and then turned to survey the area before he shut the door.

"Holy shit. Creed, did I just see that?" Mark's eyes were huge, but I couldn't stop shaking.

"That was Leader Caleb. But I saw him. On the ground that night..."

"Shhh." Cross put his hand over my mouth and stared at the house wide-eyed. "We can't be seen."

"Do we chance getting closer?" I asked when he removed his hand.

Cross shook his head and ran a hand over his face and tugged on his beard.

"I can't believe it. I thought for sure The Source was gone. Dead. I hadn't thought *anyone* survived that night, and then I find you guys. And fucking Caleb. And that horrible piece of shit Stephen."

"I think I knew," Cross said. "Deep down, I think I knew The Source had survived. Because in the aftermath, I still felt...different, like I had after my initiation."

A couple of faces were illuminated by phones inside the house, and the dim light from the kitchen allowed us to see what was going on.

One by one, the four men had their throats cut, and The Source placed a hand over the wound and something nuclear occurred. I'm sure there was some scientific name for the process we'd just witnessed…maybe it was merely processing.

Until the brilliant flash of light and the screams.

The bodies were gone, and as they led The Source from the house, now glowing, we once more felt a wave crash over us.

"Well, Creed, you're the one who was so hot on being absorbed back into The Source. I guess we know how that looks now."

I held a hand to my mouth, not sure if it was to hold in my own scream, or just from shock.

Did they know we were watching?

The three of us remained frozen as the SUV drove slowly away, so as not to call attention to their movement, and disappeared into the night.

"Holy shit, what just happened?" I jumped out of the bushes and began pacing.

"We gotta get out of here."

Just then, there was an explosion from the house that knocked the three of us onto our asses several feet from where we'd been hiding.

Apparently, they were covering their tracks.

The three of us looked at each other—then ran for Mark's truck. He fumbled with the keys trying to get the damn thing unlocked, and Cross quietly urged him to get us the fuck out of there.

Before I knew where we were going, they drove back downtown, past the bar, and into a neighborhood with apartment buildings. Mark pulled into a covered spot and turned off the truck.

"I can leave. I can—"

"You're coming inside," Cross said. "We gotta stick together after that shit. We need a fucking plan." His eyes were wide and he was shook. No longer was he the cool "I do what I want" Cross.

I followed them up the steps to their apartment, which wasn't much more than what you'd find in a cheap hotel room that rented by the week; two queen-sized beds, a mini-fridge and a bathroom. They brought their gear up from the van and put it under the table next to the windows. There was a bicycle standing against the wall and clothes in stacks piled on top of the dressers.

"It's not much, but it's home. For now."

"Although," Mark said, "maybe it shouldn't be. Maybe the three of us should get the fuck out of dodge."

"No," I said. "I'm not leaving Roman's family unprotected. And I have commitments."

"Commitments? Brother, did you not see what we saw? The Source is *alive* and sucked the *fuck* out of those four bastards. They deserved it, but I don't want to be anyone's Slim Fast shake, are you picking up what I'm putting down?" Cross shuddered and plopped down on the edge of one of the beds.

"The two of you are free to go. I understand, but I'm not leaving."

I turned for the door, and Mark stepped in front of me.

"Wait, Creed. Don't leave," he said. "I don't want to lose you, too. Even if we eventually split up again, I feel better knowing you're out there." He pulled me in for a hug, and I went, feeling his profound sadness. Him and Cross had energy signatures that were sharper, clearly delineated. Like the difference between getting hit with a spray bottle or a hose on jet power.

I patted Mark's back and turned to look at Cross. He looked equally distraught.

"I need to find out what the police know. Roman mentioned another lead...some woman who worked with an organization. He knows more. If I tell him the truth—"

"You know, I might flaunt The Way by getting up onstage and pretending to be a vampire, and I might role play with some sexy bartenders, but Creed...now that I've seen what I seen..."

"If The Source wants us gone, I don't think we have much say. But I can't help but think that following The Way, living the way we were taught, might have some sway with The Source. Maybe they're holding The Source against their will? Maybe The Source shut those guys down because they weren't following The Way?"

Mark and Cross looked at each other with skepticism.

"Brother, I don't know if I want to find out."

"Fine," I said. "But I've gotta do this. If anything, I need Roman to understand, and I need his uncle to know what they're dealing with. I'll keep your names out of it. I will not out you."

Cross stared me down. This was the true test. They could decide to shut me down, protect themselves. Or they could let me do what I needed to do. I was ready to fight either way.

"Calm down," Cross said, running a hand down his beard. "I feel you getting all riled up over there. I'm not going to stop you. I won't interfere. But Mark and I will need to confer as to whether or not we stick around."

I glanced at Mark, and he nodded. "I'm sorry, Creed. I'm not sure I want to risk the little bit we have."

I patted his shoulder, still worried this was a show and they weren't going to let me leave. "I don't blame you. But I've spent the last fifty years working toward finding a resolution to what happened to our friends. I owe it to Muse. And now that I've found Roman, I can't risk him or his family being hurt because of my past."

"Understood," Cross said, standing from the bed. "Keep us informed. If we can help, we'll...consider it," he said, making eye contact with Mark.

I nodded to them and sucked in a breath. "I'm grateful that we reconnected. I feel so much better knowing you survived. Gives me hope. If I don't make it out of this, please...take care of yourselves."

They grabbed me up in a big hug and squeezed until we were all laughing and teary. I hated saying goodbye, not knowing whether I'd see them again. It was strange, I hadn't known they were alive two days ago, but now that I knew, I hated being apart.

I said my goodbye and ran down the steps of their apartment. Then I stalled.

Was I really ready to do this?

I needed to take care of one more thing before I talked to Roman.

22

CHAPTER TWENTY-TWO

R oman

It was a long night. I was still at the station when Vanessa and Sterling got the call that there had been a house explosion on East Cliff and fire department personnel had classified it suspicious. They found a partial ID for Dominique LeMonde, the BioBourne employee with ties to Monaco. They were still searching the house for remains when we left the station at three a.m.

My head was killing me, my stupid tinnitus acting up ever since leaving the bar with Rey. I tried to be helpful, but Vanessa had to call my name three times before finally resorting to "Junior" when I didn't hear her. All the late nights, the stress, and the heartache had taken a toll. She told Rey to take me home and that she'd call if anything came up, although the trail had run cold.

Rey stayed with me at the house and threatened to take me to the doctor tomorrow morning if I was still ringing. Officer Dicknaldo would not be swayed.

I crashed hard, but a knock on the door woke me while the sky was still gray outside.

My heart ground to a stop when I opened the door to find Lexi… with Rhonda.

"I'm sorry to just show up, but I told you I'd let you know if I heard anything."

I gestured for her to come in, and Rhonda pulled away from her to run at me. She leaned heavily against my leg.

"How—"

"Creed came to my place last night. He said he's in trouble, and he asked me to watch Rhonda for him."

Rey came down the stairs in his boxers and halted. "Lexi?"

"Hi, Rey. I'm sorry to come over so early, but I didn't know what to do, and I certainly don't know how to take care of this much dog." She laughed nervously and tucked a piece of hair behind her ear. "She practically dragged me up your steps."

I took the leash from Lexi and guided her to the table. "Want some coffee?"

"Sure," she said, but she was distracted. She sat down and shoved her hands in her hoodie pocket.

I set a bowl of leftover grilled chicken on the floor for Rhonda and she ate it daintily, not scarfing it like most dogs do.

"So he just gave you the dog and said see ya?" Rey asked as he returned, pulling on a sweatshirt, and thankfully he'd thrown on sweats.

"He did. He said he had to run, and he gave me Rhonda's leash and a bunch of money, said he'd be back for her if he could. He also said that if I saw you, Roman, I should tell you he heard what you said last night, and he's sorry."

Rey and I looked to each other. "He was there?"

Lexi shrugged. "I don't know."

My heart apparently forgot it was supposed to keep a sinus rhythm as it was now bouncing around like the ball over the lyrics on the screen at karaoke.

"Lexi, did he say anything else? Is he leaving?"

"No, just that he might not be back and he wanted to know Rhonda was okay. But Roman, I'm scared for him. And there's something else." Her eyes were wide. "The night your lola had her episode? When I came in and he asked me to give her the insulin?"

"I remember," my heart now hurtling like the fucking ball in pong, slamming against walls, freefalling, floating through the air. "He had to check on another patient. I stopped him in the hallway."

Lexi nodded. "Mr. Fletcher. I went to find Creed. I knew he was going to see Mr. Fletcher because I'd asked him to when he showed up for his shift. I opened Mr. Fletcher's door without knocking, which I never do, but things were so chaotic." She blinked a few times and looked between me and Rey.

"What happened?" Rey asked.

She shook her head. "I don't really understand what I saw. I don't know for sure. They were sitting on the couch together and...I know this sounds totally unbelievable, okay? I know it does. But Creed was, like, bent over Mr. Fletcher's arm, and when he lifted his head, Mr. Fletcher pressed it back down...and I saw Creed...*bite* him."

My knees gave out, and I fell back against the wall. "What do you mean, he *bit* him? Where?"

"It was on the inside of his wrist. I don't know what was happening. I closed the door as quietly as I could and then I ran back to the nurses' station, kind of freaking out. I saw Mr. Fletcher afterward, much later, and he was singing and snapping his fingers as he walked down the hall. I asked him if he was okay, and he said he had too much energy to sleep and he wanted to grab a book from the library. He was smiling. He was so *happy*, and normally Mr. Fletcher is kind of serious. I've never heard him singing before."

"Fucking weird-ass motherfucking shit," Rey muttered. "So after we saw you, after the attack, you went straight home?"

She nodded. "I went home, showered and went to bed. Creed showed up around an hour ago with the dog and...he was *crying*. He hugged her, and then he ran away really fast before I could ask him any questions. God, I am so worried about him, but I don't know what to think after what I saw, you know? He's my best friend, one of the most amazing people I know. Why would he *bite* someone?"

Rhonda finished her food and turned to me, her reddish-brown eyes staring deep into my soul. She sat on her haunches and stared at me, and when I didn't react, she pawed at my leg and whimpered.

"Come here, girl," I said. I slid down the wall and opened my arms to her. She covered my face with kisses and then lay with her head in my lap.

Creed. What have you done?

"Look, I'm not really supposed to have dogs at my apartment, but I will—"

"Rhonda's staying here," I said, petting her head. "And we're going to find Creed. I'm so pissed at him right now, but I'm not about to let him get hurt."

I looked up at Rey and dared him to contradict me.

"We'll find him, pamangkin," Rey said, using the Tagalog word for nephew, which meant he was serious, or seriously upset. "I promise."

I nodded and focused on Rhonda, who gave a big sigh.

"I'm sorry, Roman. I appreciate you taking her. It seems like she's happier here, anyway. All she did was give me dirty looks." She laughed and then wiped a tear away. "If she wasn't Creed's dog, I would have called Animal Control. I was scared to death."

Rey put an arm around her. "We'll take care of her. You need me to run you home?"

She wiped at her eyes again and Rey handed her a tissue. "Thank you. Actually, if you wouldn't mind. I walked over here."

Rey called out to me that they were leaving, and I'm sure I said goodbye, but I was still running through what she'd told us.

He bit someone.

The attacks.

He'd been furious at those guys, but acted like what they were doing was a personal affront.

Him being unsteady on his feet after caring for Lola. He admitted that he'd healed her with his energy.

"Why does it hurt less when I'm with you?"

"Rhonda, come on, girl." I grabbed my laptop and led her over to the couch. I patted the seat next to me and she hopped up, resting her head on my thigh. "I'm feeling some déjà vu here."

I pulled up my notes from the interview I did with Carolina Villanueva in Bilbao. Her mother had reported her missing to the police, and they'd found her hiding in the train station. She'd had her head shaved and was wearing all white when they found her. I'd met with her and her mother over several afternoons. She had night terrors and trouble sleeping, so afternoons were the time she felt like she could talk, she'd explained.

Translated from Spanish.

RSA: Can you tell me a little about the program?

CV: Yes. I met Leader Lorraine on my campus for school. She came to talk to nursing students about job opportunities. She told us about a research program they had where they wanted college students to participate in studies involving healing, and that if we were interested, they had a training program. They paid room and board and tuition was free if you were selected. Mama had been struggling to pay for my school, so I thought this would be a good opportunity.

RSA: You moved to the La Mente campus and began studying. Can you tell me what the center was like?

CV: We were in sessions fourteen hours a day with breaks twice a day for eating. We learned meditation and how the body uses energy, what that looks like, how different energy is perceived by the body. That was the first six months I was there. The days were long, and I was tired because I couldn't sleep well in the dormitory—

RSA: Do you think you can tell me a little more about that?

CV: Yes. It was a large gymnasium with bedrolls. We weren't allowed any personal items, only our clothing and our sleeping things. There were at least sixty of us in this room, men and women, and the Leaders did not allow us to talk, but when they left, the others would talk, or do other things, and it did not feel safe to me, so I didn't sleep.

RSA: And do you think you can tell me about the experiments?

CV: The experiments were terrible. When it was your turn, you were taken to a room that was mostly dark. People would come into the room and crowd you into the corner. If you were lucky, they didn't speak to you, they just pressed against you and held you in place until you thought you might scream or pass out. Sometimes it was cold, sometimes it was too hot, stuffy. And some of the people would say things to you and laugh at you, and when it was men, they would tell you things and…"

RSA: It's okay, you don't have to speak any more on this.

CV: There was one man who came in, and he would make you see things in your mind. I don't know how he did it, and sometimes I thought I was going crazy. Or maybe I was asleep and having a nightmare, but then I'd feel the brush of clothing against my skin, or feel someone's breath on the back of my neck, and I'd know that the terrible things I saw were because of him. He would show me things…sexual things…torture things…

RSA: And how long were the cycles of experiments?

CV: They would keep you there for days in a room by yourself, and you never knew when it was your turn, there was no regular schedule.

RSA: Did anything else happen during your time there that made you want to leave?

CV: One of the girls who slept near me, Anna, she told me that there was to be an initiation soon, and that some of us would be chosen to move to the next level of training. She was excited to do it, she said she didn't know what was involved but that she would be able to heal people with her mind. I thought she'd spent too much time in the experiments and that she wasn't well, but she was determined. She said once they initiate you, you can learn about Exchanges, and then you could survive without food.

RSA: And that made you want to leave?

CV: They were already keeping us hungry. They did it on purpose, I think, to keep us at their mercy. To keep us needing them. I noticed once when I was getting my food that there was a door at the back of the kitchen and people came in and out, but there didn't seem to be a lock. I started to watch the Guardians who watched us while we slept and while we were in class, and there were times of the night when they went outside to the courtyard. I thought maybe if I could get into the kitchen, I could get out. So I tried it. I was so afraid when I got outside that I almost went back in. But then I saw light coming from the courtyard. I looked through the bushes and watched as they brought Anna into the light, two of the Guardians, and instead of the white we always wore, she wore black. And there was a person in red standing next to fire and...

RSA: It's alright.

CV: They took her clothes off—and they bit her. The Guardians and Leaders who had been watching over us. They bit her on the shoulders and arms, and then the person in red pressed a hand to her mouth and when they pulled their hand back, Anna had blood on her mouth. I ran. I didn't want to see any more. I thought I would die if I stayed there. I thought they were killing Anna. I thought they would kill *me*.

RHONDA SIGHED and pawed at my leg, pulling me from my thoughts.

"What does it all mean?" I ran my hand through my hair and fell back against the couch as Rey came in.

"Hey, I'm gonna head into the station and see what they got out of that house last night. You want to come with?"

"I want to find Creed," I said. Rhonda sat up and looked at the door with her ears up. "I need to know..."

"Maybe Lexi was wrong," Rey said. "Or maybe she saw something easily explainable?"

"I want *him* to explain it to me." I rubbed at my head again. My ear had been ringing all morning, but it was louder now. Rhonda leaned against me, pushing me back into the couch.

"Maybe you should stay here and get some rest. Let me find out what's going on, and then when I get back, we can make a plan."

I nodded, but I knew I wouldn't be able to rest. I read through the rest of the interview with Carolina, then read the notes from the other folks I'd talked to.

It was raining when I woke up on the couch with a heavy weight pinning me down.

I opened an eye to find Rhonda staring at me.

"You let me fall asleep?"

She stretched and dug her doggy elbows into my gut before she gracefully left the couch and stood by the door expectantly.

"I suppose you want to go for a walk?"

Her stare told me all I needed to know.

AND OVER THE next three weeks, we developed a routine. Eat, walk, teach, walk, eat, sleep. We walked the beach, we searched the neighborhoods, we hung out on the Boardwalk, she came with me to campus when I needed to teach in person, and sat beside me during my online courses. The only place I didn't take her was Puesta Del Sol, because I figured folks might freak out if they saw her. She was quite imposing, and people definitely gave us a wide berth.

But no one stayed farther away than Creed.

I'd texted, I'd called, I'd prayed every time I went to the home that he would magically appear, even though Lexi told me he took a leave from work. Told the bosses he had some personal issues to work out, but I knew the truth.

Somehow Creed was mixed up with the people behind the attacks, and he was either hiding...or searching.

But the attacks had stopped. While that was a good thing for the community, no one felt we were out of the woods yet. Vanessa and Sterling had hit several dead ends, though the FBI was still investigating the BioBourne company and working with INTERPOL. I'd met with them and shared my research, but we all felt there was something right in front of us, keeping the true intentions of the organization hidden.

And Bloody Brilliant apparently cancelled the rest of their shows and skipped town.

Had Creed left with them?

Was he really gone?

Rhonda and I moped over him together, and I started to worry when her appetite seemed to fade. I tried different foods, even made her steaks and bought her beef ribs to chew on, but she'd barely take in a little, and then she'd lay on the rug in front of the vent.

Dammit, Creed. Where are you?

23

———

CHAPTER TWENTY-THREE

C reed

I HELD out as long as I could, but I had to make one final trip to
Puesta Del Sol before I made my final move on Stephen and his
collaborators.

It took me three weeks, but I finally came across their house in
the woods off of Highway 17.

It happened by accident. I'd been on the beach at sunset, looking
for the young man and his spiritualist friends, thinking it couldn't
hurt to ask them if they'd been approached. But as I'd hidden under
the pillars of the Boardwalk, waiting to draw aside the young man I'd
spoken with, Stephen and his collaborators—the same ones who
murdered the four bullies—approached them as they were getting
started with their evening meditations.

The young man I'd talked to had smiled at first, but then he'd
stepped away from Stephen and shook his head. He gathered his
people and they made a hasty retreat. Stephen talked to the others

and then I followed them to the same Mercedes SUV parked near the Boardwalk. I'd used the last of the money I had saved to buy a beat-up motorcycle, knowing I'd have to be able to follow them, and I kept my distance, tailing them as they left the Santa Cruz city limits for the mountains. I'd had to fly past when they turned down a hidden one-lane driveway, but I circled around and parked the bike in the bushes, hoping I'd be able to find the SUV.

It was too easy.

The house was a monstrous, modern architectural behemoth with a living roof and all the windows. I chuckled when I realized it looked an awful lot like the Cullen house in the *Twilight* film and thought how perfect for this guy to take on the vampire cliché.

There were two other cars there and two more arrived while I was watching from the outside. I hated not being able to get closer, but if The Source was inside, they'd likely be able to sense me.

Another car pulled up and this one caught my attention.

It was a McLaren, and when the man parked and got out of the car, I felt the same sick energy coming off of him that I'd felt whenever Stephen was around. He popped the trunk and lifted a woman out with ease, despite the fact that she was fighting against her binds.

"Ah, Timothy, I see you found your missing wife."

He carried her up the steps toward Stephen with no effort whatsoever.

"She thought she could run, but I knew she'd go right back to her sister. Thankfully my brother-in-law was easily persuaded to return her to me."

"The Source will be pleased. Come inside."

The man carried the woman into the large foyer and Stephen followed with that creepy smile of his. My fucking skin was crawling even despite the distance.

Three more men in suits led The Source forward to greet this Timothy guy. There was talking, and then the group walked out of the lighted portion of the house and I lost sight of them.

I knew there was no way I could handle this alone. Mark and Cross were hesitant to get further involved and were making plans to skip town, maybe they had already. Rey and Vanessa were on the trail, but I worried they would get hurt, especially if they tried to deal with The Source.

The Source. Gone was the benevolent leader I'd found so captivating during my time with the cohort. I couldn't believe they were going along with Stephen's nefarious activities. How could they have let their teachings become so perverted? I was so disappointed, discouraged. I'd been ready to dedicate my life to The Source and their teachings of The Way, and now that I'd seen what they'd become...

No, I wouldn't question my decisions. There had been too much good in my life.

And if I was meant to leave it behind, so be it.

But I needed to be at my full strength, whatever happened, and I owed closure to the people who meant so much to me. I left the house in the woods and planned to drive straight to the police...but the Mercedes pulled in behind me, way too close to be a coincidence.

Before I knew it, I was sliding down the embankment, the bike toast and my body beat to hell.

LEXI GASPED when I entered the front doors of Puesta Del Sol.

"Creed! Oh my God, what happened to you? Where—"

"I can't stay, Lexi. I'm only here to resign and say goodbye."

"But you can't leave," she said, her big brown eyes filling with tears.

"I can't stay. There are people looking for me, and I don't want to chance them coming after me here."

"But Creed—"

I pulled her in for a hug and held her as she cried, fighting my own tears.

"I know. I hate it too. I need to see Mr. Fletcher, and then I'm going to swing by Yvonne's and give her my resignation."

"No—"

"I know, I'm sorry, darlin'. And thank you for taking Rhonda, is she okay?" I hated to even ask. I'd felt like I was missing a limb without her.

"She's okay, she's—"

"Creed! I've been trying to call you." Yvonne came out of the office and hurried to my side, which caught the attention of some of the residents who were in the library, and my hopes of getting in and out quickly were dashed. I took her by the arm and held up a finger to Lexi.

"I'll see you before I go."

I hated watching her cry as I practically pushed Yvonne back into her office.

"Creed, what's happened to you?"

"Yvonne, I really wish I could explain it, and I wish I didn't have to leave."

She blanched and started to shake her head. "You can't. How could I ever replace you?"

I handed her my ID and my keys and a letter directing her to donate my last paycheck to the Alzheimer's Society. I had to get out of there, but she started to tear up.

"Creed, you know you will always have a job here, so please keep us in mind."

"Thank you, Yvonne. This has been my home, my very favorite place ever. If it's humanly possible, I will come back."

I left her office feeling the weight of her sadness and the piercing pain from Lexi. I couldn't dwell here long, however, or I'd be overwhelmed with well-wishers and my resolve would weaken.

I went for Mr. Fletcher's room and found him in bed reading a book. His whole face lit up when he saw me, and he sat up.

"Creed, son, where've you been? What happened to you?"

I knelt next to his bed. "Mr. Fletcher, I'm so sorry, but I'm in a bit of trouble and I have to leave town. I didn't want you to worry—"

"Of course I'm worried! What's happened?"

Mr. Fletcher was the only one I could tell the truth because he knew my secret.

"There are people like me. Bad people who destroyed my cohort fifty years ago and killed my best friend. They're here, in town, and I need to deal with them and then get as far away from here as I can so they don't retaliate against the people I care about."

"Creed, you be careful. This world is a better place with you in it. I hate to lose you."

I knew it was about more than the Exchange for him, but I hated to think he'd begin to diminish after I left, that the new lease on life he'd experienced recently would prove to be a last gasp.

"I wish I could stay. Hell, I wish I could take you with me. I'm sure you'd be amazing in battle."

Mr. Fletcher laughed heartily, and I heard the fluid in his lungs. It broke my heart to think of him suffering. Was I being selfish? Should I just give up my quest and stay?

But then I thought of Stephen's evil grin, and I shuddered.

"There was a time I would have made a great partner in battle, but now I'm an old man wishing for a little more time."

He gave me a pleading look, and I smiled. I would do this one last kindness for him and get what I needed to face my enemy.

"You've been a true friend, Mr. Fletcher. I am grateful."

He put a hand on top of mine and then turned his wrist over. "For old time's sake."

I nodded, released the pheromone, and closed my eyes.

"Blessed be."

I pressed my lips to his wrist and pierced his skin as the door creaked behind me.

"Creed, step away."

I sighed and released as much healing energy as I could into Mr. Fletcher. I made sure to take the moment necessary to heal all traces of my bite, knowing I was caught anyway. Why hurry? Mr. Fletcher relaxed back against the pillow and was out like a light.

I held my hands up as I turned to face Reynaldo. Rey's hand hovered over his duty weapon and his posture was coiled tight, as if he were ready to take me down.

"Am I under arrest?" I asked.

"Creed, we've been looking everywhere for you," Rey said, and he wasn't hateful. I'd expected anger from him, but what I got was even worse.

"If I'm not under arrest, I need to leave. I can't let them find me here."

"You're not under arrest, Creed, but you need to come with me," Rey said.

"I can't do that. Please, let me go—"

"Rhonda needs you. She won't eat anymore."

Tears burned my eyes and a sob broke free. "No," came out in a whisper.

"Creed, come back with me," Rey pleaded. "We can protect you—"

"You can't! I can't let anyone else get hurt. I can't." I could barely talk, my throat was so full. I gauged whether or not I could take him by surprise, just barrel through him to the door or go out the window, but Rey's hand was back on his weapon.

"Don't." Rey stepped forward with a hand out. "Don't make me hurt you."

"Please. They'll kill all of you to get to me."

Rey put a hand on my biceps, his grip strong, but not enough to hold me if I fought him.

"Which is why you need to tell us what you know. Come with me."

I nodded, sucking in a breath. "But take me to the police department, not to your house. I don't want to put Roman in any more danger. They've seen him with me—"

"He's at the station. With Rhonda. Come on."

He kept a hand on me until we got into the hallway. "Don't run, Creed. Don't make a scene."

I nodded. I said goodbye to everyone I saw, grateful that Frances and her sisters weren't among the crowd. Lexi gave me a look of such heartbreak, and I hated myself for hurting her.

"I'm sorry, Lexi."

She crossed her arms over her chest and glared at me, anger and pain emanating from her tiny body in waves.

"Do I need to put you in the back?" Rey asked.

"No," I said quietly. He opened the passenger side door for me to climb in and then shut it behind me. When he climbed into his side, he stuck the key in the ignition and sighed.

"You know, you're lucky I'm not beating your ass for the hurt you've brought to my door. My auntie, my nephew...the dog... You better help me fix this shit with EVE, and then you need to clean up your mess, goddammit. I hate tears. I hate weird, but I hate tears even more, and there have been plenty going around because of Nurse Creed." He cursed under his breath and pulled his patrol car away from the curb. "Fucking Nurse Creed."

"I'm sorry, Rey. I am."

"For what? The assholes going around bullying people? Biting people? Making everyone fall in love with you? What?"

"All of it," I said as I gazed out the window at the hazy night. The fog had rolled in pretty thickly and it was tough to see past the streetlights.

"Yeah, well, you're gonna be sorry when Roman gets hold of you. I've never seen him so mad, and that's saying something."

"I'll bet." I deserved it. All of his anger.

We pulled into the lot and I followed Rey into the back entrance. He led me to a conference room with frosted windows and sat me in a chair outside. "Sit. I'll tell them you're here." Through the haze, I could see four people inside but couldn't make out who they were.

I sat on a hard wooden chair and enjoyed the pain of the slats digging into the scratches on my back from the spill on my bike. It reminded me of my purpose.

Rhonda darted out of the conference room and ran for me, lifting up to put her paws on my chest. I nearly lost it when I hugged her and felt her ribs. My poor girl. What had I done to her? If I'd have known about the shelf-life of the Exchange...

Before anyone noticed, I punctured my finger and gave her a few drops of my blood, hoping, praying it would keep her comfortable until I could figure out what to do. I couldn't leave her. I couldn't stay here. I wished I could just take her and run away. I wished I could—

"Creed?"

"Detective Cabral," I said, standing to greet Vanessa. She seemed concerned but not angry with me. Rey hadn't been angry either. How could they not be? I never should have gotten involved with Roman.

"We'd like to brief you on our current situation and ask you once more to help us. A woman's life is at stake."

I stood and reached for Rhonda's head. As always, her strength gave me courage.

"I'll tell you whatever I can."

"No, you'll tell us whatever we need to know, Creed. Otherwise, you'll be spending some time in jail.

CHAPTER TWENTY-FOUR

R oman

I BRACED myself when I heard his voice. Knowing he would be entering the room and actually seeing him were two different things.

And what I saw was not at all what I'd expected.

Creed had always seemed larger than life. He always wore a smile. Even when he was worried, his face had a soft quality to it—as opposed to my perma-scowl—that always put me at ease. He carried himself relaxed,

That was three weeks ago.

The Creed before me now was wiry. He'd lost weight, his clothes were dirty and there were lines in his stark face that I didn't recall seeing before. He looked...hard. Weathered. His eyes were sunken in and darting about the room, on alert. Even his wavy hair, so soft to the touch, always brushing his shoulders and curling against his cheeks, was brushed back off his face and looked unkempt, at least for Creed.

I still wanted to pull him in close and hold him until my heart stopped pounding with fear...and need.

I loved him, and it was killing me to see him suffer.

He made eye contact with everyone else in the room seated around the long conference table—Sterling, Captain Rojas, the FBI agent Todd Barringer—before he looked to where I was standing against the wall.

I could practically hear his apology as we stared at each other, me pleading for him to trust us, him looking for an escape route.

Captain Rojas cleared his throat and all attention focused on him.

"Mr. Lowell, thank you for coming. I want to reiterate that you are not a suspect in any of the attacks, nor are you being interrogated for any crimes. However, we have been led to believe by Officer Cabral and Mr. San Angelo that you possess a unique insight into the people behind the attacks that took place on the Boardwalk and the attempt on Donna Hicks's life, as well as her abduction, so—"

"Donna Hicks?" Creed asked, frowning. "I'm afraid I don't know who that is."

His accent was much thicker than usual, probably because he was exhausted. He moved slowly as he took a seat across from the captain, next to Rey.

Vanessa placed a picture of Donna in front of him.

"Let's catch you up," she said. "The four men who committed the attacks around town—"

"They're dead," Creed said, swallowing hard.

"They are believed to be deceased, yes," she continued. "They were all employed by BioBourne, a Silicon Valley company where Donna Hicks is head of research and development. Mrs. Hicks had been working on a way to replicate the blood of a...person of interest, we don't know who—"

"The Source," Creed said quietly.

Vanessa blinked and looked to Rey, but she remained composed.

"Mrs. Hicks and her husband Timothy are members of a private organization called EVE, or Elite Ventures Enterprises, does that ring a bell?"

Creed shook his head. "No, ma'am." He seemed genuinely confused.

"The current CEO of BioBourne, according to Mrs. Hicks, is the founding member of EVE, Mr. Stephen Adams."

That got a cold glare from Creed. Before he began to talk.

"Formerly known as Stephen Allman, born April 1, 1948 in Abilene, Texas. Graduated University of Texas, Austin, 1968, moved to the Haight Ashbury in San Francisco later that summer and was recruited to join The Gateway of the Sun, a spiritual community focused on healing and meditation. He lived with the community until 1971, when he and three of his associates mutinied against the leaders of the community, killing several members in the process."

The room was silent except for the shuffling of papers as those gathered wrote notes, scrambled through files, anything to try to figure out what the hell Creed had just shared.

Vanessa was the first one to speak. "How do you know this?"

Creed folded his hands on the table in front of him and glanced at me once before looking back at her. "Because I was there."

The paper shuffling stopped and those gathered, other than Rey, sat back in their seats, disbelief evident on their faces. Rey, however, remained focused, his body turned in the chair toward Creed, and I wasn't sure if it was out of support, or if it was in case Creed tried to make a run for it.

"Creed, if you need medical attention—" Vanessa began.

He shook his head. "If you really want me to talk, I'm going to tell you things you won't believe."

He stared at his hands and twisted his fingers while the law enforcement personnel murmured their thoughts to each other.

I couldn't tear my eyes off of Creed. I wanted to go to him, but I was frozen in my spot, in my position as a witness.

"Mr. Lowell," Agent Barringer said. "What can you tell us about the Source?"

Creed swallowed and ducked his head. "Telling you about The Source goes against everything I was taught, everything I've been trying to accomplish for the past fifty years. And it will likely get me killed." He glanced up at the FBI agent. "If you compel me to talk, I'll do so. But then you have to let me go. I won't let anyone else get hurt."

Vanessa blanched. "Fifty years? How is that possible?"

Barringer held up a hand to Vanessa. "May I?"

She shrugged and stepped back from the table and Barringer leaned forward. "Here's some information that might influence your decision, Mr. Lowell. Stephen Allman created Elite Ventures in 1978 as a shell corporation to fund bio research in the field of genetics and synthetic blood. He was allegedly killed in a car accident in Texas in 1985.

"Since then, similar learning environments to Gateway of the Sun have been documented around the world. Stephen *Adams* was born in San Francisco on April 1, 1986. No school records or work history have been located prior to the formation of Elite Ventures Enterprises, or EVE, in 2005 in Barcelona, Spain. EVE has been suspected in a couple of high-profile embezzlement cases, which never made it to court as the accusers mysteriously disappeared. Adams has been questioned by authorities in California and New York, has warrants for his arrest in Spain and Monaco. He received a speeding ticket in Santa Cruz last year.

"Am I gathering that you believe Stephen Adams and Stephen Allman are the same person? Is that what you're confirming?" Barringer asked. He slid two photographs across the table to Creed, who sat up straighter as he looked them over.

"It's the same person. Stephen Allman killed my best friend. I will never forget his face."

"Mr. Lowell," Barringer said. "I want you to trust me when I tell you that I can protect you. I have been authorized by the FBI to form a task force to work on cold cases connected with unexplained phenomenon. I have contacts who operate outside the parameters of the federal government. They specialize in protecting people from those who use their abundant powers irresponsibly."

Creed tilted his head and squinted at Barringer. "So you know what I am?"

Barringer smiled. "I've only recently learned the truth about people who have particular gifts, but yes, I sensed it the moment you walked in this room. I know you're different. I don't know much about your *particular* difference, but I'm very interested in learning from you."

Creed sat back in the chair and shook his head. "And this is exactly why I'm not keen on telling you anything. You'll focus more on figuring out what makes me tick than you will on stopping Stephen from hurting more people."

"No, Mr. Lowell," Captain Rojas said. "I have a woman missing who was supposed to be safe from harm after she cooperated with Detective Cabral. We believe her husband, Timothy Hicks, and this Stephen Adams have kidnapped her, and I want to get her back safely. That's why we need you to talk. Anything else," he said, glaring at Agent Barringer, "is fairytale shit I'm not interested in. If you can help us save this woman, you'll be free to leave...town."

Creed's shoulders hunched a bit and he nodded. "Fine. Thank you. I'll tell you what I know. First, the four men from the attacks are dead. I saw them die. They were killed by Stephen Adams, and I was a witness."

"You were there?" Rojas asked him.

"Yes, sir. I followed them to the house and was...watching from across the street and through the front window of the home when Stephen and his minions arrived. The men had their throats slit. Stephen and the others left. A few minutes later, the house blew up."

He said it all so matter-of-factly that I had to keep my jaw from hanging open in surprise.

"Do you recognize any of the others who were with Stephen?" Captain Rojas slid two sets of pictures in front of Creed.

Creed looked them over and pointed at one and his eyes flared. "This is Leader Caleb. I don't have a last name. I assumed he was killed in the mutiny but recently learned he was involved." Creed gripped the edge of the table. "He must have been the one to give Stephen access...he must have." Creed pushed back from the table and blew out a breath. "May I have a moment?" His hands shook as he pushed his hair back. "Is there a restroom?"

"I'll take you," Rey said.

I had to follow. It was breaking my heart to see him so distraught. Rey opened the door for him and said, "I'll wait out here," but I wasn't giving him that space. I pushed through the door after Creed.

He walked straight to the sink and turned the water on, leaning over and splashing his face.

"I'm sorry, Creed."

He wouldn't look at me. His posture was that of a much older man with the weight of the world on his shoulders.

"You have nothing to apologize for, Roman," he said. His voice wasn't warm like I remembered it. It was hoarse and weak. "I never should have involved you in any of this."

"How did you involve me?" I asked him. "The only thing you did was make my lola fall in love with you. And make *me* fall in love with you."

He stood up straight and looked at me in the mirror. "Roman—"

"No, don't say anything. You have more than enough on your plate. Let's get through this, and then I'm taking you home with me."

"Roman, haven't you been listening to me?" He turned to face me and threw his arms out in despair. "These people are dangerous and they'll kill you if they know how much you mean to me! They've taken *everything* from me. I can't let them take you!"

I approached him slowly and reached for him, afraid to spook him.

"They won't hurt me." I grasped his waist and tugged gently, giving him enough space to pull away.

He melted against me and shudders racked his body, his too thin body. I pulled him close, fighting back tears of my own.

"You don't have to do this alone, Creed. I swear to God, I won't let anyone hurt you."

He clung to my back and exhaled against me. He was all hard angles, so thin compared to three weeks ago.

"What's happened to you?"

He pulled back and wiped at his face.

"I'll tell you, I promise. Just let me get through the rest of this before I collapse. I can't talk much longer before I'll stop making sense." He stepped away and into the stall.

"If you need to stop—"

"No, I want to tell them what I know. At this point they're the only hope I have of stopping Stephen."

He flushed and stepped out of the stall, washed his hands and then stood before me.

"I'm so sorry, Roman. I wanted to keep you away from all of this."

"I know you did. And I'll be pissed at you later. Come here." I pulled him in tight, and this time he felt a little stronger. "I'm so worried about you. What do you need?"

He barked out a laugh. "This." He inhaled against my neck, rubbing his nose back and forth. "You. You make me feel better."

I squirmed a little. "I want to know how, though, Creed. Will you tell me?"

He pulled back and sighed. "You're doing it right now, being strong for me." He closed his eyes and breathed in through his nose. He pressed his hands to my chest and they felt...warm, warmer than the skin of his lower back, where my hands were resting just under his t-shirt. "Your energy is so...different than when I met you. Back then, you fed me with your sadness, your anger. Now, it's pure strength and..." He paused, his eyes filling with tears. "And love," he whispered. "I haven't felt that in so long." His chin quivered, and he sobbed.

"I *do* love you, dammit. Now stop." I pulled him against me and held him as he cried, but instead of weakness, his grip was strong, like I remembered. He grabbed fistfuls of my shirt and he took deep breaths to center himself.

"The last person who loved and trusted me was killed, Roman. I'm terrified you'll be taken from me."

I cradled his jaw in my hands. "Then let's work together and take these guys out, once and for all."

"So brave," he said, then he sucked in a breath.

Rey opened the door. "Everything okay in here?"

"Guess we're taking too long," I said, brushing my lips over his.

"I'm right here, Creed. Take what you need from me. For strength. And then let's go home."

"Home," he breathed and let his eyes flutter shut. "I kinda don't have one of those anymore. I gave up my lease three weeks ago. I thought I would be gone by now."

"Well, you're not, and you're not leaving, so let's do this and get on with our lives. Together. Got it?" I don't know where all this boldness was coming from, where I had the gall to decide that was how things were going to be, but it was what I wanted, what I could see coming to fruition. It was part of that "fast forwarding" I'd wanted to do earlier, when I could only see a distant light at the end of the tunnel, and I wanted to be there now.

Perhaps that was part of what people called manifesting your desires. I wanted Creed in my life. I wanted life to get to a place of peace, and dammit, I was going to make it so.

"I kinda love this side of you, Professor."

And there it was, Creed's smile. A little dimmer than the one I desperately needed to see returning, but I'd take it.

CHAPTER TWENTY-FIVE

C reed

I CAME out of that restroom not quite a new man, but one ready to do battle, sort of. And it was all thanks to a grad student still trying to find his way in this world with a powerful sense of intuition to guide him. I was still weaker than I'd been in many, *many* years, but I had resolve.

Perhaps he knew I'd needed an intervention at the moment I entered the restroom, that I'd contemplated an escape, or that I'd feared I was ready to collapse, never to rise again.

I'd spent the past three weeks isolated except for tracking Stephen and the others, and therefore I'd been starving. I desperately needed energy. I hadn't realized how strong my time working at the home had made me until I made the attempt to see Mr. Fletcher earlier out of desperation. I was depleted, and I'd begun to imagine the type of demise Cross and Mark had described to me.

I entered that restroom fully believing I might not make it out, but then Roman came to my rescue with that special brand of energy that always soothed my weary soul. I'd been through so much in my long life that I knew better than to ignore the signs.

Roman had been brought into my life for a reason, and just like the old saying that if you let love go and it comes back to you...you know, all that? I'd let Roman go countless times and he kept coming back.

That meant he was mine.

"You okay?" Rey asked me as I left the bathroom, but he looked to Roman.

"I didn't bite him, if that's what you're asking, Officer Cabral." I gave him a smirk and he threw an arm across my chest to stop me.

"Look, I don't know what the fuck I saw back at the home, but I better not see that shit around my family, you get me?"

"What are you talking about?" Roman said, getting between us.

Rey glared at me in that "I don't want to kick your ass but I will if you make me" way he did when he was on patrol.

"What he's talking about is that he saw me with Mr. Fletcher, doing an Exchange, which I will explain to you and the others." I turned to Roman. "And then I will not hold you accountable for everything you just said in there if you want to leave—"

"Creed, I swear to—"

"Okay! Let's get to it." I clapped my hands together and walked back into the conference room with a little more spring in my step.

This time Roman sat next to me at the conference table, with Rey watching me like a hawk.

"Now, where were we? You want to know about The Source?"

Barringer, the FBI agent, was something or someone more. The man had an aura about him, an energy signature that wasn't typical. He kept tight control over his emotions, and therefore I knew he must have had some sort of psychic training, but not like what I'd been through.

Beside him sat the captain, Ross Sterling the detective, and Vanessa. She was trying very hard to keep her emotions in check but she was worried about Roman, and very worried about Donna Hicks, the woman who had been abducted.

"We want to know anything that can help us," the captain said, his frustration bleeding from his pores. His large biceps and deltoids pulled at his dress shirt as he crossed his arms over his chest, and I knew if I looked under the table his knee would be bouncing up and down rapidly.

Sterling, however, appeared calm. Too calm. He knew something more than he had shared with the others, or else he would be nervous.

They all would scoff, be shocked, and then be sorry they ever took on this case. That I knew for sure.

"Whatever is shared regarding the Exchange or The Source should never leave this room," I began. "In fact, you'd all be better off never hearing about it. Having this knowledge will put you and those you love at risk."

I waited a beat to see if any of them would leave. Of course they wouldn't, they were cops. They wanted the truth, the whole truth and nothing but. They didn't know how much they would regret that once I told them everything.

"I can't find anything concrete on this person they call The Source," Agent Barringer said. "But I've heard mention of them in diaries entered as evidence through INTERPOL."

Roman's head whipped around at that.

"They gave you access?"

Barringer smiled. "Yes, Dr. San Angelo—"

"I'm ABD, Agent Barringer."

He shook his head. "Not after this, you won't be. Maybe it's premature, I'm sorry, but I'm very familiar with your work, and you and I will have a lot to discuss after this case." He nodded at Roman, and then looked at me expectantly.

"For the past fifty years, I thought I was the only one left. When I fled the commune on the night of my initiation, I believed everyone else had been killed. I wasn't aware there were any other beings like them...or me, I suppose. Not until I ran into an old associate who assured me that there are others—and before you ask, my associate was not involved with any of this and prefers to remain anonymous. I will do them that courtesy. But they did inform me that the night of the mutiny, some survived and escaped, not just me. Now I can gather that Stephen escaped with The Source and Leader Caleb."

My pulse sped up just thinking about that night. Images of violence and blood sickened me, and if it hadn't been for Roman's energy, a lifeline in this painful scenario, I wouldn't have been able to continue.

"From what I know," Barringer said, pulling me from my fog, "The Source was first mentioned in records dating back to the Romans and the conquest of Gaul and Britannica. It was a term used by the Druids, who believed that souls were immortal and were passed from one being to another."

I smirked. "Well, then. You know more than I do, Agent Barringer. All we were taught was that The Source was an ancient being who had defied death or degeneration through the practice of manipulating negative energy and spiritual healing. It was only at my initiation that I learned the truth."

"I want to know how it works, the Exchange," Barringer asked.

"Had you heard the term before?" I asked.

Vanessa cleared her throat. "From Donna Hicks. She mentioned it was part of the initiation but she didn't know what it was. They didn't allow her to go to her husband's initiation."

I said a silent apology to Cross and Mark.

"There were four Guardians with The Source for the ceremony, four Leaders, and four Learners. The Guardians were there for protection and, from what I'd been told in preparation, in case anything went wrong. The Leaders were there to observe, to bear witness. The Learners, we were told that we would be initiated. Once we were given the blessing of The Source, we would have an Exchange with them that would alter our body chemistry, making our work as healers much more powerful. We were assured that it would be relatively painless, that it was the necessary step in the next phase of our learning." I shuddered, and Roman placed a hand on my arm.

"And I'm guessing it wasn't," Barringer said.

I shook my head, my eyes stinging. "No, it wasn't. I was the third to receive...the Exchange, and if I hadn't been so in shock at what happened to the others, I would have run before Stephen acted. He..." I dug the heels of my palms into my eyes, wishing I didn't see red when they were closed.

"Mr. Lowell?" Barringer prompted me. "The Exchange?"

All the years that I'd suppressed even thinking of that night made my tongue heavy, my throat thick.

"I thought the Guardians and Leaders were supposed to observe, but when it was the first initiate's turn, the Guardians held them down and...the others...bit them. And then The Source, they...took blood inside of them, and then forced their blood into the initiate."

I was purposefully vague. I really didn't want to go deeper but I could see Barringer's curiosity.

"What was that like for you?" he asked.

I dug my nails into my palms. "It was excruciating. The most painful experience of my life. We'd been taught to release a pheromone, a natural chemical all humans have, in order to make the person comfortable and make the Exchange painless. We learned how to express it on command before manipulating a person's energy, but for the initiation, they said we needed to experience the Exchange without anything to ease our suffering so we would never forget...that we would never take without permission. We were taught to take only what we needed to survive and to give unto others what they required."

Roman sat up a little straighter and guilt crashed over me. He was getting a taste of what he'd signed up for when he chose me, and damn, but I hated once more that I'd brought him into my world. Best intentions and all that...

"So how is this Stephen different?" Vanessa asked.

"Certain kinds of energy feed us differently—"

"You mentioned energy before," the captain said. "What do you mean by that?"

This was my opportunity to come clean. I wondered if they would actually believe me.

"Think of it this way, sir. When you are in the process of apprehending a suspect, how does that feel for you?" I looked around the table. They looked at each other with frowns.

"You get an adrenaline rush," Rey finally said. "The more they fight, the more pumped you get."

"Right. You feed off their energy, you adjust your behavior based on how they respond to you. You live in a reality where you're constantly on edge, never sure how people are going to behave, and that is draining after a while, isn't it?"

All of the officers nodded and shifted uncomfortably in their seats.

"I'm kind of the opposite. Someone is angry? Aggressive? Good. The more the better. I take it in and it feeds me. Negative energy *gives* me energy, instead of draining me, if that makes sense? The more energy I take in, the more positive energy I'm able to respond with. That's why I work with the elderly. Sundowning...you know the term? How patients who are experiencing dementia have a shift in the afternoons and evenings? They become agitated, upset, their symptoms are worse. When I'm there, I take it in, take that extra negative energy away from them, and they feel better."

The others in the room sat there staring at me with no way of comprehending what I'd just said.

"It's true. I've seen him do it," Roman said. "And when he's not there, the patients lose a little ground. I've seen it with my lola." He glanced at me and cleared his throat. "I can't explain it either, but I know he's not lying."

"Can you show us?" Barringer asked.

"I'm not sure," I said. "It's not exactly a situation you can set up... Well, actually, that's not true. That's what you asked me originally, about how Stephen is different. He realized while we were in our cohort that he could create the necessary scenario to feed."

"The attacks," Vanessa said.

"Yeah. He started that stuff in our cohort with his minions. Bullied people, cornered them and terrified them. He has a gift that was unique among us. He did it once to my best friend. He can plant images in your mind, whatever he wants, and instead of using his gift for good, like maybe giving people peace during their difficult times, he shows you terrifying things, and then feeds off the person's terror. Over and over in a loop—"

"The fear study," Roman said, looked to Vanessa.

"Donna said she was being kept away from it, but they were doing experiments using fear to create energy, and that was part of what made her try to leave the first time."

"La Mente did it too. One of the women I interviewed told me about the days of torture they were all put through. It wasn't meant as a teaching tool, it was how these sick bastards fed themselves, grew stronger."

Anger poured off of Roman, and I siphoned it.

He turned to face me, his eyes wide. "You're doing it now."

"Your pulse rate has slowed, your blood pressure is back to normal. You can measure it."

The captain snorted. "Okay, whatever, this woo woo bullshit is a waste of time. We need to find Donna Hicks and we need to catch these bastards. What can you tell us that will help?"

"I've spent the last three weeks trying to track them but I kept missing them. I finally tracked them to the house off seventeen this afternoon. I spotted the Mercedes G-Class near the Boardwalk and followed them. I kept my distance—we can sense each other and I knew The Source would feel my presence. They were carrying boxes out of the house like maybe they're closing up shop. I didn't recognize anyone other than Stephen. And there was some guy named Timothy who showed up who was carrying a woman over his shoulder. She was tied up, but I didn't see her face. Perhaps it was the woman you were looking for. There were too many people there, including The Source, for me to confront them, so I was coming back to town to see you, but they spotted me and when I tried to evade them, I crashed my motorcycle." I shrugged, and Roman grabbed my leg.

"*You what?* Jesus, Creed." His worry was bittersweet. It fed me, but I didn't want it. I hated putting him through this.

"I'm okay." I really wasn't. Without my frequent energy infusions from the patients at work, I was growing weak. The road rash on my side where my jacket and shirt were pulled up by the impact wasn't healing as fast as usual, and my hip ached, plus my back had been scratched to hell by the bushes down the embankment. Thankfully I'd been wearing a helmet.

I placed my hand over his and tried to give him a reassuring smile.

"We'll send officers out to the house, just to be sure they're really gone," the captain said. "Do you have any ideas where else they might be? Anything at all?"

I shook my head. "I've been racking my brains. The only thing I thought of, and this is a stretch, but...Samhain is coming up. At the commune, we celebrated the eight Pagan festivals. I remember the Leaders teaching us that The Source drew strength from ley lines, and there's one that runs through the Santa Cruz Mountains and up to Mt. Tamalpais. Our commune was near Loch Lomond. I thought maybe they might return to that area for the ceremony?"

The officers looked at each other.

"We don't have anything else to go on at this point. Look, it's late. We've got an APB out on the Mercedes and Stephen Adams and his crew. We're monitoring all activity at BioBourne, which has been dormant since Donna went missing." The captain was frustrated. "All of you go and get some rest. Mr. Lowell, we appreciate your cooperation."

I stood up with everyone else, and I reached across the table to shake his hand. He glanced down at it and back up at me.

"I'm sorry I couldn't do more."

He reached for my hand, realizing he was being silly. "I'd appreciate it if you'd stick around. Maybe you'll think of something else, or we will."

"Not ready to escort me to the city limits yet?" I winked as I released his hand, and he rolled his eyes.

"Surrounded by comedians." He shook his head as he left the room but I could tell he wasn't really upset.

Roman, on the other hand...his mind was spinning, and I knew he had a ton of questions for me.

"Let me take you two home," Rey said, putting on his jacket.

"If you could just drop me at a motel, I don't want to impose—"

"Shut up," Roman said. He handed me Rhonda's leash and put a hand between my shoulder blades, guiding me out. Truthfully, I needed his strength. My legs were ready to give out, my side ached, and I probably needed to sleep for about a week. I needed an Exchange, too, but that wasn't going to happen.

They walked me out to Rey's F150 and I stood by while Rhonda found a discreet piece of grass to do her business. I petted her neck and tried to give her some energy, but I swayed and Roman caught me.

"Come on, let me help you in."

I wanted to protest but I was not at my best. I accepted his boost into the backseat of the crew cab, and then he lifted Rhonda up to sit next to me. He didn't even strain under her weight.

"Rey, wait up."

Agent Barringer and Vanessa walked up to the truck.

"I know you all need some-shut eye, but I was hoping I could come by tomorrow? I have some things to discuss with you both, if you don't mind."

"Sure. Bring coffee and donuts," Rey said.

Barringer laughed and waved, leaving Vanessa to give me a death stare.

"I don't like the idea of him going home with you," she said to Roman.

"I don't like it either, Detective Cabral." I hated the possibility of putting them in danger.

She scowled for a moment longer then rolled her eyes. "Fine. Call me if anything weird happens. I'm going to see Tita Frances, and I'll tell her you'll be by tomorrow, alright? All of you. She's been in a state about her Nurse Creed being gone, and she's having more episodes. It would do her good to see you, even though I don't trust you as far as I can throw you."

She was about six inches shorter than Rey, who was about four inches shorter than me. But she had no reason to trust me, and I respected her. She exuded strength and kept her emotions closer to her chest than her brother and nephew.

"See you tomorrow," Rey said. "Don't worry, I've got this,"

She frowned at him. "You better." She mumbled something in Tagalog as she walked away.

"Ouch," Roman said, laughing at his uncle.

"Weird. I'm sick of weird. Too much weird. Alright, who wants Betty's?"

"Good call," Roman said, and I knew he was still talking, but once I put my arms around Rhonda, I was out.

26

CHAPTER TWENTY-SIX

R oman

WE GOT BACK to the house with the burgers to find Creed and Rhonda still sleeping together in the backseat. Rey tried to lift her, but she lowered her ears at him, so I stepped in front of him and took her leash from Creed's wrist. She happily followed me up the steps to the house. "I'll come back for him," I said, but Rey had already tossed Creed over his shoulder and was carrying him up the front steps.

"Where do you want him?" he asked me.

"I, uh..."

I wanted him in my bed. I did, despite the fact that there were serious issues we needed to work out.

"Excuse me?" Creed lifted his head and then it lolled to the side.

"Yeah, hang on." Rey knelt down and put Creed's feet on the ground, and Rhonda ran to his side. "You need to eat, dude. I shouldn't be able to toss you over my shoulder this easy."

"Thank you. I know. I would love a shower if it's not too much trouble."

"Come here," I said, putting my arm around his waist. He leaned against me as I walked him into the downstairs bathroom. "Do you need help?"

"No, thank you," he murmured, sitting on the toilet. "I don't like being here, Roman. I don't want to put you and your uncle in danger."

"You want to stop this guy, don't you? Because if he shows up here, that's a perfect opportunity for us to catch him."

He hunched his shoulders again. "And I can't do this alone. But it's not just Stephen. If others like me find out that I shared information about us...that part of the myth about, well...vampires, I guess, is true. I only just learned. I thought I was alone."

"Do you think... *Do* you consider yourself a vampire, Creed?"

He shrugged. "I don't know what else you'd call it. Apparently I need blood to survive. I was told that once I stop, *I'll*...stop. I thought... For fifty years, I followed the teachings of The Source and believed that I could sustain myself with the energy of others and the very occasional Exchange. I thought I could stop, that I would begin to age and eventually die like a normal person. That isn't the case. I don't know what to do, Roman."

"You're going to shower, that's what you're going to do, and then we're going to figure this out. Together, okay? Shower, let's eat, and then you can sleep. I'll bring you some clothes." I grabbed a towel from the cabinet and put it on the counter, then went to the door. "Rhonda, come on."

She'd plopped down on the fuzzy rug by Creed's feet and apparently wasn't going anywhere.

"She's fine. I'll be out in a bit. And Roman?"

"Yeah?" The heartbreak in his expression killed me but I was a mess. I didn't know which way was up other than I loved him. So much.

"I mean it. I love you, but if at any point you can't take this—"

"I'm going to say this one time and then I'm just going to ignore you. There is no *I* in you and me. Now you're going to shower and eat. Then sleep." I closed the door, needing space from him before I exploded.

"He okay?" Rey asked as I plopped down at the table.

"No, he's really not. But what is okay, even? After what he's been through?" The smell of the burgers hit me, and I devoured mine in three bites before Rey could even get his out of the wrapper.

"The thing is, it's not that weird, when you think about it." Rey sat there chewing, looking off into the distance.

"What do you mean?"

"The whole blood and energy thing. Like, when he explained the thing about chasing down a perp, he kinda made sense." He took another bite and did the whole thoughtful chewing again. "I don't know. The blood thing is weird though. When I walked in and saw that..." He shuddered.

"What exactly did you see? What happened?"

Rey exhaled. "Lexi texted me when he got there, and I was nearby. I jammed over and she told me where to find him. I opened the door and...he was kneeling next to the bed, next to the old man. And he, uh...he'd..."

"He what?"

"He saw me bite him. Mr. Fletcher. On the wrist."

I turned to find Creed in a towel standing there with his hands on his hips. He wasn't much more than skin and bones, and he was covered with vicious scratches.

I stood so fast, I knocked my chair over. "Creed—"

"If y'all don't mind, I'd appreciate if I could..." Creed listed to the side and almost fell.

Rey got to him before I did. Rhonda trotted over and licked his face, but Creed only moaned.

"Take him to my room."

"He needs a hospital, Roman. Look at him."

"No, please," he whispered. "Just need to lie down."

Between the two of us, we got him into my bed and he fell asleep.

Rhonda hopped up on the bed and curled against his back. She'd slept like that with me every night since he'd disappeared.

"You sure we shouldn't—"

"Can you call Lexi? Ask her to come check his vitals?"

"Yeah, let me call her."

I sat next to Creed on the bed, watching him sleep, hating the shadows on his face. I brushed his hair back from his cheeks, noting how sharp they were.

If I was to believe him, to fully accept him, I had to also accept that he was somewhere in his seventies, that he'd been in a commune back in the nineteen-seventies, and that he's stayed young by manipulating energy and drinking blood. That somehow he'd been a part of a group similar to the one I'd studied, but that he was good, that he didn't torture people, that he actively fought *against* that.

I had to believe he was inherently good...and that was the easiest thing to accept of all.

A while later, Lexi knocked softly on the door and she listened to his heart, took his blood pressure and pulse, and took his temperature. She gestured for me to follow her into the hallway.

"He looks terrible," she said, "but his vitals seem okay. His blood pressure is low and his coloring doesn't look good. He needs fluids and food, but he probably needs rest the most."

I thanked her and, she thanked us for letting her know he was okay.

"He's my best friend," she said. "I can't believe this is happening."

"I know."

She went back out to talk to Rey, and I closed the door to my room. I stripped out of my clothes and put on my lounge pants to crawl in bed next to Creed.

I didn't understand exactly how he absorbed energy, but I planned to be there when he woke to make sure he had what he needed, whatever he needed.

If it was blood, so be it.

· · ·

AROUND THREE IN THE MORNING, Creed woke me, thrashing in the bed.

"Hey," I said, pulling him into my arms. "Shhhh, it's okay, Creed. You're okay."

"Muse," he murmured. "Muse, no. Please!"

He buried his face into my neck, and I held him tightly, our legs intertwined. I stayed awake as long as I could in case he woke once more afraid, but eventually sleep won and pulled me under.

"Roman."

Creed's movement dragged me from sleep near dawn.

"I'm here. What do you need?"

He ran his hands up and down my sides, clutched at my back, seemingly desperate to get closer to me.

"Roman," he said again, and then he kissed my neck.

I moaned and held his lips to my throat, sensation overwhelming me. He tangled his fingers in my hair.

"Goddess help me, Roman, but I need you."

"Yes, Creed. What can I do, what do you need?"

He pressed his forehead to mine and tried to slow his breathing. "Turn on the light, please."

I rolled over and turned on the Himalayan salt lamp that I kept next to my bed. I liked to think it helped me sleep better, though it hadn't helped much lately, as my worry for Creed had kept me awake for hours every night.

I rolled back to him and his haunted eyes were open wide. He was very much awake.

"What's wrong?" I asked him.

"There's nothing wrong," he said, his voice shaky. "But I won't do this, won't do *any* of this, without your consent. It's one thing to hear me talk about an Exchange in abstract terms, and another for you to offer yourself to me without fully comprehending what the ritual is about."

I pulled back slightly and held his hand in mine. Lying next to each other, sharing a pillow, our legs intertwined, I knew I would do whatever he asked, but I wanted to honor him by hearing him out.

"You can tell me anything. I want to understand."

He blew out a breath and closed his eyes for a moment.

"The gift of your essence is one I don't take lightly. Your energy has been a blessing since the first time I met you. It has sustained me, but it has also shown me the man you are, how honorable and brave you are. The fact that you trust me so implicitly makes me long for you, makes me want to do right by you in all ways."

He squeezed my hands and exhaled again.

"Whatever it is, Creed...tell me."

"What I do, I do to survive. I would never hurt you, Roman."

"I understand. You take only what you need to survive, give unto others what they require. I heard what you said. I'm not afraid."

He smiled. "The part that concerns me, with you, is the use of the pheromone."

My eyebrows rose. "How do you mean?"

He reached up and brushed his fingers over the crook of my neck. "Let's just say that I haven't been able to control myself very well with you, and it's had a physiological effect on you. I want you to know that before I use it."

"Like what? What do you mean?"

"The first time was that night about a month after I met you. We were in the library. And the second time was the night I ran into you and Rey, when I was with Lexi? Do you remember?"

I did vaguely remember feeling...odd in his presence. "You mean, like, being turned on in your presence? Because I hate to tell you, Creed, that's nothing to do with any pheromone. I've wanted you from the very beginning, and the more you ran that sassy mouth of yours, the more I wanted it on my dick."

Creed burst out laughing, which was not at all what I'd expected.

"I didn't think it was that funny—"

"The only funny thing is that I felt the same way about you. No, do you remember feeling anything else? *Above* the waist?"

I frowned and thought for a moment. "What? My tinnitus? That was you?"

"I'm afraid so. I think it somehow affects you differently because of your brain injury. I'm worried about trying it again—"

"For Christ's sake, Creed. You're really going to hold back because I get a little dizzy around you? Get over it and get on with it."

His grin faded and he looked…nervous.

"Creed?"

"Sorry. I've just never done it like this, with someone, in bed."

I leaned forward and ran my lips over his. "So we take it slow. All right? You take what you need from me, whatever you need, and then we go from there."

He gazed into my eyes and smiled. "You are truly a blessing, Roman San Angelo. Do I have your consent?"

"Yes. Take what you need."

He paused for a moment, breathed in through his nose, and then his pupils dilated. "Blessed be." As he released his breath, I was surrounded by that fragrance that was so Creed. Sugar cookies, or something very sweet. I breathed him in…and my ear started to ring, but there was no way I was going to ruin this moment. I focused on his movements and tried to ignore the slight dizzy sensation.

Creed took my left hand in his and turned it palm up. He pressed his lips to the inside of my wrist, and I felt a shiver run the course of my entire body, flooding me with warmth and pleasure. It was like the tingles you get as your body builds toward orgasm, but better. This didn't feel like it would end when I came. Every synapse in my body was delightfully turned on and telling me, "get comfortable, this is about to get good."

He lifted his head, his lips still pressed to my skin and his eyes opened.

"Are you ready?" he asked me.

"Fuck yes," I said.

His lips turned up at the edges, I felt a little pressure, a tiny bit of a sting, like the good kind though, like someone pulling your hair in the middle of sex, just enough to let you know you were alive.

And then he sucked—and I felt the pull go straight to my dick.

"Oh, God, Creed!"

He did it again, and my hips bucked. Once more and I groaned, little fireworks going off under my skin everywhere.

He licked once more, and then kissed my wrist.

"That's it?" I asked, nearly breathless and desperate for...more.

"Three pulls. That's what I was taught. It's enough to sustain us."

I gasped as my body continued to throb, as I shifted my legs and leaked precum, the sensation so much, and yet the only contact was from my flannel lounge pants.

"Well, fuck, Creed. What if *I* want more? What if I want you to do that again?"

He laughed, but I grabbed his hips and brought them in contact with mine.

His eyes flared. "What if I want you to fuck me first?" He blinked those big amber eyes of his, now softer than before, less afraid, less cagey. His whole face was a little softer. If he'd had that much of an effect from three pulls, what if he took a little more? Would that help him get his strength back?"

"Are you sure? Are you up for it?"

He took my left hand, which he was still holding, and brought it down to cup his swollen cock, throbbing like mine. "Please, Roman."

That was the consent I needed to remove his towel and my pants. I reached for my bottle of lube and rolled him over onto his back.

Rhonda grunted once and hopped down from the bed, making a show of her irritation as she found the folded quilt I'd left for her to lay on next to the floor vent.

"She'll get over it," he said.

I coated my fingers and gently, so carefully, prepared him to take me. We stared into each other's eyes the entire time, and I felt like I was seeing into his soul, every touch, every stroke, every penetration elicited a new level of pleasure from him, a new sound, a new plea.

"Please, Roman! Please."

"Yes, Creed." I pushed his legs up and I knelt before him. I used the lube on myself, making sure to take as much care as possible so as not to hurt him, but it was killing me to hold back. "I want to be inside you. But I want you to do that again. Can you take it from my neck?"

The worried look was back. "I'm afraid I'll lose control. I don't want to hurt you."

"You won't," I said. I pressed against his hole, and he melted into the mattress with a moan. I pushed in slowly and he tensed up, his breath coming in pants.

"I can't...you feel so good, Roman...it's so...good." He squeezed his eyes shut and relaxed all at once, allowing me to slide all the way in, his body rippling around me, accepting me.

"I can't breathe," I murmured close to his ear. "I can't—"

"Yes, you can." He kissed my lips, my chin, my throat, and then that special place where my neck met my shoulder. "Now move."

CHAPTER TWENTY-SEVEN

C reed

ROMAN WAS everything as he gripped my shoulders, lifted his hips, and then thrust his cock deep inside me. We both gasped, our eyes wide open, as he found the perfect rhythm, the perfect angle.

He cried out for God, he praised me, he ran his fingers over my face and stared into my eyes, pleading with me, loving me. He completely gave up his need for control. He let go, let himself take pleasure from me, let me love him.

"I want you...to do it again, Creed. Please. It makes you stronger. It's good for you, and *fuck*, it's so...good...please, Creed."

I laughed as his whole body started to shake.

"I love...how...you think I can focus on anything when you're... fucking me—"

"Fuck, Creed, now, please!" He slid a hand under my head and lifted it to his neck while his hips bucked against mine.

"Roman," I breathed against his skin. *Blessed be.* I tried to do everything right, tried to give just enough pheromone—"

"Oh God, Creed!" he cried out, and he lost his rhythm, his body shuddering.

And then I bit him, harder than I intended, but I didn't have a lot of control. And his sweet, sweet life force flowed onto my tongue and the world stopped for a split second as everything became clear, everything was in harmony, everything was perfect, pure pleasure.

Bliss.

"I'm coming!" Roman's body froze and he cried out a long, guttural moan.

I had just enough presence of mind to close the wound on his neck before I joined him, spilling onto my stomach and his as our bodies pressed together.

We lay there like that, sweaty, panting, covered in spend, kissing lazily for what seemed like forever.

"I can taste it," he said, licking at my lips. "It's not...weird. I thought it would be weird. It's not."

"It's you, Roman. It could never be anything but perfect to me."

He pulled me into his arms as he rolled us over onto our sides.

"You're amazing, Roman. Who you are, what you do, how you *feel*. I can't believe I almost let you go."

He pressed his lips together. "Yeah, what was that about?"

We laughed together, and Rhonda hopped back up onto the bed next to Roman, nudging him with her nose before she lay down with her chin resting on his ribs.

"It was about me being desperate," I said. "I'm sorry. I didn't mean to hurt you, or you," I said, petting Rhonda. "I'm sorry, girl."

She yawned and closed her eyes.

"I get it, Creed. I do. But please, promise me, swear to me you won't do it again."

I lifted my hand to his cheek. "I will be by your side for as long as you'll have me. I just hope it doesn't get us both killed."

He kissed my hand and placed it on top of Rhonda's head. "Me too. Now, let's get some more sleep before I take that ass again. Fuck, Creed. I can't believe I almost let *you* get away."

"Let?" But I was too tired to argue with him. I couldn't imagine a world where the two of us weren't together like this, never wanted there to be such a world.

I just hoped to hell we could be enough for each other to remain safe.

We woke later to the sound of Rey banging around in the kitchen and Rhonda whining at the door.

"I suppose I should take her out," I said, sitting up.

"No, you stay in bed," Roman said. "You don't have any clothes, and I kinda like that." He pulled the covers up and grinned. "You're looking better too. That nasty bruise is way better." He'd been quite unhappy with me when he'd seen the wounds from my accident. He'd muttered something to the effect of being glad the stupid bike was gone.

"Sexual energy is probably the most powerful of all," I said. "Makes me strong."

"You mean I really *should* keep you in my bed? Sounds good to me."

I fell back on the pillows with a laugh. "It certainly feels good to be in a real bed. I'm too old and spoiled to be sleeping in bushes and parks anymore."

Roman paused with a shirt in his hand. "Don't do that again, please?"

I held up my hands. "Okay. Besides, it's colder here than it was in San Francisco."

He pulled the shirt over his head and laughed. "You mean back in 1968? You were really there?" He sat on the bed next to me while I stretched my arms over my head.

"I was. Handing out flowers in Golden Gate Park, singing and dancing naked—"

"And trippin' balls?"

I pushed at his knee. "Yes, we dropped acid and smoked a lot of weed. It was a wild time, all right?"

"I bet. You know I want to hear it all, right? All of your stories, the good and the bad. Maybe I'll make that a requirement before you get clothes."

I liked this bossy side of Roman a lot. It was nice not to have to be the one in charge. I was willing to let him take care of me...for a while. It made him happy, so I'd go with it.

"I want to hear all of your stories, too," I said, reaching for him.

He leaned down to kiss me, and probably would have crawled back into bed if it hadn't been for Rhonda's insistent bark.

"That's my cue," he said, and he sprang from the bed. "I'll see what Rey's banging around about and get us some breakfast going. Stay there and look pretty, would you?"

That got a groan out of me. "Not sure I could move if you made me. Damn." I was definitely sore and tired, but in the best kind of way.

Roman winced. "I'm sorry. I should have gone easier on you."

"Don't you dare," I said with a salacious smile. "I loved it."

He paused in the doorway as if he wanted to say more, but instead his cheeks flushed and he took off after Rhonda.

I let myself fall back into restorative sleep. Between the sex, Roman's blood, and not having to sleep with one eye open, I crashed hard. I vaguely recalled Roman coming in and telling me he needed to run by Vanessa's, something about his auntie Bernadette and cousin Emmanuel, and then Rey came in to say he'd been called into the PD, but that Roman would be back soon.

So when I woke up to a quiet house hours later, the sky dark, I shot out of bed.

Rhonda wasn't in the room, and I heard her crying and scratching at the door.

I opened the bedroom door and she rushed to my side. I called out for Rey and Roman, but there was no answer.

I rummaged through Roman's dresser and found a sweatshirt and sweats that mostly fit, and I grabbed socks and my shoes.

I didn't have a phone any longer, it died when I dumped my

motorcycle. I looked around and discovered that they didn't have a house phone either.

"We gotta go, sweetheart," I said to Rhonda. I took her outside, and she did her business, but she kept whining.

"I know. I'm worried too." I looked around the neighborhood and noticed a streetlight out and lots of cars parked on the street. It would be easy for someone to watch the house undetected. They could be watching now. They also could have been watching when Roman left.

"Shit. Come on, girl. I'm going to leave you inside. Don't destroy Roman's house."

She went to lay on the rug by the floor vent and curled up tight, staring at me with big eyes.

"I promise, I'll be back this time."

I don't know if she believed me, but *I* had to believe me.

I closed up the house, leaving the window to Roman's room unlocked in case I needed to get back in. Rhonda would guard the house for sure.

It was a three-mile walk to the police department from Roman's, and I jogged most of it. When I arrived, I went into the front desk and asked for Detective Vanessa Cabral, which meant waiting. I went back up to the desk after twenty minutes and asked if the desk sergeant could let her know it was Creed Lowell waiting, and if she wasn't available, perhaps Captain Rojas or Detective Ross? She did not seem pleased and said she'd see what they could do.

After another thirty minutes, I went up again. I was agitated and there was only so much energy I could consume from the angry folks there to complain.

"I'm sorry to disturb you—"

"They're in a meeting in the conference room, and I can't just barge in there—"

"Creed, Jesus Christ, get in here!"

Rey held open the gate and frowned at the desk sergeant.

"Thank you," I said, sending her a little healing energy. Her acid reflux wasn't going to get better working the front desk, that was for sure.

"Where the hell have you been?"

"I woke up and everyone was gone, so I came over here. I don't have a phone."

"Well, we've got trouble, dammit. They're fucking gone. All of them. Vanessa's pissed and I'm losing my shit."

Anger rolled off Rey like the crashing waves that had battered the Santa Cruz coastline to the point that many houses were in danger of toppling into the ocean. Rey's fury was in danger of toppling *him* over the edge.

"What do you mean, gone?"

But I knew what it was as soon as he sat me down in a chair and Vanessa ran over.

"I sent Roman over to check on Bernadette because neither she nor Emmanuel were answering the phones. Now all three of them are missing. Patrol officers are out looking for them, the Mercedes, any sign of Stephen or his minions."

I sprang up out of the chair. "Then we have to go! Let's go to the house off seventeen, anything. If I can provoke them, get them to come after me—"

"Let's go." Rey said, checking his weapon and grabbing his keys.

"Wait!" Vanessa handed me a Kevlar vest. "Captain benched me here, but it's killing me. Maybe I shouldn't have went off on him." She shrugged, but her hands were shaking. "You guys be careful and call me as soon as you know something."

"Yeah," he said as he beat feet for the door. I appreciated that Rey was a take-action kind of guy. He didn't get hung up on semantics.

He led me out back and into the lot, and we were almost to his truck when I was hit by a hundred pounds of Doberman.

"Rhonda! How did you—" I bent down and held her wiggly, whimpering body close. She sniffed at my neck and licked my face. Would she ever trust that I wouldn't leave her again?

"Once we found *her*," Cross raised his eyebrow at me, "we figured she could find you." He fucking knew something was up with Rhonda. Goddess, could this pit get any deeper?

Cross and Mark stood back a bit, still in the shadows. Rey stiffened at my side.

"Rey, meet my friends. You did come here as friends, right?"

Cross quirked up one side of his mustache. "We had one last show in Aptos and then we were gonna hit the road. I think you can imagine our surprise when the most unwelcomest of guests showed up."

"Stephen," I breathed. "What did he say?"

Mark cleared his throat and gestured to Rey. "You tell him?"

"What I had to," I said, stepping closer to Rey. "I told them what I knew about The Source and Gateway of the Sun." I hoped they got from that statement that I hadn't outed them. They would have to make that choice. Of course, them being here probably clued Rey in. "I was trying to help. So what did he say?"

"Well, he clearly doesn't know we're in collusion with you, because he told us he needed us for the Samhain ritual. Sounds like he's short on folks who follow The Way after his friends got toasted, and The Source insisted there be four Leaders and four Guardians, as per usual."

I blanched. "Have you done this with them before?"

Mark swore and wrinkled his nose. "Hell no. *Fuck* no. We told you we hate that guy, and we haven't seen The Source since the same night you did."

Cross smirked. "But we might have agreed to help them out."

"That's all nice and everything," Rey said. "But they might have my sister-in-law and my nephews, so you better get to the fucking point."

"The point," Cross said, appraising Rey. He was definitely intrigued by the cop, which was all kinds of interesting, but this was not the time for him to try to seduce anyone. "Is that I came here thinking they had Creed, too, so the fact they don't is a win for us."

Rey stared at him, and then flicked a hand out as if to encourage him to continue. "Is that it? I'm sick of this fucking weird-ass shit."

"Right?" Cross said, rolling his eyes. "This ritual shit is *so* 1971."

"Cross," I said, irritated with his flippant attitude. "What did you agree to?"

"To meet them at a picnic site deep in the park at Loch Lomond. It's on the line, which means more power for The Source."

"Shit."

"Exactly. But I think if we have the element of surprise on our side, maybe we have a chance."

"There's something else," Mark said, and Cross nodded.

"Yeah. The Source isn't right, Creed. There's something off with them."

I frowned. "That seems pretty obvious, but how do you mean?"

"We watched Stephen leave and followed him out to the car. There were three men waiting with The Source, and they all had a big argument."

"Yeah," Mark continued. "I don't think Stephen has a full handle on things. The Source kept saying over and over, 'If it's not right, this will be the end. Too much has passed. Without the four, the ritual will fail and it will end.' Any idea what that means?"

I thought back to my studies and to the rituals we'd practiced. Mostly we meditated, but the Leaders and Guardians would carry on late into the night. I was there for two Samhains, but the mutiny occurred at the autumnal equinox of my third year, and because of the mutiny, I didn't learn the rest. Leader Bree led a class on preparing for the eight rituals of the year, but I didn't recall anything about "the end" of anything.

"Remember Leader Bree's talk about Samhain? How the veil is thin and the spirit world is closer than ever? The Source taught that their power was an accumulation of all the beings that came before them, that they needed the spiritual infusion of those that came before as part of the rituals."

Cross stroked his beard. "Question is, are they planning to snatch some spiritual energy from the other side, or are they planning to *make* some spirits, if you catch my drift."

"Fucking hell, can we just get on with the part where you take us to them?" Rey's stress had my skin twitching with the need to act as well.

"Hold your horses, policeman. Hey, do you still ride horses in this town?"

Rey sprang forward and pressed Cross up against the car with a forearm against his throat. Mark reached for Rey, but Cross held out a hand.

"No, I was out of line. My apologies, Officer Cabral."

The fact that Cross allowed Rey to pin him to the car at all was a shock, but there was some connection between the two that went beyond masculine challenge, beyond an energy exchange. Not exactly feral or sexual... It was surprising, and I could tell Mark felt the same as me.

"My family is in danger, and I don't have time to fuck around with a bunch of vampires, or whatever you are. Now are you going to take us there, or am I going to knock your head into this truck until you fucking cooperate?"

"Easy, cop," Cross murmured. "Violence is not necessary here." He breathed in through his nose and his eyes fluttered closed. "You are so good when you're pissed. Lost my head a bit."

Rey blinked a couple of times, and then loosened his hold, stepping back from the much larger man.

"Fucking weird shit. Okay, what do we do?"

28

———

CHAPTER TWENTY-EIGHT

R oman

I FOCUSED on my breathing so I wouldn't freak out and scare Bernadette and Emmanuel any more than they already were.

I showed up at their house to see what was going on, and immediately knew something was up.

When I pulled up mid-afternoon and noticed the porch light was already on and the garage door was open partway, that was odd enough. I just had this bad feeling. I texted Vanessa to let her know I was there before getting out of the car.

I walked in the front door and smelled something...sweet. Too sweet, like a vanilla air freshener that tried to smell nice but had that chemical undertone that made you wrinkle your nose.

Two men stood in the doorway to the kitchen dressed in suits.

"Professor, come in and have a seat, please."

I felt calm but alert as I sat on the couch next to Bernadette and put my arm around her. My ear started ringing and immediately, I thought of Creed.

These men are like him.

That was what the stench was about. Creed always smelled like cookies to me, and it always got stronger when we were close, and when he'd explained to me about the pheromone, he'd said it smelled unique to each person. I'd teased him that he should have smelled like peaches. But now I figured no one had a choice, because who would choose to smell like this godawful stench?

Emmanuel and Bernadette sat on the couch side by side, staring at the man who'd spoken, but they didn't seem afraid.

"What can I help you with?" I asked him.

He smiled with a little head tilt, as if he was surprised I could string words together.

"Well, Professor, I'm afraid I'm on a bit of a time crunch at the moment, but I will tell you that I need the three of you to come with me to meet someone very important, and there's no time to waste. Today is a special day, and we need your help. All you need to do is escort your aunt and cousin into our vehicle and we'll be on our way, shall we?"

Bernadette and Emmanuel started to stand, and though I wanted to as well, I threw my arm out to hold them back.

"Why should we go with you?"

He tilted his head to the side again, and I swear I saw his pupils dilate.

"Because it's what I desire you to do. Or, we can try this."

In a split second, I saw Emmanuel with a rope around his neck hanging from the rafters of the exposed-beam ceiling in my auntie's living room.

I gasped and shot up out of my seat but...my hand was still on Emmanuel's abdomen. He was still beside me with that blank expression.

"Or, perhaps this will get you to move?"

The man was suddenly at Bernadette's side with a huge knife, which he used to slice open her belly and release her innards onto the floor.

I cried out, but then she was still next to me, breathing normal, and when I squeezed my eyes shut and opened them, I realized it was all visions. They weren't real. The man was still standing where he'd been the whole time.

"You must be Stephen," I said, my heart pounding in my chest, though my limbs felt sluggish. Creed had said he could put images into someone's head. God, what a terrifying power to have.

"It's very nice to meet you, Professor. But we must go." He held his hand out, and Bernadette and Emmanuel pushed past me.

Creed had never said anything about the power of suggestion, or any sort of brainwashing like this, but then, he'd been away from this man for fifty years. Perhaps Stephen had new tricks up his sleeve that Creed wasn't aware of.

I still had command of my senses, so at least I knew that I could protect my aunt and cousin, but I didn't like the idea of getting into a car with them. I followed Bernadette and reached into my pocket to hopefully hit the call button on my phone. I didn't know if it worked, but I figured it was the best I could do.

They walked us out the front door, and I hoped to catch the eye of someone on the street, but there was no one around, which seemed odd. Vanessa's neighborhood was usually a happening place, with lots of nosy neighbors working in their yards or sitting in their open garages watching the goings on. Emmanuel complained about it frequently, especially when the neighbors would rat him out to his moms for driving too fast, or when he'd bring girls over while his moms were at work. Perhaps Stephen was masking the fact that others were around. If I couldn't see them, could they see us?

They led us to a Maserati, which I was surprised I hadn't noticed on arrival. No one on their block would drive such a fussy car. This was strictly a sedan and small SUV street.

The guy with Stephen held open the back door for us, and Bernadette and Emmanuel slid in. I made eye contact with Stephen over the roof of the car. He knew he had me. There was no way I was going to let him take them without me. Still, I remained rigid. My body fought me, swaying toward the car, but I kept my feet planted.

"You don't want to do this," I told him. "People with more power than me will come down on you like a tsunami. You won't get out of this unharmed."

"How very matter-of-fact of you. I know full well what I'm dealing with, and your people do not compare. Get in. Let's go."

This is crazy. Neither of them appear armed. I could grab my aunt and cousin and run for it. I had to try. I reached in for Bernadette's hand.

"Tita, we need to go. Emmanuel."

She yanked her arm back and started screaming, staring at me as if I was the boogeyman coming to take her away. She clung to Emmanuel for help, and he too seemed afraid of me.

"They'll see whatever I want them to see. Trust me. Get in the car, Roman."

I climbed in, seeing no way around it, and as I sat back, the two men in the front seats turned around and shoved cloths in our faces. Chloroform, most likely.

The last thing I remember was Emmanuel's frightened cry, Stephen's chilling smile, and then darkness.

I woke up naked on the floor in a dark room with a single bare bulb hanging from the ceiling. This was way too cliché, but I knew I was in trouble. My ear was ringing so loudly I could barely hear anything. The door opened, and I scrambled to my feet and into a defensive pose, but immediately I was knocked back and held against the wall by an unseen force.

Stephen entered, followed by a person draped in layers of red fabric.

"This is Professor Roman San Angelo, and he is a companion of Learner Creed."

The figure glided forward and lifted their hood from their face and exposed a...kind expression upon an attractive face. Their hair was shorn nearly to the scalp and their bright blue eyes were so wide, their pupil merely a pinprick of black. They were slender and only about as tall as Vanessa, but I knew better to discount anyone's strength because of height.

The hair rose on my arms in an unpleasant way.

A kind expression does not equal a kind being. And being was the right word. It didn't feel right to consider them human.

"What do you want? Where is my family?"

The figure took in my physical appearance and a look of discomfort came over their face before they trained their gaze on my face.

"My apologies for your treatment. It is necessary that we have the correct number of participants for the ritual, but I did not wish to see anyone mistreated." The figure turned and frowned at Stephen. "Why is the man unclothed?"

Stephen bowed and then straightened. "My apologies. I have corrected the situation."

The Source turned back and smiled at me this time. "Wonderful, you've received the vestments. When evening arrives, you shall receive a small meal and then we shall travel to the ritual site. Do you have any questions about what is to happen? I gather you have been instructed—"

I opened my mouth to protest but my vocal chords were...paralyzed. I couldn't make a sound.

"Yes, the professor and his family have received instruction on what will take place. Now, let's get you back to your sanctuary so you may rest."

The Source looked from him to me, and seemed frustrated.

"Leader Stephen, I should like to spend time with the professor. It has been so long since I have spoken with an academic—"

"There isn't time. The sky grows dark and you must prepare."

The Source seemed almost childlike as they pouted. "I hope we will have time to talk afterward. I always enjoy learning other perspectives and it has been a long time."

They looked to Stephen and glided past them out of the room, and it was then I realized the truth.

"You're manipulating them."

He lost his smile and became...agitated. "You have no idea what it's like. The Source must be kept. They could level this entire area, cause a catastrophic earthquake or worse. For fifty years, they've been my responsibility, and now, thanks to Creed's interference and those four fools, I have no hope of ever being free!"

"You certainly don't have a hope if you're kidnapping people."

He glared at me and shook his head. "You have no idea what you're talking about. I'll be back when it's time."

He shut the door, and I cursed, furious to be trapped here. Naked. I looked around the room and then closed my eyes, trying to focus on getting my tinnitus to stop so I'd be ready to face anything these people threw my way.

"Roman! Roman!"

I rushed to the adjoining wall.

"Emmanuel, it's me, I'm here! Are you okay?"

"Yeah, I'm okay, but where's my mom? What happened?"

Shit. Emmanuel was a mouthy kid just like me. I didn't want to take the chance that he'd upset the delicate balance here.

"Hang in there, okay? Don't believe everything you see. This guy Stephen is bad news, and he can make you see things that aren't there. Did they take your clothes?"

"No, they didn't touch me."

Weird. "Good. Do you have your phone? Or shit, what about your Apple watch?"

"My phone's gone, but I have my watch."

"Text Rey and Vanessa, make sure your location is on. Do you have service?"

"Barely. I'll keep trying."

I pressed on the walls around the room, trying to find any weakness. They were covered with, like, pressboard, the kind we had in the university classrooms so people could hang stuff. I wondered if we were in a school building somewhere?

"Roman, what the fuck is going on?"

I sighed. "I don't know everything, but it has to do with the attacks in town...and my boyfriend."

"Boyfriend? Since when do you have a boyfriend?"

"Since now. He's...it's Nurse Creed from Puesta Del Sol. Now listen—"

"No way! Does Lola Frances know?"

"I—not yet. Listen, *focus*, Em. I need you to remember, not everything is what you see. If you see something that scares you, close your eyes. If you can still see it with your eyes closed, it's not real. Okay? Ask me if it's real if you can't tell. Now, can you hear your mom? Go around the edges of your room...wait, what do you see?"

"It's...like a classroom. There's a chalkboard. And...hymnals. Like, it's like a Sunday school place or something."

"Okay, maybe we're in a church. See if you can find anything else in the room, like a location, and keep trying to send texts from every corner of the room. Something is bound to get through."

I must have been in a storage closet of some kind. Hopefully Emmanuel could get a message out.

I paced around the room and felt my chest tighten, my pulse racing. If I kept this up, I was going to pass out. I crouched down in a corner, my back against the wall, and I closed my eyes, focusing on my breathing, and thought of the one person who always made me feel better.

Creed. Please find us. I'm trying to hold it together, but I'm not as strong when I'm not with you.

Hurry.

CHAPTER TWENTY-NINE

C reed

"GOD BLESS THAT KID," Rey said. "I'm never giving him shit about his electronics ever again!"

We traveled in a caravan toward the location Emmanuel had shared with Rey via his watch, deep in the Santa Cruz mountains. Vanessa realized he had his watch on, and that he could send messages even if they took his phone. A jumble of texts came through with random bits of information, but it was enough for us to piece it together.

I rode with Rey and Vanessa in her SUV, which she insisted she would drive. Mark and Cross were in Mark's truck ahead of us on their way to the spot where the ceremony was supposed to take place. It was near a church camp, not too far from where our original commune had been, although those buildings had all been burned to the ground in the mutiny. Ross, Barringer, and Captain Rojas were in an SUV behind us, ready to provide backup.

"Let me clue you in on a few things that could happen," I said, wanting Rey and Vanessa to be prepared. "Remember, Stephen can make you see shit that's not there. Also, apparently one of the people with him can drain energy on command. They confronted me at the home one night a few weeks ago and one of them was able to not just absorb my excess energy, but to really yank a big chunk out of me. It was such a violation. It goes against everything we were taught. Be aware because he may have some very powerful people with him."

"So what can we even do against that?" Vanessa asked.

"If you start to feel tired or weak, don't ignore it. Tell someone and get the fuck out of the way so you don't get hurt." Reynaldo was checking all of his weapons, loading and reloading them, checking the magazines.

"Yeah," I said. "That's about it. But if you see something that's upsetting, close your eyes. If you still see it, it's not real."

"What kind of upsetting?"

I sucked in a deep breath. "Stephen did this once to my friend Muse. He showed her images of him raping her. Another person, he showed them their lover being gutted. He's thorough, and he's cunning. He seems to know what scares people."

"Let him fucking try," Rey snarled as he slammed a mag back into his weapon. He asked Vanessa for hers, and then did the same with both her duty pistol and the backup she kept strapped to her ankle.

We pulled into the trees a few hundred yards from the church, which appeared abandoned. Only a couple of windows showed dim lighting. Cross and Mark continued on to the picnic area parking lot, which was walking distance from the church building.

"Creed, you stay with Vanessa," Rey said. "And I swear to God, I'm trusting you with my goddamned family's safety, so don't fuck up."

"Enough, Rey. Just stay close, Creed. Don't be a hero."

"I won't. But I can tell you, they likely won't be armed with guns. There will be a ceremonial knife, at least. But they are physically powerful." I shook my head. I didn't like this scenario at all. I hated bringing the uninitiated into this fight because I had no clue how to protect them. "My biggest concern is The Source. I'd heard stories about how powerful they are, but I don't know everything they're capable of. You'll be able to feel them as you get closer."

"What the...more fucking weird shit. Fine. Stay close," Rey said.

We creeped around the back of the building, but there was no one in the vicinity.

"They must have gone to the ritual site," I said. "I can't feel anything."

Vanessa looked at her GPS and started walking. "It's this way. Stay close together."

Our backup left in the car when they saw us walking into the woods. The plan was, they would approach from the parking area where Mark and Cross were headed and hang back unless we needed them.

There was a clear path from the church toward where this picnic area was supposed to be. The darkness was smothering, the only light coming from the sliver of moon reflected on the lake and a few buildings on the far shore. We clung to the tree line as we walked for what felt like hours but was probably only twenty minutes. Every minute spent dreading what we were walking into picked away at my courage.

I was terrified of what we would find as I ran through my memories of the last ritual I'd ever participated in.

1971

Cross, myself, Stephen, and one other initiate were led by Leader Bree into a circle in a part of the woods we'd been forbidden to explore. There were markings on the trees and a stone slab in the middle of the circle. The stone had dark stains on its surface, but in the twilight I couldn't fathom what I was seeing.

Leaders Caleb, Lauren, and Quinn stood around the stone chanting softly, with candles in their hands. A few steps behind each of them stood four Guardians with their hoods pulled low so I couldn't make out their faces.

Leader Bree directed us to kneel in front of the stone as we waited for The Source. I'd been so excited to finally interact with The Source, as they were always on the periphery and accompanied by Guardians. When they came forward in their crimson robe, my heart fluttered with excitement. I knew my life was about to change, that I was about to witness a miracle, and I was elated. All of my hard work and sacrifice had been worth it.

"I present these learners to you for initiation," Leader Lauren said as The Source approached.

They nodded and pulled their hood back, finally revealing their true face. So beautiful. So peaceful. Tears filled my eyes from my gratitude. I'd been chosen, deemed worthy by the Leaders, and now I would receive a blessing from The Source.

"Learner Cross," Leader Lauren said. "Come forward to be received by The Source. After tonight, you will be known as Guardian Cross."

He stood slowly, as we'd been instructed, and approached the slab. The Leaders took his hands and helped him to lie upon its surface.

"As you have been instructed, the pheromone will not be used for your initiation. You will feel every sensation and be of your own free will and unhindered of mind in order to receive this blessing. Do you agree to follow oath of our kind?"

"Yes, Leader Lauren," he answered, and then he spoke the words we'd been taught. "Give unto them what they require. Take only what is necessary to survive."

"Blessed be," was declared by all present.

The Leaders pulled open the black vestments covering Cross's chest, and I remembered them saying that not all of the initiation was pleasant, but then The Source gave off such a calming and pleasant energy, I thought, how could that be?"

"One who is called Cross. I take from you and give unto you the essence necessary to fulfill your duties. The Exchange is the most sacred act of healing, and with it, you must always take the greatest care. Do you accept and consent to this Exchange?"

Cross looked up to the sky and nodded. "I consent."

The Source smiled...but then the energy around us changed. A frigid breeze blew through the trees and Cross fidgeted on the slab. The Source held their hands over Cross's chest and closed their eyes. Suddenly, I noticed beads of red on Cross's chest growing darker, and then running down his sides. I gasped as his blood was literally pulled through his skin and into The Source's hands.

Cross's face tightened and he grimaced, his breath coming in pants.

"Leaders and Guardians, accept this initiate into our community, as have I."

And I watched in horror as the pink-robed figures came forward and began to lick and suck from Cross's chest. He strained against invisible bonds as he squeezed his eyes shut. When they began to bite him, taking more of his blood, he finally cried out.

I looked to The Source, ready to shout for them to stop, that they were going to kill him, they were hurting him. This was not The Way, we didn't hurt people...

The Source looked upon me with affection—and suddenly I realized that everything I'd been taught, this cause I'd dedicated myself to, was something much darker, more sinister than I could have ever imagined.

There was great power here. And power corrupts.

"Guardian Cross, welcome to The Source."

The Source opened their palm and blood flowed from a wound into Cross's mouth. There was so much blood, on his body, on his face...

The Leaders and Guardians finished with Cross and lifted his unconscious body from the slab, laying him on the grass on the other side of the stone. Stephen was taken next, and he withstood the initiation without any cries, without a reaction, while I sat frozen, terrified of what was about to happen. When they took Stephen off the slab, I was compelled to stand and move forward. I say compelled because after what I'd just seen, I couldn't have made my legs move if I'd even tried.

I lay upon the slab, still questioning myself, wondering how I'd ended up here, when The Source began to speak. Their words were drowned out by a rushing sound in my ears. I know I repeated the oath and gave my consent, but I don't recall my brain commanding my mouth to say things, and then it was *my* blood, and then they were biting *me*, and the blood was in *my* mouth.

As I lay on the grass, unable to move but capable of witnessing, an explosion rocked the compound. Suddenly screams filled the night sky. The hold on me was released and there was a flurry of activity around me. A group of Learners rushed in out of the darkness and while Stephen and another approached The Source, who was cowering from the fire. The Source was led away while Stephen spoke to them, telling them there had been an accident and they needed to escort The Source to safety. Knowing Stephen's ability to make others see what he wanted them to, I wasn't surprised that The Source followed with no argument.

The other three of us who had been initiated stumbled to our feet and ran for the dormitory only to be confronted by Stephen's lackey.

"What is going on?" I shouted.

"We are the bringers of change. Join us or die."

I started to question him, but Stephen returned, held up a hand and then ordered his followers to act. One of the men grabbed the last initiate and slit his throat, which sent the rest of us running.

Muse. Had she escaped? I had to know, couldn't just leave her. I continued on toward the dormitory, seeing Stephen and his followers take down one soul after another with the ceremonial knives. The Guardians were nowhere to be seen. When I got to the buildings, they were engulfed in flames, the other Learners crying for help as they burned to death. I kept to the tree line, out of sight, and that was when I saw her. I ran to her side, even though I knew it was useless. She was covered in blood, her eyes open and fixed. She'd almost made it out of the compound.

It took a split second for self-preservation to take over.

I ran into the woods, weakened from blood loss and going into shock. I ran and ran until the gray morning light allowed me to see that I wasn't being followed. I cried my heart out there, feeling the absence of my fellow Learners' essence. I couldn't sense The Source either. Were they slaughtered along with the rest? Would I know? So many questions...*where can I go? How will I survive? What is the point?*

"CREED, THIS WAY."

Rey whispered and gestured for me to move behind him. I'd been frozen in my spot by memories of the worst night of my very long life...

"Hey," Vanessa whispered, waving her fingers in front of my face. "What's wrong?"

"This is...they're set up to do an initiation," I whispered back. "We can't let them—"

"It's okay. We'll stop them. Once they're all set, we'll move in."

We crept closer to the site, and it was the worst déjà vue.

Only this time, the Guardians each held a knife to the throat of the four "initiates."

Roman, Bernadette, and Emmanuel, as well as the woman they'd shown me a picture of, all stood in a line, waiting to make their sacrifice, dressed in black, their eyes dazed as if they were in a trance.

I brought my hand up to my mouth.

No. Please don't let him be hurt. Don't let any of them go through this.

Three Leaders moved to their places in the center, but they'd apparently had to improvise and were using a picnic table instead of the stone slab. They lit their candles and waited.

A rush of power rolled over me, spreading goose bumps along my flesh and sending tingles up my spine. I hadn't felt that level of power for fifty years...

Stephen came forward, guiding The Source, who wore their red hood covering their face. Stephen held onto their arm and then stopped. He removed their hood and took his place amongst the Leaders.

The Source's face was always a shock to behold, their ethereal beauty still made my heart flutter, but my terror at the potential catastrophe about to happen overruled any admiration I still had for the being.

The Source tipped their head back and raised their arms. "Blessed is the Goddess who is with us on this sacred night, and who has given unto us the new initiates. Come forward, Guardians."

But immediately, their serene expression twisted in anger when they saw the knives.

"Stop that at once!"

They held out a hand and pushed it down, effectively causing all of the Guardians to drop their knives—and the cops their weapons.

"Shit," Rey whispered as he bent to pick his up, only to find that it wouldn't move. Neither would his leg that had the backup piece.

A magnetic field. Of course. The ley lines gave the Source more power on this special night, and now the cops had been rendered useless.

"We have spectators," the Source said, further angered. "You interrupt a sacred ritual. Show yourselves."

The cops were all stuck, but not me. I walked forward into the clearing while Vanessa and Rey whisper-shouted for me to stop.

They couldn't help me now.

As I grew near, The Source's expression softened.

"Guardian Creed. We are truly blessed. Come closer."

I moved with trepidation, unsure what The Source's reaction to me would be.

I was shocked when they pulled me into an embrace, and I got a load of their latent power buzzing just below the surface.

"Always one of my favorites, one of my strongest initiates. What happened to you, Guardian Creed? You disappeared after your ceremony. I knew you persevered, but I could never see you or reach you. What happened?"

Is it possible they don't know?

I glanced at Stephen, who had moved closer to the Guardian holding Roman.

"What did *Stephen* tell you happened?"

The Source glanced from Stephen to me. "What do you mean? After your ceremony? We went on to work with our next group of recruits at the next commune. Stephen became my escort and we went together, leaving Leader Bree in charge of the commune we left behind."

"That's what he told you?"

"That's what happened." The Source didn't sound as confident, that rich voice that coated my insides like honey had the slightest tinge of uncertainty.

"Stephen and his minions killed everyone there and took you away," I said, trying to sound calm. Stephen shook his head when I spoke. "They've been keeping you all these years, away from the truth."

I caught Mark's eye where he stood with Cross behind the circle. They were poised to move in protection of the initiates, who at least were no longer threatened with knives.

"Creed, you are mistaken," The Source said, their voice softer. They stroked my cheek and held onto my shoulders. "That is not what happened. Now, if you would join us, I would be delighted, but it is crucial that we continue this ritual, as Samhain is beginning and the veil is lifting. Without the new blood and the infusion from the spirits... We can't have that. It is crucial we continue."

They tried to smile, but there was fear in their deep crystal-blue eyes as they stepped away from me and approached the picnic table.

"Bring the first initiate."

I placed a hand on The Source's shoulder, cringing at the thought I might lose that hand. "I can't let you do that."

They turned on me and the ground began to shake...violently. "You can't stop the ceremony, Creed. There will be...consequences."

"Creed, you need to step away."

I looked to Roman, and saw Stephen's hands around his neck as Roman fought to breathe. I gasped, but closed my eyes. Still there. "Stephen, *you* need to stop this. Your use of terror is not The Way. It's not right."

The ground continued to shake, growing with force as The Source became more stressed. The Leaders gazed around in fear, moving toward the water and away from the trees, which had begun dropping debris. But the water sloshed violently against the shoreline, growing more agitated by the second.

"Stephen has been manipulating you," I shouted to The Source over the chaos. "He's hurting people and you're the only one who can stop it!"

"Stephen?" They reached for him to help, but Stephen was wrestling with a now lucid Roman. The backup officers and Rey and Vanessa came rushing forward, all of them moving toward the Guardians who held the initiates.

"No!" The Source shouted as they held onto the table to keep from falling. They waved a hand and knocked everyone to the ground, except for me. "Creed, I don't know what to believe, but this ritual must happen *now*!"

"You can't! These initiates are not able to give con—"

"Silence."

They threw me with a flick of their hand and I flew backwards, hitting a tree before sliding to the ground. My vision grew fuzzy, just as the four initiates were pulled toward The Source as if there was an invisible tether about their waists.

Roman was chosen to be first.

"No! Roman—"

The Source held their hands up and brought them down fast, and the weight felt as if a boulder had landed on my chest. I had no choice but to watch the violation of my beloved...

30

CHAPTER THIRTY

R oman

I'D READ accounts of people awakening during surgery and having to witness their flesh being cut, their innards rearranged, having to see it happening but being unable to speak, to move, that helpless feeling of pain being inflicted while you're unable to stop it.

It was one of my greatest fears. Thankfully, I'd never had to go under the knife for any reason. I'd had broken bones set, my head injury healed after months in a dark room with no screen time.

I didn't think I'd ever heal from this.

This person they called The Source was literally turning me inside out. I was forced to watch the blood leave my body and be absorbed by them. I hadn't agreed to this. I sensed the being was frantic as they attempted to complete their ritual, as if there was a monster chasing them or death was right on their heels. Perhaps that's what it all meant. If The Source was unable to take in the blood, they would lose power and *they'd* be the one absorbed.

I tried to hold on, but I was slipping away, my life being squeezed and pulled out of my very pores. Time passed in a surreal manner as I was treated to some of my less-than-stellar memories, moments when I'd treated my life like garbage. Who knew that life flashing before your eyes was less nostalgic and more punitive?

Shame washed over me for all the times I made my lola worry, and for not being there when my parents were slaughtered while I was out smoking weed and running old ladies off the sidewalks on my skateboard. I was ashamed that I'd been unable to protect Bernadette and Emmanuel from these cruel people.

And then it was over and the memories pulled away from me like a TV flickering off, leaving me in darkness. Cold darkness. Shaky, windy darkness. Crackling sounds and a loud rumble filled my ears, and I thought, *well, this must be what it feels like to get sucked into Hell.*

But then I opened my eyes and saw the redwoods thrashing overhead, and I felt the bits of debris pelting my skin like fingernails on a sunburn.

"Roman, stay with me!"

Reynaldo's voice filled my head like so many times before, but instead of chiding me, he sounded terrified, desperate even. I guess for once the mess I was in wasn't due to my fuck-up. Maybe upon my death, I was no longer Junior with a chip on his shoulder, but finally Roman Emmanuel San Angelo the Second, a man capable of standing on his own two feet. Or nearly that man.

Another voice shouted over the din, this one tugging at my heart.

"There is another way, you don't have to do this! Please!"

Creed. The agony in his voice filled me with rage. I'd sworn to him he would be protected, that he could trust us, but he'd been right. We couldn't have known what this being was capable of. Even Creed hadn't been sure himself.

"Guardian Creed, you must let this take place. Please do not force my hand—"

"Creed," Stephen said. I will not hesitate to end you. Do not get in our way."

"Stephen, step back." The Source stepped in between I have

doubts about your sincerity. We will discuss them when this is over. I won't have your influence ruining this ritual." The Source flung their hand and Stephen stumbled backwards, but remained standing. He shook off the force and headed after Creed once more, but The Source spoke again, their voice reverberating in my chest. "You are not fit to be a part of this ritual. If you cannot banish this hatred from your heart, You'll force me to punish you."

The Source placed a hand on his chest and he sucked in air. He choked and began coughing violently. His face paled in the moonlight and he appeared to...Agee. Right before our eyes.

"What have you done?" Stephen held his chest, his eyes wide." He charged The Source, but Creed shoved him back. Stephen's loss of focus allowed others to intervene.

Vanessa tackled Stephen and nearly had him face down in the dirt. Somehow Creed's interruption and Stephen's behavior had allowed Vanessa a brief respite from the mind-control or whatever was interfering with her ability to move. He caught her with an elbow to the face, but when he tried to get up, he had to bend over and catch his breath.

Vanessa flipped off her back and landed on her feet, delivering some blows to the head that further incapacitated him. The two of them struggled, and thank goodness my tita was highly trained in martial arts. Stephen grew weaker by the minute. When it seemed that she'd gained control, she shouted, "You're under arrest—"

Stephen threw her off of him, and she scrambled to regain the upper hand. She dove for him once more and managed to get him in a sort of sleeper hold, one I'd seen her use on tito before. Stephen's eyes went wide as he gasped for air.

"You don't understand, let me go!" He begged and pleaded, his voice straining under her hold. "Let me go or you'll—"

"I've already seen you threaten my wife, son and nephew. Enough with your bullshit!"

He protested more, seemingly shocked she was able to subdue him, but when she yanked her arm tighter, he passed out. His body went slack and one of the other cops took over and pulled his arms back farther and secured them with a zip-tie.

"Try that scary shit, asshole," she shouted over his motionless body. "You have no idea what I'm capable of," she growled, giving him one final push as she stood and waved over Detective Sterling. Only then did she run to her wife and family.

At that point I was fading fast, but when I realized my family was safe, I turned my head and saw the FBI agent I'd met holding The Source as Creed pleaded with them. The other cops detained the rest of Stephen's people. They didn't seem to fight back once Stephen was out of commission. Vanessa escorted Tita Bernadette and Emmanuel away to her car.

"Em? Bernadette?"

"Roman!" Rey knelt beside me, pressing a cloth onto my chest. "Direct EMS over here," he shouted. "The blood won't stop!"

I tried to lift my arm, but no luck. "Rey?"

"Shhh don't try to talk. Help is on the way."

"Em and B—"

"They're fine. Creed was able to stop them from being hurt. Just relax, Junior. God, so much blood…"

I wiggled my fingers, but they were numb, and I didn't have the strength to roll over and sit up.

"Rey, I'm sorry I was such a shithead. Please tell Lola I'm sorry, and Vanessa—"

"Shut up. The paramedics are here, now shut up. You're pissing me off, Junior!"

For the first time in my life, I saw my uncle cry, and it was the last thing I remembered before the ringing in my ears took over and everything went black.

DREAMS HAD NEVER BEEN KIND to me. When I was a boy, I had nightmares almost nightly. My parents talked to doctors, and they all said something similar. "They're night terrors. He won't remember them. They're worse for you to witness than they are for him." But that wasn't true. Then after they were murdered, guilt became the main theme. I woke up every morning to beat myself up for all the things I'd fucked up in my life. Therapists told me to forgive myself, to write a letter to my parents. They sent me to grief counseling. The thing that healed me? Bashing my head on a rock in the ocean. The recovery was so miserable that I felt like I'd suffered enough. It was time to move on.

These fragments of my life created my mistrust of all things related to authority. There were only two things I trusted in my life: what my grandparents told me, and that everyone else was full of shit. I didn't even fully trust my aunt and uncle because they liked to mess with me, and then they both went to work for The Man.

But then I found Creed, and I knew that he was good. I knew he loved me. I knew that if we could just skip ahead in time to after all this bullshit was settled, everything would be fine.

But it seemed we hadn't yet reached the after part.

I woke up from a terrible dream, drenched in sweat, in a hospital room with Bernadette and Emmanuel arguing next to the bed. When my mouth chose to cooperate, I said the nicest thing I could think of.

"Why does everyone in our family have to argue about everything?"

Bernadette squealed and dove for the bed, nearly knocking out my IV in the process. Nurses came running in, and Emmanuel had to pull his mom back from the bed so they could fuss over me.

"Where is everyone? What time is it?"

"Mr. San Angelo, I need you to lie still so we can check your vitals, and then the doctor will be in to examine you."

"But...what's happening?"

"We'll tell you everything," Bernadette said, "just let the doctors check you out."

I might have been a dick to the medical staff, but everyone was avoiding eye contact and speaking in hushed tones, and it was thoroughly pissing me off.

"Mr. San Angelo, your body has been through a serious trauma.

The attack left you with severe blood loss. You're lucky the paramedics got to you when they did, and that your boyfriend was a match for your blood type, or else you might not have been so lucky."

I had no idea how to respond to that, so I sat there with my mouth hanging open.

"Is that what we're calling it? An attack?" I finally muttered, confused.

"You experienced hypovolemic shock, Mr. San Angelo. We're unsure of the amount of damage done to your heart, but you've been in a coma for eight days—"

"*Eight days*? But—"

My chest burned and my breathing became shallow.

"You need to avoid any and all excitement for the near future. We'll do a full evaluation after you've had a few moments to speak with your family."

"Where's Creed?" I asked Bernadette. "Where are Rey and Vanessa—"

"Do you have any questions for me?" the doctor asked. "I know this is a shock."

"Yeah, how long do I have to stay here?" My mind was flooded with all of my responsibilities...Lola, teaching, my dissertation.

Where's Creed?

"Hey, Junior. Glad you decided to join us."

Rey came strolling in, decked out in his uniform and a grin on his face.

"That I can't tell you until we've done a complete exam, Mr. San Angelo. I'll leave you to talk to your family." He and the nurses left with Bernadette and Emmanuel, which was good, because I intended to kick Rey's ass.

I tried to push myself up and swing my leg over the side of the bed, but nothing cooperated.

"Whoa whoa whoa, Junior. You can't get outta that bed, not for a bit."

"No kidding," I muttered, looking under the sheet. Catheter, monitors, IV...this was no joke. "Rey," I said, my voice cracking. "What the fuck happened? Where's Creed?"

Rey lost a bit of his grin, and he moved closer to the bed, leaning in a little closer. "I'm sorry, man. Here," he said, pulling out his phone. He pushed a couple of buttons and pushed it into my hands, which were weak. So weak. "I was instructed to call as soon as you woke up."

FaceTime rang and rang and finally the screen popped up...with Agent Barringer smiling at me.

"Mr. San Angelo! So good to see you up and around. How are you feeling?" He stood, and I could tell he was walking with the phone.

"Confused as hell. Where is—"

The phone shook as if someone snatched it out of his hand, and there he was.

"Roman—"

"Creed!"

His smile finally calmed my heart that had been pounding since I'd heard the word "coma."

"Blessed be," he breathed, and he touched the screen. "Are you really awake? Roman, I miss you. I'm so sorry."

"Are *you* okay?" I asked. "What happened?"

Rey cleared his throat. "I'll give you two a minute." He squeezed my shoulder and then patted it in a move very unlike him. He left my room, closing the door behind him.

I clutched the phone with both hands and waited for Creed to get settled. He'd moved outside, and I could see trees behind him. When he finally stopped walking, his eyes were full of tears.

"I feared I'd never hear your voice again. How are you feeling?"

"Like shit," I said, then I laughed and wiped at my own eyes. "Did you really...give me your blood?"

Creed smiled sadly. "We're a perfect match for each other, even on a molecular level, it seems." His smile faded and he took on that haunted look. "But don't worry, it's not the same as, you know... You're not like me. It takes more than that."

"I don't even care," I said, although that opened a whole new can of worms. "Where are you?" I asked him.

He looked around and held the phone close to his face. "A non-government sanctioned safehouse. I'm not allowed to know where. After the situation at Loch Lomond, Barringer arranged for us to be whisked away to this location for...containment purposes."

I frowned and felt my ear get fuzzy, like my tinnitus was coming back.

"I need to see you, Creed. I need to understand what happened to me."

He licked his lips. "It's not safe for you to travel yet, according to your doctor. Hopefully by the time it is, this situation will be... contained, and you can come here, or I can come to you." He winced. "It's *killing* me to be away from you right now."

"What do you mean by contained...or can you tell me?"

"It's not safe over the phone." He wiped at his eyes and blew out a shaky breath. "If it were at all possible for me to be there, I would be holding you right now. I hope that when you learn what happened, that you'll forgive me. I hope that you'll wait for me...but I'll understand if you can't forgive me for letting you be hurt."

"Creed, what are you saying?"

"I am...needed here. What happened at the lake, I have to make sure it doesn't happen again. I need to be sure there's no more danger. But I *will* find a way, Roman, I promise, and then we'll be free to start a life together...if that's still what you want."

"Of course it is, Creed. I thought I made myself clear."

His pink-stained cheeks were all the answer I needed.

"I am yours. You know you have my heart."

"Good. Then it's settled. I'll be here, you know, learning how to use my body again, and you'll—"

"Roman, I'm sorry—"

"Don't be. Frankly, I don't really want you seeing me like this."

"I'm a nurse, Roman. It's what I do."

"Not with me, you don't."

He growled at me, but then we both laughed.

"Will you at least give me permission to communicate with your doctor?"

"Of course. But Creed, don't worry about me. I'm going to be on my feet in no time, and then I'll come to you."

"We'll find a way to be together, Roman, I swear to you." He smiled hopefully. "I'm not about to give up the best thing to ever happen to me."

"Good. I won't be *given* up."

"Good. Then it's settled. You focus on getting well, and remember that...I love you, Professor."

My eyes fluttered closed. Those words, coming from him, were a balm for my soul. Knowing he was on the other side of my recovery made me determined to get out of this bed and mobile so I could go to him and remind him how much he loved me.

"I love you, too."

"You need to rest. I promise, we'll be together soon. And when you can, have Rey call this number—"

The phone disconnected.

"Creed? Creed! No. Rey! Rey, get in here!"

A monitor started beeping behind me, and my face flushed. I lay back on the pillow and shut my eyes as the doctor and nurses all surrounded the bed. I wanted Creed. I needed him. I always felt better when he was near. Why couldn't he be near?

"No excitement, Mr. San Angelo. You absolutely must not overexert yourself."

"I got this, Doc." Rey took the phone from me and slid it in his pocket.

It took me a few minutes for my breathing to slow to semi-normal. When the doctor felt I was stabilized, he agreed to come back after I'd had a chance to talk to Rey.

"What's happening? Do you know where Creed is?"

He walked over and shut the door. "The FBI agent has taken Creed, those musicians, and The Source to a safehouse to debrief them and to deal with the fallout. He didn't want to go, Roman. You have to know that."

"I believe you." And I did, even though there was a selfish part of me that wanted Creed here, that thought he should be the one to bring me home. "What about the others?"

Rey smiled. "In another undisclosed facility in solitary confinement. From what I hear, they are begging to confess and Barringer's got people working on...ahem, *with* them."

I wasn't a violent person by nature, but I really hoped he meant the former. "So what happens now?"

"Now, you take the time to rest and get well. Vanessa is working on the case against Stephen with the district attorney, while we try to find the rest of the people involved with the takeover of BioBourne. Timothy Hicks is still at large. He wasn't at the lake." He pulled on his duty belt. "I'm back on patrol, though. I'm done with special duty. This way, I can see Tita Frances and keep an eye on you."

"How are B and Em? Are they okay?" I felt awful that they'd been dragged into this mess.

"They don't remember any of it," he said. When I frowned, he shrugged. "Really. Vanessa had them talk to the department shrink, who thinks that it's a trauma response, or perhaps it was some mind control hypnosis thing or they drugged them before you got there."

"Anything is possible, I guess. Was Creed hurt? How did he stop it? The ritual?"

Rey frowned. "No. The person who did this to you, they recognized Creed. I don't really know how he got through to them. I was too busy trying to keep your ass alive."

There was something he wasn't telling me, and I had so many questions.

"Look, I have the number for their secure line, we can call him another time, but I want you to know, he didn't have a choice, Roman. Creed had to go. He saved us all from that...thing."

That didn't surprise me. He was a strong man, strong of character, heart, mind. And he was always going to sacrifice himself. I knew that.

And he loved me.

"He would be here right now if he possibly could."

"You believe that?" I had to ask. Rey suspected everyone. It was not just his job but part of his nature.

"I do. Your auntie and your cousin are safe because of him. You're alive because of him. I believe in him."

Then I would too. I didn't want to imagine a life without Creed, now that I'd found him, so I would wait and do my best to be patient.

"Alright, then. Get that doctor back in here and let's get this recovery on the road."

CHAPTER THIRTY-ONE

Creed

"THIS HURTS." I pulled Rhonda near me and held her until she squirmed to get away, holding her tennis ball in her mouth. She loved dashing back and forth across the massive fenced-in lawn at our secret location. She also loved all the people she had to fuss over her. Mark especially loved to play fetch with her, and she loved to lay in front of Cross while he played guitar.

Most of all, she loved her swims with The Source in the indoor pool. Whoever designed this place had thought of everything, including a wade-in pool, so she didn't panic like she had the one time she'd jumped in a hotel pool after me and couldn't climb back out over the edge. She swam alongside The Source and she seemed to grow stronger every day, almost puppylike.

Unlike me.

Whether it was the toll of the events on Samhain or the lack of energy to consume out here in the woods, away from people who actually needed healing...I was fading. And while Cross and Mark had taken nourishment from The Source, I'd refused.

I was angry. Angrier than I'd ever been in my life, including after the events fifty years ago that set this whole disaster in motion.

Muse, I'm sorry. This wasn't at all the way I'd planned to avenge your death.

"I'm sorry, Creed," Barringer said, and I believed he really was. "I wish we could chance it for you to talk longer, but with Timothy Hicks still on the run and the potential psychic fallout from the disaster at Loch Lomond, we need to lay low. My people have their feelers out, Roman is being guarded, and as soon as he's well enough to travel, we'll give him the option—"

"What, to be whisked away from his life to join our fucking monastery up here? No fucking way. He's gotta finish his degree. He's got his grandmother. *Fuck!*"

I kicked at a rock and paced away from him.

"You have given up so much of your life in pursuit of justice for the fallen at Gateway of the Sun. You thwarted a terrible tragedy and saved the life of your boyfriend a week ago. It's understandable that you'd be frustrated."

Fury threatened to boil over my surface, but I hated to explode all over Todd. He'd done everything possible to intervene in this situation and resolve it in a way that protected Roman and his family, and I should have been grateful.

Instead, I was trapped.

"I didn't intend to become a prisoner," I snarled at him.

"Creed, you know that's not—"

"I can't leave, Todd. I'm trapped here when I'm needed elsewhere."

"You're the only one who can heal The Source."

Ah, the truth of the matter.

The Source had become tainted by Stephen's evil. He'd used his nefarious talent on The Source for fifty years and convinced the sheltered being of his fucked-up agenda. He lied to them about why they needed to continue the medical research, including what they were doing with The Source's blood. I offered myself in exchange for the others, let The Source know the "initiates" were not there voluntarily, that they knew nothing about The Way and that they would be breaking the covenant if they continued with the ritual. They'd been literally brainwashed, and now it had become my responsibility to deprogram them and find out the truth about their behavior during the ritual. What hadn't they told us? Why were they so panicked?

They'd nearly drained Roman of his lifeforce, so I did the only thing I could think of.

"There's another way. I'll show you," I'd said to them. Something in my tone made them listen, and when I gave my consent for an Exchange, they were distraught by what they learned.

When the maelstrom died down, Cross and Mark had kept The Source calm while I ran to Roman. The paramedics determined he would never make it to the hospital without an immediate transfusion. None of the others present were a match.

My blood was type-less as a result of my initiation. I could save him.

They managed a field transfusion, taking three pints of my blood before they loaded him into the ambulance. All I'd had the chance to do was kiss his cold lips, say a prayer to the Goddess to spare his life, and let him go with all the healing energy I could muster. When I staggered away, Todd hustled me over to a dark SUV, loaded up Cross, Mark, and The Source, and let Captain Rojas know that he would be in touch. The only way he got the captain to agree was to leave him Stephen.

I prayed that wasn't a mistake.

"They were all...*wrong*. The Source was supposed to be a benevolent leader, that's what we were taught, but what I sensed from them was all wrong. Stephen lied to them this whole time, manipulated them by showing them a world that wasn't true. He showed them that fear and evil were necessary, but that wasn't The Way."

"It seems as though the lessons you learned were truly the way you were *meant* to be taught, and during their time with Stephen, The

Source was corrupted. If we can't find a way to correct this situation, we'll have to keep them contained permanently."

"And how do you propose we do that?" I asked him. "You saw how much power they wield. Is it possible to make them fit into this world? Is it possible to keep the world safe *from* them? And what if others learn about their power and like Stephen, want to use that power for their own gain. Sure seems like this Hicks guy intends to do that."

The one bit of information Todd had gotten from his associates—who I learned were not government officials, not law enforcement—was that Stephen had recruited Timothy because of his specific connections, that he'd been ready to kill himself and The Source because none of their experiments were working to replicate The Source's blood and he'd grown desperate to get away from the whole operation. Stephen claimed Timothy was greedy for the power he thought he could get from The Source, and that he was truly the threat. How much of that could be believed, I had no clue.

Todd looked at the ground and shook his head. "If anyone can make a difference, it's you, Creed. Couldn't you teach The Source to heal the way you do? The way you've helped countless patients over the years?"

"Maybe. If I can get past the whole 'you nearly killed my boyfriend' issue."

"I'm sorry, Creed. I can't imagine how you've dealt with all of this for fifty years. I will say that Mrs. Hicks sends her gratitude. She thought she was going to die. She's agreed to testify against Stephen and company. She wanted to thank you but we've placed her in protective custody. I know that it doesn't fix anything for you, but I wanted you to know. I'm here, though, if you want to talk about anything."

I did, but I wasn't ready. Everything was too raw. I was back to where I'd started months ago, when I thought I would find Stephen and destroy him and then settle in Santa Cruz and live out the rest of my existence, aging naturally until it was time for my death.

Boy, had I been wrong. On all accounts.

"How is Roman?"

I'd almost forgotten that Todd was still there.

"He's awake. He said he'd allow the doctor to give me information about his condition, so maybe next time I talk to Rey—"

"We just need to be careful, Creed. We don't know if he's being watched. We've got someone from our organization posted in the hospital, and we'll keep him safe until you can be with him again."

I nodded. "I'm glad you said 'can' and not 'maybe'."

Todd sighed. "I'm sorry it has to be this way, Creed. I really am."

I held up a hand. "It's okay. Everyone's gotta have a purpose, don't they?"

"And yours, apparently, is to save the world."

I barked out a laugh. "If I'm going to do that, you're going to need to find me some energy, Todd. I'm running on fumes."

He grinned. "I do have a surprise for you." Todd turned and gestured with a hand toward the house, and we started walking together. "One of my associates paid a visit to Puesta Del Sol, and there was a very concerned patron who wished to see you."

"Who—"

We stepped through the doorway into the sunroom, and there sat a familiar face that always made me smile.

"There's my favorite nurse."

"Mr. Fletcher!"

He stood achingly slowly, and I sensed that his hips were causing him terrible pain. He was weaker, but that sparkle hadn't left his eye. We embraced, and I couldn't help the tears that spilled down my cheeks. His presence and his trust in me emboldened me to my task.

People like Mr. Fletcher were why I'd followed The Way after the tragedy that befell my cohort. I wanted to heal people, that was my purpose, and I wanted to protect those who needed it.

"I feel better already," he whispered to me, patting me on the back.

"Me, too," I said, wiping at my eyes.

"When my colleague explained to Mr. Fletcher that you were in need of a friend, he didn't hesitate to tell the staff at Puesta Del Sol that he would be 'transferring to a private facility.'"

I turned to face Todd, my eyes wide. "He's staying here?"

Todd nodded. "What better way for you to heal The Source than by showing them the good you do with your gift?"

"But Mr. Fletcher? What about your family?"

"I told them you'd transferred to another facility and that I wanted to keep working with you. I told them I was coming here for an experimental treatment." He winked at me, and I couldn't help but laugh.

"Sounds like a plan," I said.

It was the perfect plan.

And with Mr. Fletcher's help, I'd be strong enough to take on the task at hand, and in turn, I could be back with Roman sooner.

I turned to Mr. Fletcher. "Are you ready to get to work?"

He stood a little straighter and gave me a salute. "At your service."

The End...

MOONWISH: SUNDOWNERS BOOK TWO COMING IN 2025

Read on for the beginning of *Moonwish...*

Prologue
  Timothy Hicks

The employees squirmed before him and he enjoyed every bit of their terror. He bathed in it, slathered it on like expensive skin products that promised to make you beautiful and didn't do shit. Once it soaked into his pores it took mere seconds to light up his synapses like one of those high-speed films of cars on a freeway.

Power. It made Timothy Hicks giddy. Made him hard, too.

He sat at the head of the table in a stark white conference room underground in a bunker owned by the company his wife Donna had made wildly successful before she became a liability. Not only was Timothy now in charge of BioBourne, but somehow he'd managed to evade the police and take the reins of the Western division of EVE, Elite Ventures Enterprises, catering to the rich, powerful... and medically desperate.

"With Adams out of the picture, my wife missing, and The Source out of our hands, we need to make a solid plan. We've got distributors lined up to carry the product to our clients and I will not default on our agreements. So somebody better come up with a plan to get EVE back on track, or there will be consequences for all of you."

One of the things he'd learned over the past decade as CEO of his previous company was that the best way to get results from one's employees was to give them everything they could ever want, and then impress upon them the knowledge that it could all be taken away. Employees should like and respect those in charge, but above all, they should fear them. Just a little. Enough to keep them on their toes.

The employees sitting in this conference room in the BioBourne bunker were terrified.

"Mr. Hicks, sir? There is the possibility we don't need The Source to continue producing our, um, serum."

Courtney was one of the few women who'd been allowed to remain on the board at BioBourne when EVE took over the biomedical research company and put Hicks in charge. She was smart, hungry, and had plenty to lose if he needed leverage on her.

Timothy knew EVE had chosen wisely when they took him on in Stephen's absence. Yes, they had accumulated a lot of wealthy and influential people in the Bay Area, but those members were old. Timothy knew that old people usually wanted more time. They were in it to find the fountain of youth or equivalent, and they believed that The Source was the answer to their prayers. If they just waited long enough for technology to catch up, they knew they could harness the power of the being they called The Source. In the meantime, they had expanded their research into other areas, including "health retreats" where clients who were members of EVE or their immediate family members were being treated for a plethora of ailments with trials of the synthetic serum created from The Source's blood. Through partners like BioBourne, EVE had the means to continue producing it as long as there was a workforce of those trained in The Way.

That's where Timothy saw his opportunity. From adolescence, Timothy knew he was special. He had a little trick hidden up his sleeve that benefited him greatly, and it was just what was needed to overcome the current hiccup in EVE's plans.

With The Source out of reach, they either needed to find the answers with what material they had already harvested, or they needed to take their research in another direction.

Hicks leaned back in his chair and linked his fingers over his chest. "And how would that be possible? We still haven't identified all of the particular elements necessary for the formula."

Courtney flicked her long, straight, black hair over her shoulder and debated whether or not she wanted to give Timothy the information she was holding on to.

Of course she shouldn't tell him, and she knew it. He had proven to be ruthless, often unscrupulous when it came to furthering EVE's mission.

"There are others who have been blessed by The Source and who practice The Way. They may not be as old or as potent, but it's worth analyzing their blood."

"And who are these others? Stephen told us the others in his cohort were slaughtered. He and Caleb are in police custody...Who else is there?"

She pulled up a file on her computer and asked to have access to the projector. He nodded at her and she connected. Onscreen popped three pictures.

"Mark Bullock, one who goes only by Cross, we don't have another name for him. And then there is Creed Lowell."

Timothy looked closely at the three men onscreen. "And what do we know of these acolytes?"

"My source at the police department says that Stephen recruited Bullock and Cross to step in at the failed ceremony."

Stephen was in way over his head by the time Timothy joined EVE with his wife Donna. He was short-tempered, prone to histrionics, and refused to let anyone get too near The Source. He kept his knowledge under wraps, so if he knew these men, knew they'd been in town, but had been avoiding them for some reason, what did that mean? Was he trying to control them? Was he intimidated by them?

The man preyed on peoples' fears, but for some reason, he'd succumbed to his own. From what Timothy had learned of the night of the ritual, he'd basically given up and put up very little fight when the police showed up.

Timothy wasn't sorry he was gone.

"Interesting. And what about Lowell?"

The corner of her lip turned up which stirred something in Timothy's groin. "According to my source, he's a nurse. He told law enforcement that he's been using what he learned from The Source for the past fifty years to heal the elderly in care homes around the country."

Hicks gazed closely at the pictures. All three images were taken outside at night with only parking lot lights to illuminate their faces. But one fact was clear.

"You said he's been a nurse for fifty years? And these other men? They supposedly were in the commune with Stephen?"

"Yes, sir," she said.

None of the three men looked a day over thirty. Lowell, in fact, looked like a fresh-faced straight-out-of-college kid. Interesting.

"Where can we find these three?"

She fidgeted slightly in her seat, the only acknowledgment that she was nervous about sharing this info.

"They were taken into federal custody at Loch Lomond and no one local has heard from them."

Hicks raised an eyebrow at her. "No one disappears completely, not in this day and age. Perhaps you could take a closer look, see what you can find out from your...source." It was good to have sources in law enforcement. It was partly why Timothy had been able to find his wife when she'd run the first time. He'd caught her, but then after the debacle at the lake, she'd been taken back into protective custody, and no one seemed to know where they were keeping her. For all he knew, she swas hanging out with The Source.

He vowed to get her back. *I always get what I want.* And right now, he wanted to keep EVE on track. They had serum to deliver to their clients and they had some big promises to deliver upon. Nothing, not the lack of The Source, his missing wife, nor any law enforcement entity would keep them from success.

"There might be a way to make them surface."

He turned my chair to face her. "And what would that be?" Courtney was trying her best to make herself useful. He appreciated her taking the initiative.

"Lowell's boyfriend is in a convalescent hospital in town."

Hicks folded his hands under his chin. "And where one's true love lies... Excellent work, Courtney. Be sure to see me after the meeting."

She nodded and unplugged the computer from the projector.

Moments after he ended the meeting and gave the group their assignments, Courtney appeared in the doorway to his current office, ready to do battle for him and EVE.

She'd given a lot of information that could be useful, and he intended to use it. He'd get what he needed from her. Maybe even more than she bargained for.

He always got what he wanted.

Chapter One
Roman

Three Weeks after the incident at Loch Lomond

The human body is a miraculous machine. Think about it. The liver can regenerate itself in as little as four weeks, the human brain can retain an amount of information equal to 20,000 dictionaries, and the circulatory system acts as a high-speed transportation system, moving 8000 liters of the life-giving, life-sustaining elixir we all need to survive around our body every day.

Blood.

I'd never given much thought to my blood until it was taken from me involuntarily. Not spilled, not withdrawn in a medical procedure...no. It had been *removed*. Pints of it. And I couldn't even be mad. Well, I could, but then I'd have to be mad at the man I'd fallen ridiculously in love with, and since he was the reason I got out of bed every day and the reason I was currently strapped with wires all over my torso while running—walking, I mean. I wouldn't be running for a long time to come, if ever— for my life, I...well I could be mad. Or at least perturbed.

"Creed Lowell, I swear, when I get out of this place, I'm going to kick your ass—"

"Mmm I can't wait."

The treadmill slowed to a stop and I grabbed for my water bottle while the nurses got the readings from my latest test and I gasped like I'd just finished a marathon. Hopefully I'd done better this time and would be one step closer to getting released from the convalescent hospital. I felt better, stronger, but I still needed to use a cane and I was nowhere near the shape I'd been in before. Hypovolemic shock is a bitch.

Creed's smile on the screen of the SAT phone made the pain lessen somewhat, though being kept away from him hurt more than I could stand.

"You're such a tease," I said between gasps for air. "You're going to be in so much trouble when I get out of this place."

Creed sighed. "Promise? How much longer, have they said?"

The thing driving me through my rehab was that I knew Creed needed me as much, if not more, than I needed him, and I was desperate to be with him again. This Facetime bullshit wasn't cutting it.

The door opened and my uncle—Santa Cruz PD Officer Reynaldo Cabral—entered with a laugh.

"Hey, Six Dollar Man, you almost done? I gotta get back." My uncle could be an asshole—my favorite nickname for him was Dicknaldo after all—but he was just as anxious for me to get out of rehab and back to my life as I was. It wasn't only because he was sick and tired of being our go-between. He had possession of the super secret bat phone that Creed and I had to use to communicate. Creed was being kept at a classified location by an FBI agent who was working with a non-governmental task force to deal with the events that put me here.

No. Uncle Rey wanted me out of here so we could all focus on finding the people who'd been wreaking havoc on our hometown and who regularly took blood and energy from people without permission.

The plan was that as soon as I was well enough to be released, I would be secreted away in the dead of night to be reunited with my lover. It sounded like the plot of a romance novel, but in reality, it was much more serious than that.

"Six Dollar...fuck off. I'll be done in a minute." I used a towel to wipe my face, cringing at the thought that once upon a time, I could run a six-minute mile, and now walking for six minutes at two point five miles per hour had me sweating buckets and wrung out.

"Sorry, Rey. It's my fault we're taking so long. I love watching him sweat." Creed winked at me, but the absence of his multi-watt smile let me know that while this rehab was physically torturing me, it was torturing him by proxy.

"No problem, Nurse Creed. By the way, Vanessa wanted me to let you know that she's sitting in on Stephen's deposition tomorrow. Agent Barringer is going to be participating remotely as well so I'm sure he'll keep you updated as much as he can."

"I'm aware," Creed said, his expression going dark. "Any word on Timothy Hicks?"

Rey shook his head. "Not yet. We've managed to get a few more names of folks involved, however, and it looks like what Stephen was saying about being a pawn may be sort of true."

"Bullshit," Creed said, but it was more of a summation than an interjection.

After my exsanguination at Loch Lomond in the Santa Cruz mountains, Stephen Adams had been captured by my intrepid aunt, Detective Vanessa Cabral. She'd barely kept herself from beating him within an inch of his existence after he kidnapped her wife and son, and yours truly. But all Stephen would say was that everything he'd done was to care for The Source, that he had nothing to do with the attacks in town, nor the biomedical and financial organizations. We knew that wasn't true—at the very least he would be charged with attempted murder, kidnapping, and the murders of the four young men who had been leading the terror campaign in downtown Santa Cruz. Stephen Adams would never be a free man again. It wasn't enough.

"I know," Rey said. "But I'm no detective so what the fuck do I know? Anyway, I'll give you two a minute to wrap things up."

He stepped back out into the hallway and I smiled down at Creed, who winced.

"As much as I love seeing you without a shirt, I'm not a fan of your current accessories."

I looked down at myself and poked at the monitors. "I don't mind it. Hopefully the nurse will like my results this time." I pulled the phone closer to my face. "How are you, though?"

Creed's smile didn't have the charm it used to, and the dark circles under his eyes worried me, though he always argued that he was fine.

"I'll be better when I can kiss you. Hold you. Who are you that you've turned me from a solitary man into one who pines after the man he adores? I may be the mythological creature of darkness in this relationship, but it's you who's put a spell on me."

If he'd been himself, if he'd smiled that flirty smile of his, I would have laughed out loud at his proclamation. But he was serious.

"There's nothing dark about you, and you know it. Babe, I'm sorry. I'm trying my hardest. If all my tests look good in the next few days, the doctors will start making discharge plans."

"I know you are, Roman. I'm just being morose. Ignore me. Please, take your time. You need to be well. I'm fine."

"You're not fine, though." I cocked my head to the side. "Have you, you know, been taking care of yourself?"

Creed smiled weakly. "Mr. Fletcher being here helps. I'm doing the best I can."

"What about…have you gone to *them*?"

The *them* I referred to was the center of this whole fucking debacle. The Source. If I were to believe everything I'd been told, they were an ancient being who had somehow figured out how to cheat death. I still wasn't too clear on the process, but there was no denying The Source was powerful.

"Cross and Mark have. I don't...I can't. I won't."

"But if it will help you—"

"I'm making do with what I have. Barringer and I are working on some additional, uh, energy resources."

"And I'll be there soon."

Creed's answering smile let me know what he wasn't able to say. He was struggling, and while he would never ask me to do anything that would set back my recovery, he *needed* from me. He needed *me*, and that was something that would continue to drive me until I was back in his arms.

"Soon," he breathed.

We could have said more, but we knew we were being monitored, and what we most wanted to say to each other was better left for the time we were truly alone.

"I promise. Stay well, okay? And hug Rhonda for me." I'd become awfully close with Creed's Doberman before the shit hit the fan. I missed her almost as much as I missed him.

Creed snorted. "Wherever she is. Traitor. She's enjoying herself way more than I am."

I gave him a sad smile and touched the screen with my index finger.

"Soon." And then the line disconnected. My eyes burned and I rested my weight on the treadmill bars, a wave of sadness threatening to buckle my pitiful knees.

I had to be strong for Creed during our infrequent calls, but returning to the status of a disabled person was infuriating and at times debilitating. I thought I'd hated it after my first near-death experience. I'd been surfing the often treacherous waves at Steamers Lane in Santa Cruz when I'd gotten caught by the undertow and my temple smacked into a rock under the surface, giving myself a concussion and the wonderful secondary lifetime afflictions of vertigo and tinnitus. Yay. Things had been much better in that department, actually, until Creed came along.

I wasn't complaining though.

See, for all intents and purposes, Creed was a vampire in that his survival depended on access to human-created energy and blood. He was no Dracula, although he was sexy as hell, but he had this chemical that he referred to as a pheromone he released that relaxed his, well I don't want to call them prey because that did make him sound like Dracula. His willing participant. The person relaxes, Creed says a blessing, he sinks his evolutionarily sharp teeth into a vein close to the surface, under thin skin, and he takes three pulls of blood. No more. He follows a very strict ritual that he was taught by acolytes of The Source decades ago. And that act, along with being a human energy recycling plant, has kept him from aging and gives him tremendous strength. He's spent his existence post-cult life taking care of elderly people in the evening when they need it most, feeding on their negative energy while providing healing energy in return. I'd seen him do it with my grandmother and it was truly a miracle to behold.

Unfortunately, not all of the people who were instructed in the ways as he was, used their power for good.

And that, my friends, is how I came to be disabled once again. I fucking hated this shit.

"You and loverboy all done?" Rey called from the hallway. "The nurses want to unhook you from your wires and you need to get back to bed."

I groaned. "I don't want to go back to bed."

Yeah, I sounded like a whiny brat, but I was so tired of this.

"I know," Rey said quietly. He stood next to the treadmill, maybe to catch me, maybe for emotional support, as the nurses unhooked all of the wires and assured me I was continuing to make improvements. They handed me a second towel to mop up the ridiculous amount of sweat I'd conjured up.

"The doctor will see you this afternoon and go over the results."

I thanked them and they left Rey to escort me back to my room. I pulled on my UCSC Banana Slugs sweatshirt and reached for my cane. *Jesus.* Twenty-five, almost twenty-six years old and I needed a damn cane to get around.

"I really think you ought to revamp your wardrobe when you get out of here. Canes are rad, dude. You could start wearing tweed and shit like a real college professor."

I rolled my eyes. "I *am* a real college professor. Or I almost was. At this rate, I'll go straight from grad student to retiree. Fuck, Rey, how the hell am I supposed to finish my program? How the hell will I ever get a job if I can't even walk down the hall without running out of steam?" I knew better than to let myself wallow because it took energy I didn't have to waste.

"You're getting stronger all the time, pamangkin. You're going to be fine. What you need is patience and I know that doesn't come easy for you."

I grunted in agreement. Rey knew me better than I knew myself. I think I reminded him of how he was as a teenager. He hadn't gotten in nearly as much trouble as I had, but then he and my aunt Vanessa had survived a childhood marked with tragedy.

Their parents died at Jonestown.

"I know, I know. I'm trying. It's just, it's been almost a month."

"Yeah…since you *died*! You seem to forget that fun little fact. You're lucky to be out of bed at all. Now be a good patient. I've got a treat for you."

He said that like he was talking to a dog and I wished I had it in me to deck him. Not really, though. I merely wanted the ability.

We entered my room, and I went straight to the bed "like a good patient." I carefully lowered myself onto the mattress, in case my arms or legs decided to take a vacation on me. My blood pressure was still prone to dangerously low levels and I continued to suffer bouts of fatigue. I'd slept more since I'd died than in all of the years I'd been in higher education. The doctors couldn't tell me how long it would take for me to get back to my previous level of fitness. They wouldn't assure me I *could even* be that fit again. Thankfully the damage to my kidneys was minimal, and I'd been able to avoid needing dialysis. Yet.

That's all we knew at the moment of my prognosis. It was a day-at-a-time scenario.

"Your roommate get liberated?" Rey asked.

"Let's get you reconnected here, Mr. San Angelo." My nurse Wilhemina removed the wires from the stress test and reconnected my heart monitor, the pulse ox finger thingie, and made sure my oxygen was within reach in case I needed it. Fucking old man shit up in here.

I looked to the empty bed next to mine and sighed. "Mr. Chu adequately recovered from his hip replacement surgery and his family picked him up yesterday." Yeah, Mr. Chu was like ninety-years-old, and even he healed faster than me. I'd been through two roommates already. "Apparently, I'm getting a new roommate sometime today."

"Hopefully they won't be put out by the sheer number of books you've managed to collect. Speaking of...Pliny the Elder, huh? A little light reading?"

"Yes! Thank you!"

Rey dug in his messenger bag and pulled out a large tome. "Ms. Beckett at the library wanted to make sure you had everything you needed and insisted that I bring these over right away." He tossed his non-existent hair and slid pretend glasses down his nose to wink at me.

"Eh, she likes Creed more than me." I accepted the book from him and my weak-ass heart sped up just enough but not too much to make my monitor start freaking out.

"You finding anything interesting in these books?"

I'd already cracked open the Pliny and was running my fingers over the page. "Yeah. Humans have been ingesting human blood for a long fucking time."

Rey cursed under his breath and hooked his thumbs in his utility belt. "Weird fucking shit. Didn't I tell you how tired I am of weird shit?"

"Uh huh." I was already immersed in the book, ready to tune everything out.

"Yeah, yeah, I know you and your books. Hey, remember tomorrow I'm busting you out for evening bingo, so rest up, hear me? Lola wants to see you."

"Uh huh."

My grandmother's move to an assisted living facility was the catalyst for the events that led me here. Creed was her nurse at Puesta Del Sol. I'm not sure who she missed more, me or him. As far as she or anyone at the home knew, he'd had a family emergency out of state. The saddest part was that with him gone, Puesta Del Sol was a melancholy place. Sure Lola and her sisters still watched their programs and played bingo, but she was deteriorating at a more rapid pace without his healing. Who knew how long we had with her, and here I was being an old man myself. Thankfully I was making progress. The sooner could get out of there, the better for all involved.

I was pretty sure Rey said goodbye before he left, but I was deep into Pliny's description of peasants running into the ring toward fallen gladiators to drink from their open wounds, how they believed the vitality and strength these warriors possessed could be gleaned through their fresh blood.

There were so many instances of humans resorting to blood drinking which they thought provided physical benefits...What if La Mente, or whatever this organization was calling itself these days, traced its practices back to these ancient times?

I couldn't wait to go over all of this with Creed. I had a mountain of examples to share with him, as soon as I was well enough.

A knock sounded on the doorjamb sometime later, jarring me from the text.

"Hello Mr. San Angelo," Wilhelmina said. "I'd like for you to meet your new roommate, Dr. Alistair Gardner."

Two orderlies wheeled in a gurney with a silver-haired, gaunt old white man with piercing blue eyes. He may have been wheeled in but he looked ready to do battle.

"Nice to meet you," I said, watching him curiously. He gazed around the room with a raised eyebrow.

"You as well," he said. I detected a faint accent.

"You two should have plenty to talk about, seeing as you're both in academia."

I smiled and steeled myself for the comments. Every older white male professor I'd met throughout my journey discounted me as a young blowhard with no substance to back it up.

"Splendid," he said. "What is your discipline?"

"Criminal Psychology. And you?"

The old man grinned. "Cultural Anthropology with an emphasis on paganism in ancient and medieval times."

It was my turn to grin. I rubbed my hands together. "Emphasis in cults and criminal behavior. Very nice to meet you."

"Now, no getting excited, Mr. San Angelo. The doctor will be in shortly to discuss your test results and if he sees you getting riled up—"

"I know, I know, he'll take my books away."

Mr. Gardner raised both eyebrows this time. "Cruel and unusual punishment. What's next? Drawn and quartered? The Iron Maiden? I know all the best torture techniques, but taking books away from an academic is barbaric."

I laughed. "Good to know you have my back."

Wilhelmina did some work on Mr. Gardener's chart and then checked my monitor.

"Your oxygen is kinda low. Let's get you hooked up for a bit, shall we?"

I grumbled, but my nurse laughed. She was used to this routine.

"I thought I'd be the grumpy old man in this scenario," Mr. Gardner said. "What's a young man like you doing hooked up to oxygen?"

I groaned and leaned my head back into the stack of pillows, my eyes falling closed.

"How long you got?"

Preorder your copy today!

AFTERWORD

I hope you enjoyed this first installment of the *Sundowners* series, a spinoff from the Gifted series. If you haven't read *Healer, Connection,* and *Protector,* you may want to see where the two, well, connect. There are Easter eggs between the two series that you might enjoy, plus there's a similar vibe: Folks who learn they have something a little extra who learn to use their power for good...or nefarious purposes, and the people who make it their life's work to protect those that need it.

If you've read the Gifted series, you may recall learning that I spent a significant amount of time studying cult activity. I also have a master's degree in Counseling Psychology. I've always been fascinated by the forces that drive people to join these organizations, and the people who believe in their cause. These two series reflect my desire to learn more and maybe, perhaps, help folks who are trying to make a new start and leave their damaging pasts behind.

Sundowners came about because I was rebelling. Yes, that's right, I'm really mature. I was supposed to be writing something else so OF COURSE this novel that I started writing in 2020 (that year that we were all in the dark times, remember?) wouldn't stop poking at me. I'd been wanting to write a vampire story, but was determined not to do it until I had something original to say. We'll see if you agree that this was the right time, the right lore, and the right story...

As for the "Sundowning,"—which is a genuine disorder—my family has experienced a fair amount of dementia-related ailments. Alzheimer's and the like are devastating illnesses for those experiencing them, and painful for the family members caring for their loved one. If you or anyone you know needs help, here are some organizations that may be helpful.

Thank you for joining me on this journey.

Alzheimer's Support: https://www.alz.org/norcal
    Cult Education: https://culteducation.com/

ACKNOWLEDGMENTS

Above all, I need to thank my former professor, William D. Russell. Thank you for the knowledge and inspiration you sparked during my days at Big G.

To ASP, wherever you are, thank you for inspiring Reynaldo Cabral (AKA Officer Dicknaldo). I miss our lunches and adventures. I hope you're having less exciting ones now and that you have found your happy place.

To the city of Santa Cruz, thank you for the years of sand, surf, and sunshine. For cheer camp at UC. For the shows at The Catalyst. For hanging in there after we lost so much in the Loma Prieta Earthquake of 1989. For one of the greatest vampire movies of all time, *The Lost Boys*. I'll be back soon.

A really cool conversation with Sue Brown-Moore and Marie Booth helped spark the ideas for this book and I'm so grateful for both of these women! Further conversations with Kim Fielding and M.D. Neu spurred on this quest to write the right vampire story for me. If it missed the spot, blame them AHAHAHA. NEVER. Thank you all for supporting and inspiring me.

I'm fortunate to have some fantastic folks that help to lift me up when I'm floundering: My beloved editor Kelli Collins, without whom this wouldn't occur, Allison, my proofreader who is a lifesaver, Rachael Herron and my cohorts in the 90 Days to Done (etc) courses, Bay

Area Queer Writers Association, Angela James's From Written to Recommenced along with Assistant Extraordinaire Dan, Bay Area Romance Writers, Inclusive Romance Project, and I absolutely can't forget The SBC Crew. I am so fortunate to have such incredible folks behind me.

My Roadies of Romance, I'm grateful for all of you, and I can't wait to hang out with my new group of pals, The Racy Reads Party Room! Thank you for supporting me and my weird stories!

And last but CERTAINLY not least, my beloved PA Rachel Hamilton who is still trying to figure out how to wrangle me. If you have any suggestions (besides Diet Coke and chocolate) for her, feel free to send them to me via messenger or rlmerrillauthor@gmail.com.

Thanks for hanging out and *stay tuned for more...*

ABOUT R.L. MERRILL

R.L. Merrill is like your local hard rock/metal radio station and Rochelle Merrill is her Adult Contemporary alter ego. Spinning feel-good stories to make you laugh and swoon, or spooky yarns to make you shiver, Ro writes contemporary and paranormal romance for grown-ups who use their words (mostly) and take care of business. She's a mom and wife on hiatus from a career in education while she explores the new terrain of mid-life adventures. You can catch her walking and gardening in her neighborhood by the San Francisco Bay, spoiling her rescue pets, and dreaming of the day she can attend concerts safely. Stay Tuned for more hits coming your way...

COMING SOON:

October 2022 - My sixth Magic and Mayhem Universe book:
Five Fanger Witch Punch

March 2023 and July 2023 - I will be contributing two novellas to The HEA Collective. They will be queer tropey romances, that's all I can tell you! If you want to know more about this project, visit https://happilyeveraftercollective.com/ and join us!

There may possibly maybe be some other releases in between, but I'm hard at work planning my schedule and just like that famous box of chocolates: you never know what you're gonna get!

ALSO BY R.L. MERRILL

Haunted Series: (Contemporary Romance)

Haunted

Fated

Bated

Jaded – (Coming Soon)

Minded Series: (Paranormal Spinoff of Haunted Series)

Minded

Blossomed

Father F'in' Christmas

A Peculiar Prom Night

Magic and Mayhem Universe: (Funny Paranormal Romance in the universe created by Robyn Peterman)

Shifted

Ghoul Me Once

Gator Me Twice

Magic and Mayhem/Shifted Collection

Fang Me Three Times

Fangtastic Four

Five Fanger Witch Punch

Hollywood Rock 'n' Romance Trilogy: (Contemporary Romance)

Teacher

Teacher: Act Two

Teacher: The Final Act

Contemporary Romance Series:

The Rock Season

Road Trip

You Fell First

The Heart Knows (Re-Releasing Soon)

A Match Made in Spain

LGBTQ Romance

Pinups and Puppies (Originally in Love Is All Vol. 2)

I Want, More – Bolder Breed Studios #1 (Originally in Love Is All Vol. 3)

Love and Pride – Bolder Breed Studios #2 (Originally in Love Is All Vol. 4)

Everything's Better With You: An MM Sports Romance

All I Wanna Do — Bolder Breed Studios #3 (Email Ro for your copy)

Under His Sheets: Accidentally Undercover – Out April 9, 2024

Feuds and Interludes: Road To Rocktoberfest 2024 - November 2024

The Banes of Lake's Crossing (Historical Horror Romance)

The Fourth Man (The Banes of Lake's Crossing) (Historical Horror Romance)

The Redemption of Nathaniel Bane

<u>The Absolution of Jonah Bane</u>

The Gifted Series: (Supernatural Suspense/Paranormal Romance)

Healer

Connection

<u>Protector</u>

Sundowners (M/M Paranormal Romance

<u>Sundowners Book One</u>

Moonwish: Sundowners Book Two (February 13, 2025)

Forces of Nature Series: (Gay Contemporary Romance)

Hurricane Reese

Typhoon Toby

<u>Earthquake Ethan</u>

Summer of Hush Series: (Gay Contemporary Romance)

Summer of Hush

Brains and Brawn

Carnival of Mysteries: (Gay Paranormal Romance, connected to Summer of Hush series)

<u>You Can Do Magic: Carnival Of Mysteries </u>(Season One, Book One)

You Can Save Me: Carnival of Mysteries (Season Two, Book Two)

You Can Make Me: Carnival of Mysteries (Season Three, Book Three Out September 13, 2025)

Anthologies:

Thanksgiving Day Parade From Hell (Worst Holiday Ever) (Gay Contemporary Romance

Valentine's Day From Hell (Worst Valentine's Day Ever) (Gay Contemporary Romance)

Salty and Sweet (Summer Fair) (Lesbian Contemporary Romance)

The Fourth Man (The Banes of Lake's Crossing) (Historical Horror Romance)

A Piece of Him (Gone With The Dead) (Horror)

<u>Breaking Bread</u>—Dark Divinations from HorrorAddicts.net Press (Horror)

Exchange (Renewal) (Science Fiction)

Tap-Tap-Tap (Impact) (Horror)

Human Sacrifice (Innovation) (Horror)

The Sitter (Clarity) (Horror)

Joy Is A Phone Call Away – A More Perfect Union (Lesbian Contemporary Romance)

The House Must Fall – Haunts and Hellions from HorrorAddicts.net Press – May 2021 (Horror)

A Kept Woman – BAQWA Presents: Horror Show 2021(Lesbian Horror Romance)

Gods of Rock 'n' Roll (Free on Wattpad)

How Bittersweet is Karma? Free on Wattpad)

Let Me Stand Next To Your Fire (Queer Cheer)

Midnight in the Renaissance Elevator

Holiday Romance

A Peace Offering (Re-release)

Love and Pride – Bolder Breed Studios #2

Once Upon a Goth Dog Solstice

Audiobooks

The Rock Season (Kiss App)

Brains and Brawn (Kiss App)

Teacher (Kiss App)

Hurricane Reese (Kiss App)

A Match Made in Spain (Audible)

Healer: Gifted Book One (Audible)

Under His Sheets (Audible Coming Soon)

You Can Do Magic (Audible Coming Soon)

Road Trip: A Rock 'n' Romance Story (Coming Soon)

Non-Fiction

Horror Addicts Guide To Life Volume 2 - Edited by Emerian Rich

Death's Garden Revisited - Edited by Loren Rhoads (Out Fall 2022)